TO BE A NINJA

BENEDICT JACKA

SIMON AND SCHUSTER

The essay, 'Ninjutsu Hiketsu Bun', on page 77,
is translated by Stephen and Rumiko Hayes, copyright © 1981 by them.
Reprinted with permission. Thanks to Ben Jones for Japanese translation
and assistance.

First published in Great Britain in 2005
by Simon and Schuster UK Ltd, a Viacom company.

Simon & Schuster UK Ltd
Africa House, 64-78 Kingsway, London WC2B 6AH.

A CIP catalogue record for this book is available from the British Library.

ISBN: 1-416-90128-0

1 3 5 7 9 10 8 6 4 2

Typeset by SX Composing DTP, Rayleigh, Essex
Printed by Cox & Wyman, Reading, Berkshire

www.simonsays.co.uk

PRELUDE

INTO THE WOODS

Ignis slid open the window and swung out onto the darkened roof. Moving silently on hands and knees, he crept down the tarmac slope and peered out over the edge.

Just beneath him, a figure was leaning against the wall. The shadows would have hidden the man's shape but for the glow of the cigarette he held in his hands. Ignis's nose twitched as he inhaled the smoke, recognising the smell: it was Pete. He would have a gun, but Ignis knew he wouldn't dare use it, not on them. Silently, Ignis pulled back, looked up towards the window again and held up one finger.

Allandra had already come out onto the roof behind him, waiting for his signal. She looked back into the window where her twin, Michael, was watching anxiously. Allandra beckoned.

Michael looked anxiously at his siblings. "*Later*," he mouthed.

Allandra shook her head. Michael hesitated. Allandra beckoned again, more urgently. Reluctantly, Michael reached back for a roll of sellotape and put it into Allandra's hand.

Ignis looked up. In the eastern sky, the first tinges of grey were showing, but the dawn was still too far away to make the house and the woods anything but looming shadows. It was time to see if Allandra's plan would work. He looked back at his sister and nodded.

Allandra turned and threw the roll up and over the house. Spiralling over and over, it vanished into the darkness and for a moment there was silence. Then, from the other side of the house, came a faint thump.

Below, Ignis heard Pete catch his breath. Footfalls, faint but purposeful, came from under the eaves of the roof as Pete started around the house towards the sound. Quick as a flash, Ignis dropped over the edge.

He landed hard on all fours, but the damp grass under his hands silenced his fall. He moved quickly aside, and Allandra and Michael came down behind him, small, dark shapes in the twilight. The three of them ran for the driveway. Ignis looked back over his shoulder as they passed the black Land Rover, but as trees cut off his view of the house, he could see no trace of Pete. A second later, they were out on the open road, shivering in the sudden cold. Ignis felt a surge of exhilaration as the house, Tawelfan, disappeared behind them. They were free.

Rhosmaen was hardly big enough to be called a village: a few dozen houses on either side of the road, clinging to the steep slopes of the valley. Above them, rocky hills rose into overgrown farmland and light forest; below, between the trees that crowded its banks, the river gleamed faintly. Ahead, in the distance, they could see the shadow of the high, forested hills around which the valley forked.

The trees closed in quickly around them as they walked. In the early morning silence, the only sound beyond the padding of their trainers on the road was the quiet whisper of the river down to the left. They passed a track that led to a house with a sign at the gate saying "The Old Vicarage", and a triangular red sign that said "Beware of falling rocks" in English and Welsh. Ignis looked up, curious. Shadowed boulders littered the slope. They didn't look as though they were about to fall any time soon.

Michael glanced back and spoke for the first time. Even though no one was in sight, he kept his voice low. "Do you think they can hear us?"

Ignis laughed, the sound loud in the cool air. "Pete's probably gone back to sleep."

Allandra put her hands behind her head and stretched. "Maybe." She shook her hair back. "But we'd better get a long way away before we stop."

"Oh, c'mon." Ignis yawned and looked around at the trees. "They're not even awake yet."

"Pete might go back inside to check on us," Allandra replied. "Or Tav might get up early. We have to make sure."

Ignis shrugged. Pete, Tav and Vargas were nowhere in sight, and they were out on the open road and free. What was the point of worrying over what might happen? But it had been Allandra's plan that had got them out, so he kept going.

The sky grew slowly lighter as they walked, the greyness changing to a dusky blue. The clouds that had covered the sky throughout the night had faded away, and in their wake stars sparkled in the clear air. The constellations glowed softly overhead, an intricate web of twinkling white pinpoints, now beginning to fade as the sky brightened around them. On the horizon all around, the hills and mountains that had been hidden were beginning to appear out of the darkness. Reaching the place where the valley forked, the children crossed a bridge over the river, passing a sign that pointed off to their right for the dam. They followed the road up into the left valley, disappearing into its thickly forested slopes. The last houses of the village were left behind them now, and the only sign of human life was the road they were walking on.

"Michael, what food did you get?" Allandra asked.

Michael rummaged in his pockets. "Let's see . . . an apple, two bunches of grapes – they're a bit squashed – and four sandwiches. No, three. And a Mars Bar."

"What kind of sandwiches?"

"One's cheese, the others are tuna."

Allandra made a face. "I hate tuna."

"Well, it was hard with him watching."

"I told you, he wasn't watching you, he was watching me. That was why I couldn't take anything."

"Well, I didn't notice," Michael muttered.

"Let's get off the road," Ignis said.

They had come to a place where the road ran high along the left side of the valley, a long way above the narrow, fast-flowing river at the bottom. Ignis led the other two down the earth and granite of the valley's slopes, and across the river at a narrow point where it could be jumped. The sky was a slate-blue now, the last stars of the night glinting faintly in the west, and the valley regaining its colour with the rising sun.

Now that they were at the bottom of the valley, they could see that it was the meeting place of two rivers, their channels forming a Y shape as they followed the slope of the valley downhill. At the intersection of the Y was a junction pool, a churning froth of water fifteen metres wide, and just above it, between the two rivers, a jumble of granite rocks that provided cover from the road above them. The three children waded through the bracken down towards the rocks, hearing the rustles of animals around them.

"Look – people have been here," Michael said. In the grass next to the pool was a circle of blackened earth and the remains of an old fire.

"Maybe people use this place for camping," Allandra said, interested. "We could—"

"Look out!" Ignis hissed. Through the trees above he had seen the flash of a windscreen. For a moment the three children froze, then a black Land Rover roared into sight. The rush of the water had drowned out the approaching engine. Ignis looked back to see Michael standing in the middle of the grass, in plain sight, staring upwards in panic. He shoved him forward, hard. "Go! Get down!"

Michael scrambled over the rocks. For a moment he looked as if he was going to slide down the boulders into the water, then he disappeared from sight down the other side. Ignis and Allandra darted after him.

They had landed in a perfect little hideaway. It was a small patch of grass, only a few centimetres above the running water of the pool, surrounded by granite. Rock walls to their left and right blocked off sight to either side, and the curve of the left wall hid them from the road. No one could see them without climbing down from the road, crossing the river, and approaching the rocks on foot as they had done.

"Did they see us?" Michael worried.

"If they did, it was because you were so slow!" Ignis

scowled. "What, were you waiting for them to spot you?"

"It's fine," Allandra said quickly. "If they'd seen us, they'd have been out of the car by now, and," she sneaked a look around the rocks, "they're not."

Ignis looked at the empty road with satisfaction. "I hope they crash and die."

"I hope they didn't take the other car as well." Michael sat down. "What if they come looking?"

"Who cares?" Allandra propped herself up against the rocks happily. "We could stay here for ever. They'd never find us."

"So can we have something to eat?" Michael asked.

Allandra gave him a stern look. "We should be rationing ourselves. We could be out here for days. Weeks, even."

"Yes, but I'm hungry now."

"Oh, all right. But only half of it. And leave me the cheese one," she added as Michael retrieved the sandwiches from his pockets.

Ignis kept lookout. The Land Rover had vanished northwards, following the road into the trees. The sides of the valley were too steep for even the four-wheel drive Land Rover to handle, and there was no road down. Satisfied, Ignis settled down to wait.

They ate, drinking from the river one at a time as the other two kept watch for the hunters. Before long the Land

Rover appeared again, returning across the valley above them, then going in the opposite direction. They sighted it four more times as the morning wore on, passing back and forth along the road. Each time, a little more time passed before it appeared again. Once it stopped and three figures emerged to scan the valley from the ridge, but Ignis spotted them early and all three children hid in the shadow of the rocks until they had gone. The sun rose higher and higher in the sky, but gave little heat. It was one of those clear, crisp autumn days, where the sky is a bright robin's-egg blue but the shadows are deep and cold.

By eleven o'clock the Land Rover had not appeared for more than an hour. Ignis pulled himself up again for another quick look around. "They've given up."

"Bet you they haven't," Michael answered gloomily.

"They probably think we went the other way," Ignis said. "Let's head up into the hills."

"If they come back while we're climbing they'll see us," Allandra said. "Let's wait till we're sure they're gone."

Ignis shrugged. It was all the same to him where they waited. They sat a little while in silence.

Allandra leaned back against the rock and sighed. "I wish we could have brought my books."

"Let's have lunch," Michael suggested.

"No," Allandra answered sternly. "We haven't got any more food. We have to make it last."

"But I'm hungry."

"Fugitives are always hungry. People who escape from prison can go for days and days without eating."

"We're not escaping from prison," Michael replied.

Ignis rolled his eyes, but his sister carried on talking. "Yes we are. We want to leave, don't we?"

"Yeah."

"And he won't let us," Allandra finished conclusively. "So it's a prison."

"No, it's not," Michael answered. "Anyway, we're going to get some food when we get back."

"We're not going back," Ignis cut in.

"But when they bring us back, they'll take our food away, anyway. So what's the point of starving now?"

Ignis looked up sharply. "What do you mean? You don't know they'll catch us."

"They always catch us."

"Well, this time, they won't."

"That's what you say every time."

Ignis's eyes narrowed. "What's your problem all of a sudden? Don't you remember last year? We got away from the house. We went three whole days without him getting close to us. If we'd picked a different shelter, we could have done it for ever."

"And what about the other times we've tried it in London?" Michael began to count on his fingers. "The time

Tav came in the room while we were trying to climb out of the window? The time you made it out the window, then landed on a garden fork and sprained your ankle? Or what about the time you took us out through the laundry door? We got halfway down the street before we bumped into Pete. It's always the same. One of us gets caught and we have to stop. And remember when we were in Devon and you and Ally thought we could just walk out the front door into the garden? It only took them a few hours to find us on the road, and when they did Vargas was so angry that he—"

"Oh, yeah? Well, if it's all too much trouble, I'll tell you what." Ignis pointed away down the valley. "Go home. Go on! It's only an hour down the road. Then you can eat as much as you want, and we won't have to listen to you complaining!"

"That's not what I meant!" Michael protested.

"Yeah?" Ignis grinned nastily. "I think you've got cold feet about the idea of escaping in the first place. If it wasn't for me and Ally, you'd never have the nerve to do it yourself. Maybe you *want* us to get caught, so you'll be safe. So why don't you save us all some time and run home? That way you can be a good little boy and he'll be pleased with you. Go on." Ignis made flapping motions. "Back home, little chicken."

Michael narrowed his eyes. "You're just jealous. You know that it's me and Ally he wants the most. He only chases you because you're part of the family, not because he really wants you around. He cares much more about us than he does about you."

Ignis jumped to his feet in a rush of anger and advanced on his brother. Michael scrambled up, fear suddenly showing in his eyes.

Then suddenly Allandra was between them, eyes blazing. "Stop it! Are you crazy, Ig?" She pointed up at the road. "They could be right next to us. All three of them are trying to hunt us down and you're going to *fight each other*? What are you *thinking*?"

Ignis glared down at his sister, anger burning inside him, then with an effort turned away. The three of them stood for a few seconds in silence.

"But Michael's right."

Ignis turned in surprise.

Allandra and Michael didn't look like twins. Although both were small and slight, Allandra stood a little taller than Michael, and while his hair was a pale brown, hers was a bright golden blonde. But they *were* twins, twelve years old and constant companions. Ignis was a year older than them both – taller, with sharper features and darker hair. The only characteristic all three shared was their light blue eyes, tilted up at the corners. Those same eyes, set into Allandra's pale face, were now clouded with worry as she looked at her elder brother.

11

When Ignis didn't answer, Allandra dropped her gaze and spoke again. "Michael's right. We do always get caught. There's no point pretending. No matter what I come up with, they always get us eventually."

"Ally . . ." Michael said uncertainly.

"So what are you saying?" Ignis demanded. "I'm not giving up."

"That's not it." Allandra took a few steps away and stared down into the pool at their feet. When she spoke, her voice was quieter.

"I'm not going back this time. I'm not. I don't care what we have to do. I just . . ." She turned and hesitated. "If one of us gets caught this time, I think we shouldn't stop."

Michael's blue eyes went wide. "You mean separate?"

Allandra nodded. Michael shook his head. "No. Ally, don't."

"No. I'm not going back, Michael. Not this time." Allandra stared into the swirling pool, the water golden brown in the sunlight. "If I do . . ." She shook her head. "If we get split up, we can meet again later. You're right, Michael. They always catch us because they only need to get one of us to make the others stop."

Michael was shaking his head, fear plain on his face. "But what if one of us ends up caught and the others get away? No, Ally, don't, please. You, too, Ignis. I'm sorry about what I said before. I didn't mean it."

Michael stared at Allandra forlornly. Allandra looked back at him, then bent down and picked up a sharp rock.

"Here." As Ignis watched, she walked to where Michael was standing and used the rock to cut a line across the granite wall. "Now scratch another line across that one."

Michael hesitated, then took the rock from her and scratched again across the granite face. The two lines formed an X.

"There." Allandra stepped back. "This is for all three of us. If we do get separated, then we'll meet back here. This mark is our promise that we'll find each other again."

Michael still looked unhappy, but he nodded. Allandra beckoned to Ignis. "You do one too, Ig."

Ignis rolled his eyes. "Forget it. I'm going to take a look around – then we'll get moving." Ignis walked to the rockface, pulled himself up – and found himself staring into a man's face.

The man was short but heavily built, with a battered, unshaven face and grizzled black hair, and his name was Pete. As he saw Ignis, his eyes went wide. He turned and shouted: "Hey! Hey! They're over he—"

As he twisted, he grabbed for Ignis and lost his footing on the granite. With a yell he slid down the rockface, falling into the pool with a splash.

Ignis jumped down. "Run!" he shouted.

There was only one way to go. They scrambled around

the edge of Junction Pool, the gorse bushes that littered the rocks scratching their clothes and skin. Ignis jumped up to the next level of rocks and pulled Allandra after him. A growing roar of water made him look up, and for the first time he saw the second of the two rivers.

White water smashed and frothed against line after line of jagged granite boulders, disappearing up into the hills. The pounding of the water on the rock made a constant, steady roar. On the far side was thick forest, but the river-bank here was formed of water-worn formations of rock, resting against each other at crazy angles. Ignis and Allandra looked at each other, and started climbing.

Rocks two metres tall blocked their progress. Ignis used the trees and bracken growing between the boulders as handholds, climbing and jumping from one rock to the next. Allandra, with her shorter legs, was finding it harder, but she struggled on gamely, Michael a step behind. Ignis paused on a flat ledge and looked out at the roaring waters to his right.

Allandra pulled at Ignis's arm and pointed back. Behind them was Pete, scrambling over the first rock. He was soaking wet, and looked very angry.

They scrambled slowly up the valley, the boulders becoming larger and larger the further they went. Pete might be bigger than they were, but he wasn't as nimble, and as Ignis glanced back he saw that the stocky man was falling further and further behind. For a moment it seemed that they would be able to get away.

Then Ignis looked ahead and his heart sank. There was another man among the rocks fifteen metres in front of them: Tav, the second-in-command.

Ignis, Allandra and Michael came to a halt by a jagged rock three metres high that pointed upwards like a knife. The slope to their left was too steep to climb. They were trapped.

"Ignis," Allandra said quietly.

"Yeah, I know. It's the end of the line." Ignis laughed suddenly, the sound swallowed by the roaring water. Somehow, everything seemed so much simpler now that their escape route was cut off. The roaring water sang to him, filling him with a wild energy. All he could do now was make a last stand, fighting until he was struck down. "I'll go for Tav. You and Michael might be able to get past if I distract him."

"No. We can all get across."

Ignis looked at Allandra in surprise. She was pointing into the river, where the white water frothed and roared, throwing spray into the air. Just a couple of metres away from them, the raging torrent broke around two or three boulders – and the boulders were within jumping distance of each other.

Ignis's eyes widened in admiration. "No kidding!"

15

Michael followed their gaze, and his eyes widened too. "No way. You are not even *thinking* about that!"

"I mean it." Allandra stared intently at the river, plotting out a course. "Three jumps, that's all it'll take. Just two rocks."

"You're out of your mind!" Michael shouted. "You'll actually *die*!"

"We can make it. It's the only way."

"No." Michael shook his head. "I'm not doing this, Ally. It's over!"

A cold voice spoke from above. "Yes. It is."

The man standing at the top of the rise dropped onto the first rock, then gripped the branch of a tree and swung to the ground. Despite his size, he moved with the grace of a panther. He had Ignis's dark brown hair and angular face, and his blue eyes smouldered as he looked down at them. Ignis backed away to stand next to Allandra and Michael, hate and fear fighting inside him.

The man's name was Vargas Havelock, and he was their father.

"This was supposed to be a holiday." His voice was tight and angry. "A few days where we could take a break before you went back to school. Now we're going to have to return home in the evening instead of the morning, and I'll have to cancel everything I'd planned for today. By performing this stupid stunt, the three of you have caused

16

me a week of work. You have no idea how much trouble you are in."

Ignis tried to sound defiant. "We're not going back."

Vargas's cold blue eyes locked on Ignis, and despite his anger Ignis quailed. "You," Vargas said, biting off the word. "You are going back, Ignis. Back home, or back into that river, but believe me, you *are* going back." Vargas's gaze flicked to Allandra, and Ignis could feel her trembling beside him. "And then all three of you are returning to London with me. I've no more time for your childishness today."

Pete and Tav had reached them, and they moved up behind Vargas, panting. Pete's rough face had an ugly scowl. "You stupid brats," he snarled. "I'll teach yer a lesson yer'll remember if yer live to be a hundred." Their father held up a hand, and Pete fell silent. The three children remained motionless, like birds mesmerised by a snake.

Then, as Pete and Tav started for them, Allandra turned and with a desperate leap launched herself at the first rock. For an instant she skidded, then found a grip with both hands. She turned back. "Michael, Ig!" she shouted. "Come on!"

Ignis looked at Michael, saw his brother hesitate. Then Michael walked towards his father, shaking his head. Tav grabbed him. "Michael!" Allandra shouted, spray whipping at her face.

17

Vargas moved forward, his eyes blazing. Ignis stepped up towards him, but Vargas struck him aside, sending him sliding to the water's edge. "Allandra!" he shouted. "*Get back here right now!*"

Ignis rose to his feet, snarling. In the middle of the river, Allandra stood up, wobbling, then turned towards the second rock. It was small and glistened with moisture.

"Ally, don't!" Michael cried.

Allandra jumped.

She landed squarely with both feet and for a moment it looked to Ignis as though she had made it. Then her feet slid out from underneath her and she fell awkwardly upon the slippery stone, grabbing at the rock as her legs skidded into the water. Ignis saw her mouth open in a gasp, but the sound was lost in the roar.

Michael was fighting against Tav, shouting, trying to get to his sister. Everyone's attention was fixed on Allandra, struggling in the river. Ignis was free to run: no one would notice. Allandra slid further, the roaring water dragging her into the current.

Ignis charged. He made a flying leap past Vargas, coming down on the first boulder with both feet. Suddenly he was surrounded by rushing water. Spray whipped at his face, nearly blinding him. Allandra was only a metre or so away. Ignis braced himself to jump again.

"I'll be all right!" Allandra shouted, her voice barely

audible over the thunder of the river. The two of them were on tiny islands in the roaring water, white spray all around them. Ignis could see his sister's fingers being pulled loose from the rock, one by one. She lifted her head. "Ignis! Get Michael and—"

Allandra's grip slipped and she vanished into the torrent. With a wordless shout Ignis dived in after her, getting a grip on her arm as the water whipped them both away towards a huge boulder. In the second before they struck Ignis pulled Allandra around, shielding her. The water smashed him against the rock, the blow landing across his back and head, and his vision exploded into stars and darkness.

Icy cold gripped Allandra, freezing her body. She and Ignis were dragged down head over heels, and she lost her breath in a cloud of bubbles. Her head broke the surface and she struggled to take a breath, but before she could a current sucked her under again, banging her legs and arms against sharp-edged rocks.

She hung onto Ignis with a death grip, clawing with her spare arm at the rocks as she glanced off them, but the current spun her past too quickly to catch herself. The world had turned into a whirling chaos of water, foam, and noise. Bumping, bruising, striking, feeling pain in every part of her body, Allandra was thrown like a rag doll down through the river, catching confused glimpses of trees, earth, and sky.

Then suddenly the current was slackening, and she was floating, drifting along the edge of a wide pool. Floating next to her, Ignis was heavy and still, his eyes closed. She clutched at the rocks of the shoreline, trying to keep them both afloat, but the deadly cold had leeched her strength. The world seemed to have become dark and distant, and the shore just in front of her was fading from her vision. She made a last feeble attempt to pull herself up, then let herself sink back into the water's freezing embrace.

A hand shot down and grabbed her. Allandra was hauled, coughing and gasping, out of the pool. Dimly she was aware of Ignis being pulled out after her, and of being set down on soft grass. A figure was leaning over her.

"They'll be here in a few minutes." The voice was quiet. "Just lie still, and you'll be found."

"No!" Allandra gasped. Coughing, she grabbed at the person above her, forcing out words. "Don't let them find us. We have to get somewhere safe. Please . . . you have to help . . ." Blackness swept in from the edges of Allandra's vision and the world faded away. The last thing she saw was a pair of strange blue eyes looking down at her.

When Pete and Vargas reached Junction Pool, both Allandra and Ignis were gone.

20

1

ROKKAKU

Creeeak.

Creeeak.

Ignis rolled over in his bed and pulled the blanket up over his ears. He hurt all over, and wanted to sleep.

Creeeak.

Creeeak.

The noise was waking him up. It sounded like someone walking across floorboards. "Michael, shut up," he muttered from under the covers.

Creeeeeeeak.

Ignis opened his eyes, ready to curse his brother, and was suddenly wide awake.

He was in a small room made of wooden boards, lying on a mattress laid out in the middle of the floor. Apart from a few pieces of furniture, the room was bare. Through the windows set in all four walls he could see trees, and sky. Afternoon sunlight was shining down onto the bed, making him blink.

Ignis sat up, wincing at the twinge in his neck. He

reached back to probe at it cautiously. His back and the nape of his neck flared in pain as he touched his skin, but there was something in between – a plaster. Another was on his arm, and two scrapes on his leg seemed to have been washed and dressed, too. Ignis stared at them for a minute, frowning, then saw his clothes folded by the bed.

As he dressed, there came another long *creeak* from under his feet. He stopped. The *creeak* came again. This time it felt as though the floor shifted. Startled, he looked around. The branches through the front window were still. Through the other windows, the leaves shifted gently in the breeze, but there was no other movement. He started to turn away, then stopped dead as he realised what was wrong. *Wait a minute . . .*

. . . how can there be branches outside all *of the windows?*

Ignis moved to the door, opened it, began to take a step out – and grabbed the doorway to stop himself, his eyes widening.

The door opened onto a tree branch. Beyond that was a ten metre drop. Ignis backed away and sat down on the bed with a thump, staring out of the door at the leaves and branches behind it.

Creeeeak . . . This time the floor definitely shifted underneath him.

"Oh, hell." Ignis crawled on his hands and knees to the

doorway and slowly peeked out over the edge.

Branches and leaves blocked most of his vision, but he could see that beneath him was a long building, flat-roofed and built of wood. Between him and the roof was nothing. No ladder, no stairs – only a few ropes strung through the branches.

The wind whispered through the leaves and the tree leaned gently with another *creeeak*. Ignis held on tight until it had stopped moving.

He took a breath. *OK . . . climbing a tree. That's all you're doing.* Then before he could think twice, he swung out and started clambering down. It was easier than it looked. The branches were worn smooth from use, and there were footholds nailed into the trunk. In only a few seconds, he turned, jumped, and landed with a thump on the roof below. Then he straightened and looked around in amazement.

The valley he was standing in was like nothing he'd seen before in his life. In front of and behind him, along the length of the valley, was a line of long, broad buildings like the one he was standing on, built on stilts over the narrow stream that ran below. There was a small gap between the end of one building and the beginning of the next, and they stretched down the valley one after the other, obscured slightly by the oak, birch and alder trees that lined the slopes.

23

Above them were dirt paths, cut slightly into the valley's steep slopes, and along the paths were the doors and windows of rooms. The rooms – if that was what they were – had been built into the valley sides, sunk deep into the earth so that only a door, a couple of windows and a little of the roof showed of each. The valley was so steep that the rooms were nearly on top of one another, the paths forming levels that rose higher and higher upwards. Steps, logs and curving tracks linked the paths to the ones above and below them.

But it was what was between the slopes that made Ignis stare. The house he had left wasn't the only one up in the air. Nearly all of the bigger trees supported either huts or small platforms, connected in midair by a network of ropes and swings. The lowest paths on either side of the valley were joined by hanging bridges made of logs. The higher levels were connected only by taut ropes, running from the valley sides to the trees, the branches, and the huts and platforms. Each layer of huts and platforms was stacked on top of the next, so that the ropes rose higher and higher until the uppermost level was in the treetops, more than ten metres above the ground and level with the highest layer of paths on either side of the valley. Afternoon sunlight shone in patches through the leaves, forming dappled patterns on the houses and ropes and leaving many of them half hidden in the greenery. It was as if the entire valley had been designed not for walkers, but for creatures that could fly – or climb. As Ignis turned slowly to look down the length of the valley, he could see in the distance the glitter of some vast body of water through the trees.

There was a thump and muffled voices from the building he was standing on. Ignis jumped. He could hear someone shouting. Hurrying to one side, he found a ladder and climbed down onto the grass. The voices from inside grew clearer.

"Keep your *centre*, damn it! Stop trying to pull him off his feet and keep your centre! Again!"

There was a moment's silence, then a thundering crash which made the building's thick wooden stilts quiver.

"No, no, *no*! God help me, what did I do wrong to get landed with the most bungling pack of students this school's ever seen? There are three-year-olds in Japan who can do this trick! Arthur, Toshiro, get over here. See if you can be *uke* without mucking it up."

Curious, Ignis stepped around the white flowers lining the stream and moved to the building's lower side. There was a set of steps leading up to an open door. He leaned his head around the corner.

The hall was long and wide, with a rubbery floor. Twenty boys in their early teens were standing around a short, bald-headed man. It was his voice Ignis had heard. All of them were wearing odd-looking black suits with slipper-like shoes and a thick green belt tied at the waist. As Ignis watched, a black boy half a head taller and twice as broad as the short man stepped forward and grasped the short man from behind in a bear-hug, pinning his arms to his sides. A shorter Japanese boy stepped in front of him.

"Right," the man declared. "Now *uke* attacks." The Japanese boy nodded and threw a punch.

The man did something very fast. Suddenly the boy was on the ground clutching his stomach, and the boy behind him was flying through the air, landing flat on his back with a crash that shook the room.

Ignis stared, certain he had been hurt badly, but as the boy sat up Ignis saw to his surprise that he was grinning. The man pulled the boy up. "Now did you see that?" he demanded to the rest of the class. Heads nodded. "Again, and this time do it right!"

Ignis ducked away, wide-eyed. Where was he?

He ran down the steps, but stopped as he was about to turn the corner. Above the trickling of the stream, he could hear voices approaching.

"Christopher!" A girl's voice, cheerful and enthusiastic. "I've been looking all over for you! You know, have I ever told you how much I appreciate you?"

"Yes . . . lots of times. Usually just when you're about to get us both in trouble."

"Get you in trouble? I'd never do anything like that.

Why would you ever think—"

"What have you done, Jennifer?"

"Done? Nothing! I just wanted to ask you a hypothetical question . . ."

The owners of the voices walked into Ignis's view. They both looked his age or a little younger, and wore the same black suits he'd seen on the boys before. The girl was slight, like Allandra, with streaked blonde-brown hair and a bounce in her step, while the boy was taller, with dark hair and eyes, slightly bronzed skin, and a watchful expression. He stopped and folded his arms. "What sort of question?"

"Well, hypothetically, suppose someone in our class – let's call him Ichiro – had said something nasty – like, oh, that everyone in the class except for him and his friends had sucky *taijutsu* – then, hypothetically, should I put a pair of slugs in his *tabi*?"

"No, Jennifer. Hypothetically, picking a fight with the toughest and best student in the class would be a very, very *bad* idea. You've done more than enough to make him mad at you already."

"Are you sure?"

"Yes! I'm very sure!"

"OK." She paused. "Here's another hypothetical question . . . what if I already did?"

From somewhere behind the buildings to the north came

a high-pitched yell. Christopher jumped, then spun to glare at the girl, whose face had broken into an expression of delight.

"*Jennifer!*"

Jennifer fluttered her eyelashes, placing her hands over her chest with a look of angelic innocence. "Who, me?"

"Are you out of your *mind*?"

"C'mon, Chris. Slimy things always get into people's shoes. It's like, a law of living in the woods or something."

"Or get put in! And if Ichiro finds out who did it, we're *both* going to—"

"Jennifer."

The man who had approached without any of them noticing was Japanese, with a lined face and greying hair. The black suit and belt he wore were faded with age. Despite his plain looks, there was something commanding about him. Christopher and Jennifer jumped, turned, and bowed hurriedly. "Um, Nishiyama-*sensei*. We were just—"

"Akamatsu's *taijutsu* class has just been disrupted." Nishiyama's voice was even. "It seems that Ichiro is claiming that someone put some kind of creature into his *tabi*. I don't suppose that either of you would know anything about this?"

Jennifer backed up a step. "Um. N-no, *sensei* . . ."

"Your father made some comments in the letter that arrived with you, Jennifer. Specifically, he claimed that

28

you could not go a fortnight without stirring up trouble. Given that you have been in Rokkaku three weeks and the incident last week with the shaving cream also happened in your presence, I would be interested to hear where you have been this past hour." His tone remained mild, but his eyes didn't stray from Jennifer's face. She gulped.

"No! She didn't have anything to do with—"

Nishiyama's gaze slipped to Christopher, and the boy hesitated. "I mean – she couldn't have had anything to do with it. Because . . . um . . ." he turned to look behind Jennifer, "she was showing the new student around!"

Ignis moved to one side to see who Christopher was pointing at, and his eyes widened. It was Allandra. She was standing behind the other two children, looking up at the man they called *sensei*.

"I see," Nishiyama replied. "Well, neither of you seem to have found her a *gi* yet, so I suggest you do so. Allandra, have you been assigned a room?"

Allandra shook her head.

"Then I expect the same goes for you, Ignis."

Ignis jumped. Nishiyama had given no previous sign that he knew Ignis was there. "What . . ." Ignis began. He had intended to ask what was going on, but as he spoke Nishiyama turned to look at him. The man's face showed no particular expression, but something about it made Ignis change what he had been going to say. "Uh, yeah."

29

"Then you can share with Shiro Yoshimatsu in the fifth set of rooms down Fox Row. Allandra, you can take the single room three down Willowherb. Both of your injuries from the river seem to have healed, so unless Dr Furuta says otherwise, I expect to see you in classes tomorrow. You have a great deal to catch up on." He turned and paused. "Oh, and Jennifer? Stay out of trouble." He walked away.

Ignis stared after him. "How did he know my name?"

Jennifer shrugged. "He's the headmaster. He knows all the students' names. Whew, that was close."

Christopher turned on Jennifer. "That was more than close! Why do you always have to drag *me* into these things?"

"Oh, stop complaining. It's not like you've got anything better to do."

"Not got . . .!"

"Ally?" Ignis asked, walking towards them.

Allandra grinned and gave him a quick hug. "Hi, Ig. Glad you're better. I went up to see you earlier, but you were still asleep."

Ignis hugged her back, then shook his head and held her at arm's length. "Wait a minute! I want to know what's going on."

"First things first. This is Jennifer, and this is her friend Christopher. They've been showing me around – uh, apart from the last ten minutes. Jennifer, Christopher, this is my older brother Ignis."

Jennifer waved. "Hiya. Did you both enrol here at the same time?"

"We haven't—" Ignis began.

Allandra interrupted quickly. "Um, Jennifer, how about you come back later, after Ignis and I have had a chance to talk? It's just that we really need to catch up."

"OK, we'll be tour guides!" Jennifer bounced away down the path, dragging Christopher with her and waving. "See you later!"

As they turned the corner, Ignis rounded on his sister. "What the hell is this place?"

"Rokkaku."

"What? No, forget it. Where are Vargas and the others?"

Allandra laughed. "Miles away. Calm down, Ig, we're safe. Vargas doesn't have a clue where we are, and he can't find us, either. We've really landed on our feet."

Ignis looked around. The steep-sided valley was nothing like the one into which they'd fled. "Where are we?"

"A mile or two northeast of the Tawi, I think."

Ignis stared at her. "What's the Tawi?"

"The river we fell into." Allandra sighed. "Just stop asking questions a second and I'll explain. After you hit that rock, we were carried downriver. Someone pulled us both out—"

31

"Who?"

"I *told* you, stop asking questions. I don't know who. But while we were unconscious, he carried us, northwest, here, to this valley, and he did it without anyone seeing. Our father's got no idea where we are, and he can't find us, either. This school doesn't appear on any map."

"School? What do you mean?"

Allandra grinned. "I'll show you." She took Ignis's hand and led him up the valley. The path they were walking on was made of packed earth, with grass and wild flowers growing around it. A few metres above them, higher up the valley, was another path, and through the trees, higher still, was another. They were passing by the rooms Ignis had seen earlier, the little houses sunk deep into the sides of the valley. Allandra led Ignis onto a small platform built over a short drop down to the banks of the stream. The valley was dotted with them, one-metre squares of wood along the sides of the paths.

"What are we—" Ignis began.

A bell rang.

Suddenly the valley was alive with young people, pouring out of the doors all around them and from the long buildings along the stream. All of them wore the same black outfits that Christopher and Jennifer had, with belts of white, green, red and black; but apart from that, they were different in every way: boys and girls, tall and short, light and dark skinned. Some were no older than Ignis, while others looked old enough to be adults. The one thing they all shared was an easy grace of movement. They weren't just walking, either. As Ignis watched, a boy on the opposite side of the valley grabbed a rope and swung easily across the stream, flying over the roof of the building below to swoop straight towards them. Ignis jumped back, and the boy came down with a thud in the centre of the platform. "Hey!" he called. "Keep the landings clear!" Then he ran past and away, springing up steps cut into the side of a tree trunk that was laid up the valley slope.

The boy wasn't the only one travelling by air. Children scaled the trees to reach the houses in the middle levels: others used the rope swings to travel between the lower platforms. At the highest levels, the ropes were being used as well. As Ignis watched in disbelief, a boy twice his size stepped out of the door of one of the high houses and *walked* along one of the ropes towards another house twenty paces away. Halfway along it, he turned, jumped backwards, caught the rope as he fell, and swung casually onto the roof of a house three metres below. In the clearings further down the valley Ignis could see pairs of boys sparring with long sticks, and below that a crowd of younger children being led uphill by an older man. Ignis turned to Allandra.

"What *is* this place?"

Allandra grinned at him. "This is Rokkaku. Ninja school."

Ignis looked at the boys and girls swarming around them. "This is a school?"

"It's a martial arts school." Allandra started leading them back down the path, keeping to the left to avoid the shouting children. "They teach regular things, but they also teach ninjutsu. It's a Japanese martial art – fighting and stealth and lots of other things. Like that." Allandra pointed to a rope above their heads where someone was walking. "Students join at eleven and stay to eighteen. Jennifer told me a bit about it while I was waiting for you to wake up. Everyone's just finished afternoon classes, that's why they're all out."

"Afternoon classes? What time is it?"

"Four o'clock. You slept through the day."

Ignis noticed they were getting sidelong looks from some of the children brushing past. Glancing down at his clothes, he realised why. He was still wearing the same sweater and jeans from before, while everyone else he could see in the valley, even the adults, was wearing one of the black suits. "What about Vargas?"

"That's the best part. Rokkaku is a secret school. Apart from the people who come here, no one knows it's here. There's no way Vargas can find it. We're safe."

They had come to the lower end of the valley. The long buildings over the stream carried on a short way further, then stopped as the stream widened and became more pebbly, disappearing down between a cluster of trees. To the right, the valley slope was covered with some kind of pink, flowery herb that sprouted up around the grass and trees. It gave off a dry, sweet smell. Scattered between the patches of herbs were doors, set into the valley sides. Allandra pointed at a door one level higher than them, then at one below. "That's your room, and this is mine."

"Good." Ignis took a quick glance around: despite the bustle, no one seemed to be looking at them. He opened the lower door, motioned Allandra in after him, and closed it.

The room was small and sparsely furnished, like the one he'd woken up in. A low bed sat in one corner, next to a table and chairs. The fading rays of the afternoon sun shone through the windows to paint squares of light on the wooden planks of the side wall. The walls were bare except for a piece of paper above the bed. The noise of the valley behind them faded away and it was quiet.

Ignis sat down upon the chair. "How much do they know about us?"

"It's not what they know, it's what they think." Allandra sat down on the bed and looked at Ignis seriously. "They think we're new students here."

35

"What?"

"Remember the person who brought us here? Whoever he was, he left a letter with us. The teachers here had read it by the time I woke up. I don't know everything it said, but it told them our names – and that we were enrolling as first years here at Rokkaku."

"Did you tell them who we were?" Ignis demanded.

Allandra looked insulted. "Of course not. I'm not *totally* stupid, Ig. I told the doctor that we'd fallen into the river and I couldn't remember anything else. He didn't ask any more questions. When I asked about you, he got Jennifer and Christopher to take me to you."

Ignis relaxed slightly. "Good. They wouldn't have been so helpful if they'd known our father was a drug dealer."

The words hung in the air. Calling Vargas a drug dealer was like calling a professional assassin a common crook: it didn't go far enough. Vargas Havelock *was* the drug industry for his part of London. How far his influence spread no one but Vargas himself knew, not even Pete and Tav, his two closest lieutenants. Vargas travelled throughout England, sometimes overseas. Ignis, Allandra and Michael had overheard snippets of deals over the years. Not only drugs. Handguns to England; automatic weapons to Ireland; other products risky enough that they were referred to only by codenames. But drugs were the biggest seller. It was drugs that had financed Vargas's rise through society; drugs that had bought him the six or more houses he owned throughout Britain; and drugs that led to the meetings with the men in the expensive suits whom they sometimes glimpsed visiting him in the evenings. Vargas knew everyone, had contacts everywhere. And as far as Ignis knew, he'd never been arrested.

Ignis yawned and winced, touching the plaster at the back of his neck. It seemed things weren't as bad as he'd feared. Still, there was no point wasting time. "Ow, I hope this gets better soon. OK, then. What's the nearest town?"

"Rhosmaen, I suppose."

"That's no good. Somewhere else."

"I don't know if there is anywhere else. We're really in the wilderness out here. But I guess if we went around the lake to the dam road, we'd find a place eventually."

Ignis nodded. "It's good enough. We can wait till sunset. Did you see anywhere we could take something to eat?"

"For what?"

"For when we get out of here."

Allandra hesitated. "Why now?"

Ignis looked at her in surprise. "Huh? Well, it doesn't have to be right now, but they'll figure out we aren't students sooner or later. Better get out before that happens."

"How would they know?"

"Well, if we stick around without going to the classes, they'll notice, won't they?"

"But what if we *did* go to the classes?"

Ignis frowned. "What do you mean?"

"They think we're students. Well, what if we *became* students? They've already given us rooms and enrolled us. And the way the teachers were before . . . I don't think they ask many questions here. They wouldn't tell our father, anyway. And we could—"

"Wait a minute, wait a minute." Ignis held up his hands. "Last thing I remember, we were trying to run away. What's the big idea?"

Allandra's eyes were bright. "Because here we've finally got a chance. Don't you see, Ig? This is the one place in the world where Vargas could never find us. No newspapers, no telephones, no police. Out there he has contacts everywhere, can track us wherever we go. Look, we always try to run *away* when we escape. We never think about where we're trying to run *to*. Can you think of a better place than this to hide in?"

"You've got to be kidding me. You think I got away from home and ran the gauntlet down that valley to go to *school*?"

"Why not?" Allandra's voice was quiet. "We have to learn somehow. Jennifer and Christopher told me stories. They said that the master ninjas, the really good ones, are almost invincible. We could stay here for a few months. Then when we're stronger than Vargas," she straightened up defiantly, "we could go back and rescue Michael."

Ignis rolled his eyes. "Oh, come *on*. Ally, I know you love coming up with these grand plans, but they never get anywhere. You know you wouldn't stand a chance against our father. And Michael probably wouldn't even want to leave."

Allandra narrowed her eyes. "That is not true!"

"Whatever. Anyway, I don't go to school in London and I'm not going to school in a forest, no matter what they teach."

Allandra let out a breath, then looked thoughtfully at Ignis.

"I'm not kidding, Ally."

"One week."

"What?"

"Try it for one week. Then if you don't like it, we'll both go."

"Ally, I told you. I'm not rolling over and playing lapdog for *anyone*. Not Vargas, and not some stupid teachers, either."

"Think about it, Ig." Allandra's voice was persuasive. "We don't lose anything. If we stay here a week and then leave, it'll still be better than running away now. By then Vargas will have given up searching around here – he'll think we've gotten away somewhere else. And if we find out that we really *can* learn something, we'll have a better chance when we *do* leave. We win either way."

"But—"

"Please, Ignis." Allandra reached out and touched Ignis's arm. "I'm not sure we'll get another chance like this. I don't want to risk Vargas catching us again. If that happens . . ."

Ignis was silent. Vargas had never made a secret of his goal for his children. They were to take over the family business. Become like him. "Grooming them," he called it. And over the last year, their father had been starting to put pressure on them to begin working for him for real. As the pressure had grown, his patience with their escapes had grown shorter, and the punishments harsher. Ignis knew that with this last escape, they had pushed their luck too far. If they were recaptured, they would get more than just a beating, more than just a session with Pete. Vargas's revenge would be dire – both for him, and for his sister, who was now looking at him with pleading eyes.

"This could work, Ig. Just try it. Please?"

Ignis looked at Allandra, and threw up his hands in defeat. "Ah, fine. One week. But that's it. After that, we leave."

Allandra's eyes flashed with happiness and she hugged Ignis close. Ignis put up with it for a few seconds, then pulled away.

There was a knock at the door. Allandra and Ignis exchanged glances. "Who is it?" Allandra called.

The door opened. Jennifer poked her head in. "Hi, Allandra."

"Oh, hi. Come in. Did you come to show us around?"

"Nope," Jennifer beamed. "We came to kill you and eat you."

Allandra stopped. "What?"

"Well, they don't feed us enough here," Jennifer began, "and the teachers don't taste very good. So we decided last week we needed a food supplement, and we thought the new students would be best, because—"

With a sigh Christopher pushed past her. "Just ignore her. We actually came to bring you your *gis*." He held up a bundle of folded cloth.

"And to warn you about the snakes under the bed," Jennifer added with a straight face.

"*And* to show you around," Christopher said, "if you can put up with my lunatic friend."

Allandra giggled. Ignis rolled his eyes and said, "Right. Well, I'll leave you to make friends. See you later."

He walked out past Christopher, ignoring the offered clothes, and climbed a steep path that took him to the row that Allandra had pointed to. The door had a 3 carved into it, and there were windows on either side. Ignis opened the door and walked in.

41

A boy was inside, sitting on his bed in an odd cross-legged position, one foot against the opposite knee and the other tucked underneath him. He looked up from the book he was reading as Ignis entered; he was tall and slim, with dark hair and eyes. He wore the same black coat and trousers as everyone else, with slipper-like shoes and a white belt. "Hello?" he asked, his tone of voice an inquiry.

"Yo," Ignis answered. There were two doors in the corners of the room. One led into a small bathroom. Ignis glanced through the other. It was a bedroom similar to this one. The bed was made. The same piece of paper he'd seen in Allandra's room was pinned on one of the walls. At the top were several words; one was "Ninjutsu".

"Can I help you?" the boy asked, politely.

"No, I'm cool." Ignis leaned against the wall.

The boy looked at him, his eyebrows raised. Ignis folded his arms and glanced around the room. There was a bookcase, half full of volumes Ignis couldn't recognise, and a small table which held a bowl of fruit and a tea set. In the corner were propped up a collection of sticks and something that looked like a wooden sword. There were no posters. Apart from a small figurine on a bedside table, the room had no decoration at all. It was so tidy Ignis felt uncomfortable.

"I don't mean to be rude," the boy asked finally, "but what are you doing in my room?"

42

"Oh, right. My name's Ignis. I'm going to be living here a while. You're Shiro, huh?"

Shiro blinked. He looked Ignis up and down. "Living *here*?"

"Just for a week." Ignis looked around. "You got a CD player we could put on?"

"A CD player?"

"No? How about a stereo? It's so quiet here it's freaking me out."

"No."

"A radio?"

Shiro shook his head.

"OK, then where's the TV?"

"I don't have a TV." Shiro looked at Ignis quizzically. "But where were you going to plug it in if you got one?"

"Into the— huh?" Ignis looked around. He couldn't see any power sockets. He bent to look under the bed and table. Nothing there. He walked to his room and did the same thing. Still nothing.

"Hey, what's going on?" he demanded, walking back out.

"Rokkaku doesn't have a lot of power. The wind generators on the lake shore don't provide much electricity, and we need all of it for the lights." Shiro nodded at the lampshade hanging from the ceiling and the reading lamp above the bed. "There are back-up generators above the kitchens, but they're only for emergencies."

"What? So what do you do all day?"

"Well – for one thing, we don't watch TV. Mr Oakley went over all this on the first day. Weren't you there?"

"I just got here."

"I can tell." Shiro looked at Ignis dubiously. "Are you sure you're a student?"

Ignis bristled. The tone in Shiro's voice seemed to suggest he didn't think Ignis was good enough. He didn't particularly want to be here, but even so . . . "I said I'm a student. Have you got a problem with that?"

Shiro raised his eyebrows, shrugged, and went back to his book.

Ignis looked around the room. There wasn't much to look at. "How come my room's smaller than yours?" he asked after a while.

"It's not." Shiro didn't look up. "This room is my bedroom and the shared room. You can use it as well."

"There's nothing in here to use." Ignis studied Shiro. "So you're Shiro Yoshimatsu?"

Shiro turned a page. "Yes."

Ignis looked at him. Shiro was tall and pale-skinned, with dark hair and eyes. "How come you have a Japanese name when you're not Japanese?"

Shiro turned another page.

"Hey. Didn't you hear what I said?"

Shiro spoke without looking up. "It's not polite to ask

44

questions like that."

"So I'm not polite."

"Yes. I noticed."

Ignis glared down at the boy, but Shiro sat quietly, reading. There was a rap at the window; Ignis looked up to see Allandra's face and walked out to join her.

"How's it going?" Allandra asked.

Ignis exhaled. "I've been in this place one hour and already I don't like it. Can we get something to eat?"

"That's why I came." Allandra pointed Ignis up the valley and they started to walk. Students were walking in the same direction ahead of them in twos and threes, crossing the bridges to head up into the trees. The sun was beginning to set, and dusk had fallen over the valley while Ignis had been inside. As they watched, sphere lamps flickered and came on between the houses, first one or two, then more and more until the valley was dotted with globes of pale light. On their own, none was bright enough to illuminate the valley, but collectively they cast a white radiance like a full moon. Each lamp had a hooded shield mounted above it that reflected the light down and sideways. From above, the spheres would be invisible. "Jennifer and Christopher told me that it's dinner time. The canteen's at the top of the valley. It lasts from six to seven-thirty."

"Then what?"

"Then everyone goes back to their rooms, I think. The lights go out at ten o'clock."

"This is ridiculous," Ignis growled.

"It beats getting caught by Vargas."

"If he's still looking for us."

Allandra's eyes were shadowed. "He will be."

Rhosmaen was growing quiet in the twilight. The black Land Rover was parked in the driveway of Tawelfan. The window through which the children had escaped was closed.

Pete stopped outside the kitchen door and swallowed. Bringing bad news to his boss made him nervous. He opened the door and walked in.

The kitchen was cold and dark despite a fire burning in the stove. Vargas was sitting at the end of the table. Icy blue eyes lifted to fix upon Pete as he entered. Pete came to a halt. Vargas waited.

"Uh," Pete began. "We've been all the way down the river. I don't reckon they went that far. I mean, we're sure. We've asked about. No one saw anything. So, uh – I guess they went up into the hills."

Vargas said nothing.

"There's a lot of hills. And it's getting dark. How about we—"

"Keep looking," Vargas said evenly.

"Uh." Pete hesitated. "It's real dark up there. We can't see much. If we just . . ." Vargas's eyes narrowed just slightly and Pete quickly changed tracks. "Right. Keep looking. You got it, boss. We'll find them." Pete backed out of the door, hurrying down the corridor into the back room. He let out a breath.

"Well?" Tav asked.

"He says keep looking."

"Hell." Tav's handsome face twisted. He disliked menial work of any kind, especially anything that involved dirtying his clothes. "More hours on that hill. They're miles away by now."

"You sure?" Pete asked dubiously.

"You think anybody would stay out in the middle of nowhere like this if they had the choice?" Tav grunted and stood up. "Fine. Let's get this over with. By tomorrow he'll have to set up a proper search. County police, probably. Then we can get out of this godforsaken place and back to London."

A voice spoke from above. "Um, Tav?"

Pete and Tav turned. Michael was hesitating at the top of the stairs.

"What do you want?" Tav said.

Michael swallowed. "Um . . . do you know where Ally—"

"Get out of here, you dumb brat!" Pete snapped. "You'll

47

know soon enough when I get my hands on them." Michael's eyes went wide and he fled. Pete turned to Tav with a scowl. "I hate these rugrats. Why wouldn't the boss let me teach that one a lesson?"

"Go ask him yourself."

Pete backed off. "Hey, man, I'm just saying. All he ever lets me do is hurt 'em a bit. He never lets me really teach 'em."

"Because he wants them whole, and you'd best not mess with that." Tav walked to the door, then looked back. "By tomorrow, we'll be back in London and Vargas'll have everything in place. There can't be more than a dozen villages they could have reached on foot from here. He'll have contacts in every one. And if they're still out along the river, the police or the rangers will find them. They'll be back soon."

"Then what?"

"Then he'll probably let you loose on the both of them, as long as you don't do any permanent damage."

Pete grinned. The motion stretched the skin of his face, showing an old scar down his left cheek and two missing teeth. His eyes glinted. "When I've finished with them, they ain't going to be running away no more. How long you think it'll be?"

Tav shrugged and pulled open the door. Pete followed him out into the darkness. "Who cares?" Tav said as they started walking down the road. "They have to surface sooner or later, and when they do he'll get them. It's just a matter of time."

2

THE NEW STUDENTS

"Wake up, Ignis."

Ignis opened one bleary eye to see Shiro looking down at him. "Go 'way."

"It's time to get up."

Ignis looked at the clock muzzily. "What time . . .? *Six in the morning?*"

"Yes, time to get up." Shiro's voice was impatient. "Come on, we're going to be late."

Ignis pulled the covers up past his head and rolled over. Dimly, he heard steps. Suddenly icy water poured onto his hair and pillow. Ignis jumped up as though he'd been electrocuted. Shiro was standing over him with an empty cup.

"What the hell?" Ignis shouted. His hair was dripping.

Shiro raised an eyebrow. "I told you. It's time to get up."

"You—! I'll kill you!"

"Get dressed first." Shiro tossed him a bundle of black cloth. "Here's your *gi*."

"What the hell is that?"

"It's your uniform," Shiro sighed. "And you probably don't know how to wear it either, do you?"

"You can take your gee and your clothes and—"

"Spare me." Shiro sighed again. "Look, I'll show you how to put it on if you'll just shut up."

There was a pair of black trousers, made of a thick, stiff canvas, and a black jacket of the same material with a red badge of Japanese characters on the left breast. A white belt like Shiro's went around the waist, tied with a special knot. The shoes were called *tabi*, and looked like a cross between slippers and boots: a close-fitting tube of soft fabric that came halfway up to his knee. The soles were made of rubber, and the front end was designed so that the big toe was kept separate from the other four. A line of thin metal tags along the side slipped into a row of thread loops, holding the *tabi* on tightly. Although the *tabi* were comfortable, the *gi* felt heavy and awkward. "This is too thick," Ignis complained as he pulled on the jacket.

"That's because it has to be tough enough for someone to pick you up and throw you with," Shiro answered. "And fold it left over right. The only time you fold it right over left is on a corpse."

Sulkily Ignis obeyed. "*Now* are we ready?"

Shiro nodded. "We're ready. Time for your first day."

Rokkaku was still dark: the rising sun was hidden by the

eastern hills. A crowd of students was massing at the bottom of the valley. Shiro led Ignis down a log and around the path to the edge of the crowd. A boy and a girl were standing a little apart: it was Christopher and Allandra. Allandra waved as Ignis came close. Clad in the black *gi*, her gold hair and white belt stood out brightly; the rest seemed to disappear into the shadows. Shiro nodded to Christopher. "Hi, Chris. Where's Jennifer?"

Christopher grinned. "Staying out of sight. After that stunt she pulled with Ichiro, she doesn't want him to see her until he's had a chance to forget about it."

"He doesn't forget that easily," Shiro replied.

Suddenly the crowd began to move. Ignis looked at Shiro. "What's going on?"

"Morning run. Think you can handle it?"

Ignis watched the first students break into a jog and shrugged. "Course."

Twenty minutes later, Ignis staggered to a tree and clutched at it for support, panting. Shiro looked over his shoulder, then loped back. "Can you keep going?"

"Give me . . . a second." Ignis sucked in air. "You do this . . . *every day*?"

"Yes. I thought you said you were fit."

Ignis glared at him. "You didn't say . . . we were going through the *forest*!"

Trees were packed all around them. They'd been running for twenty minutes, and Ignis was pretty sure that they hadn't crossed a single bit of flat ground since they'd set off. Everything was either up, down, around a tree, or all three at once, and his lungs felt as though they'd been dipped in acid. He had only Shiro to trust that they were going in the right direction – the others had vanished out of sight long ago.

"Well, if you can't handle it, go back."

"Listen, you . . ." Ignis snarled, but Shiro was already running up the hill. Taking a deep breath, Ignis forced himself forward.

As he came over the crest of the hill, the trees suddenly stopped and there was nothing but stumps. Dead branches were littered underfoot, making running harder, if anything. Allandra was sitting on a stump in front of him, panting. Shiro was standing nearby. He didn't even look out of breath. Ignis finally staggered to a stop, staring out over the scene before them.

Shiro pointed forward. "Llyn Garedig."

Laid out below was a vast expanse of water. Llyn Garedig was a reservoir, a man-made lake created by the dam that formed a grey line at the far end of the valley. A long embankment made up three-quarters of the dam's length; at the far end, a spillway dropped down out of sight, spanned by a concrete bridge. There were no beaches: the edges of the valley dropped sheerly into the lake, giving the huge expanse of dark water a strange, dramatic appearance. Over the eastern hills ahead of them shone the first rays of the morning sun, reflecting off the lake and turning its waters into a glittering panoply of silver and white. The sky was blue, clear, and cold, with the last stars of the night fading in the west.

Even though Ignis's legs and lungs were burning from the run, the view still took his breath away. He stood staring at the beauty of the scene before them. He'd never seen anything like it before.

Allandra stirred. "OK, it's great. When do we start training?"

Shiro had been looking out at the view, a relaxed expression on his face. He looked down at Allandra and shrugged. "Soon. We've finished the warm-up." He loped down the hill in long strides.

Ignis and Allandra looked at each other in disbelief. "The *what*?"

As soon as they got back there was half an hour of stretching, with a teacher guiding them through a series of positions that they had to hold for a minute each. Nearly everyone in the class was more flexible than Ignis, and he had to struggle to match even the slowest of the other students. Then they split up for breakfast, heading for the canteen. It was the biggest building in Rokkaku, built over the stream and into both sides of the valley, at the upper end of the school. The food – rice and something that looked like fish-balls – was strange to Ignis, but he was too hungry to be picky.

The bell chimed as he walked out of the doors into the morning sun. Shiro was nearby, and Ignis walked over to him, yawning. "So, what's next?"

"Lessons."

Five minutes later, at the opposite end of Rokkaku in one of the valley-side houses, Ignis leaned from his desk to hiss at Shiro, "*Maths* lessons?"

"Uh-huh."

"What's going on? I thought this was ninja school? Why are we learning stupid—"

"Ignis, if I could have your attention, please?"

Ignis jerked upright. The Maths teacher was looking at him, eyebrows raised. "Did you have something to say?"

"Uh, no."

"Good. Then you can demonstrate the next problem at the board."

Ignis looked at the signs on the whiteboard – none of which meant anything to him – and groaned. At the end of the lesson, the teacher called him to his desk and gave him a sheet of algebra problems to solve for the next day.

After Maths came History, and after History came English. In each one Ignis found himself behind, and he was given a History chapter to read and a long poem to produce a spoken report on for the next day.

"When am I supposed to do all this?" he demanded of Shiro at morning break.

"In your free time. Classes finish at four, so you have plenty of time for homework."

"Homework? Since when is there homework?"

"Every night, unless you get it done during the day. If you have trouble with Maths, ask Christopher, he's the resident Maths genius. Better do it later, though, the next lesson's starting."

Like the first three, the lesson was in one of the bigger buildings cut into the sides of the valley. "Doesn't anyone use the ones up there?" Ignis asked Shiro, pointing at the houses in the trees. "That was where I woke up."

Shiro looked up. "The high houses? The sixth-formers live in some of them, and the teachers live in a few more. The rest are used as classrooms, but only for the upper years. But there are always a few spare or being rebuilt, so if someone shows up unexpectedly like you, they often get put in one of them. You were lucky to see them – we're not normally allowed up there."

"Who's 'we'? And who says?"

Shiro raised his eyebrows as they filed into the class-

56

room. " 'We' means our class, the first years. And the ones who say so are the teachers, unless you want to be put on kitchen chores."

The teacher wasn't in the classroom yet, so Ignis took the chance to get a good look at the rest of the first-year class. A knot of Japanese boys were talking quietly under their breath against the opposite wall, while a bigger boy with a stiff, controlled manner leaned back on his chair. When he spoke, the others fell silent.

"Hey," Ignis said quietly to Shiro, "is that Ichiro?"

Shiro gave a single nod and looked away. Ignis looked at him in surprise, then shrugged and turned to Allandra, who had entered and sat down on his right.

"Hey, Ally. How come you're in my class?" Allandra was a full year younger than him.

Allandra grinned. "This is the beginner's class. It doesn't matter what age you are."

Ignis took another look around. There were twenty-seven in the class in all – twenty-nine, counting him and Allandra. About a third were Japanese, the rest were a mix of British and other nationalities. Most looked a year or two younger than him, although there were two or three that could be his age. There were only a few girls. Everyone wore the same black *gis* and white belts.

Jennifer hurried in late, out of breath, bringing the number up to thirty. Ichiro narrowed his eyes as she passed. The teacher bustled in just as Jennifer sat down.

He was a middle-aged man, with a mop of grey-white hair and a pair of glasses perched on his nose, behind which two round brown eyes looked out amiably. Although he wore the same *gi* and black belt that the other teachers did, on him it somehow looked less like a martial arts uniform and more like a set of scholars' clothes. He was the oddest mixture of disarray and good nature Ignis had ever seen. His name was Mr Oakley.

"Ah, there you are. Forgive me for being late, there was an essay that quite held my attention." Even his voice was scholarly. "How are all of you?"

"Tired!" a girl piped up from the back of the class.

"Tired? Oh, yes. You were learning *sanshin* in *taijutsu* class, weren't you?"

"More like not learning it," a voice muttered from somewhere.

"Ze'ev wouldn't let us go no matter how long we trained," Christopher complained. "It wasn't till after dark that he said we could stop. And we still have to go back again on Saturday."

Mr Oakley chuckled. "Yes, Ze'ev isn't one for soft practice. I did give you advance warning of that, class, as you should recall. In comparison to the sort of training Ze'ev went through, what you did yesterday was a walk in the park."

"But why do we have to do it anyway?" Christopher persisted. "I mean, sanshen—"

"*Sanshin*." Mr Oakley held up his finger. "*Sanshin no kata*. The three hearts form."

"*Sanshin*," Christopher said patiently. "I thought we only learned things that were effective? I mean, when's someone going to walk up to you and try to hit you in the ribs when you're sticking your hand in the air?"

Mr Oakley waved his hand. "Never, of course. But that isn't why you're studying the classical forms. After all, it's rare that you'll be expected to perform a quadratic equation in real life, but that isn't why you study them in Mathematics. Hmm. You haven't started learning quadratic equations yet, have you? No, no, of course you haven't. For a moment there I thought you were the fifth-year class. There's a boy there who was asking something very similar about the *shimewaza* technique that was demonstrated last year at the Tai Kai. None of you were there, were you? I really must arrange for you all to go next year. There's a simply wonderful—"

One of the boys coughed.

Mr Oakley blinked. "Oh, yes. *Sanshin*. What you have to remember, Christopher, is that you're only at the beginning of a long course. It's principles you're studying, not techniques. Now, you will almost certainly go your entire life without using one of the five *sanshin no kata* in

59

earnest, but by practising them you learn ways of moving and holding yourself that you will build on in later training. You could easily study more specific techniques which would be more practical to try and apply in combat, but if your training wholly comprised that you'd always be relying on your opponent to attack in a way which you'd been trained to deal with. If you learn the principles behind the techniques, on the other hand, you can adapt them as you see fit. It's rather like constructing a house. Do any of you know anything about building? No? Honestly, I wonder what they teach you these days. When one's building a house, the first thing one has to establish is good foundations – it doesn't matter what they're made of, just as long as they're solid. Then you can build the rest of the house on those. If you try to build the house first and put in the foundations afterwards, then what happens? Not only do you get a shoddy construction, but it takes you twice as much work just to keep it from falling down."

Christopher leaned forward, his dark eyes intense. "But why do you always have to learn these things through something useless? Why can't they teach us how to move with techniques that would actually be useful?"

Before Mr Oakley could answer, Ichiro stood up, bowing. "*Sensei*."

"Yes, Ichiro?"

"*Sensei*, is it not true that *Kancho* Nishiyama has

approved the first-year training requirements?"

Mr Oakley nodded. "Yes, Ichiro, he has."

Ichiro nodded and sat down. Another Japanese boy stood up. "*Sensei*."

"Yes, Hiroshi?"

"*Sensei*, will you be spending this lesson suggesting changes to our training regime?"

"No, Hiroshi, I will not be 'suggesting changes' to your training. I am giving you an explanation, not a set of instructions. In any case, Nishiyama mentioned to me yesterday that the level of knowledge amongst students of the martial arts regarding their predecessors had declined in comparison to past centuries."

Ignis frowned, trying to figure out what he'd just heard. Mr Oakley's eyes rested on him. "You appear puzzled, Ignis. By the way, how has your first day been?"

"I won't know for a while," Ignis answered.

"I look forward to your opinions. Did you not quite follow?"

"No."

Mr Oakley smiled. His eyes crinkled as he did, making his face look rather like a walnut, and Ignis had to bite back a laugh. "Ah, I see you have not yet been tutored in Japanese reserve. What Nishiyama meant by that comment was that he thinks I spend too much time letting you argue about *dojo* training and not enough on teaching

61

the history of ninjutsu, which is, in theory at least, the purpose of this class. And on that subject," Mr Oakley looked around, "how many of you would be confident in explaining the origins of the groups that between them influenced the founding of ninjutsu, a subject upon which you would all be eminent experts had you read the chapters I set you on Monday?"

Four or five hands crept up. One was Christopher's; the rest were Japanese.

Mr Oakley sighed. "About what I expected. Well then, listen. The first group enter the story with the fall of the T'ang dynasty in China in the eleventh century. Fleeing the collapse, small groups of warriors, scholars and monks reached the remote provinces of southern Japan. They brought military, cultural and religious ideas from all over Asia – from Tibet, India, and even eastern Europe. Their influence was pivotal in creating the second group: the Shugenja, practisers of a religion called Shugendo. They were mountain priests, Animists, with a reverence for nature and animals, similar to the American Indians. You do know who *they* were, don't you? Good. These two groups, combined with older traditions among the Japanese peasantry, developed into what we now call the ninja. Remember, though, that the ninja of those days did not think of themselves as ninja. As far as they were concerned, they were just people with views that differed from those of the majority. The ruling class of Japan at that time were the samurai, and ninjutsu developed as a highly illegal counter-culture to the accepted beliefs of the majority of Japan. Over time, the ninjas' ways and methods of survival came to be known as *Shinobi*, then as *ninpo*, and finally, by the name we use now, ninjutsu . . ."

"Well, that was weird," Ignis commented as they left at the end of the lesson.

"Actually, I liked him," Allandra said hesitantly. "Not that I know him, but . . ."

Ignis shrugged. "I guess."

"Whew, we're clear!" Jennifer jumped in next to them. "Ichiro has English language, so we're safe for a bit."

"If he has English, what do we have?" Allandra asked.

Jennifer grinned. "Japanese. You'll love it."

Ignis put his hand over his eyes.

". . . And then he asked if I even knew what a subject and an onject were, and when I said I didn't, he gave me this to read!" Ignis hefted a grammar textbook. It was lunch hour, and he, Allandra, Jennifer, Christopher and Shiro were sitting around a table in the canteen. The big room bustled with activity, students calling out and waving to each other over the racket and jostling for space at the packed tables.

"Object," Christopher corrected with an amused look.

"You think yours is bad?" Allandra complained. "I got set enough Maths problems to keep me busy for a week. You got off easy."

"Didn't you do all this stuff at school?" Christopher asked, absentmindedly blocking Jennifer from stealing a forkful of his rice.

Ignis slammed the book down on the table. "No! We hardly even went to—" He stopped abruptly. Explaining why they had left half a dozen schools and been taught only by a series of private tutors, none of whom had lasted longer than a month, would raise questions he didn't want to answer.

Jennifer giggled. "You look like the *neko* when you bristle like that." She made another approach at Christopher's lunch, only to be intercepted once more. "Oh, come on, Chris. I'm hungry."

"What's a *neko*?" Ignis demanded.

"You've already eaten all your food. Leave me mine." Christopher pushed his tray further away from Jennifer and looked across at Allandra. "You still have the evening, you know."

"The evening?" Allandra looked dismayed. "I thought after four o'clock was free time?"

"Oh yes, free time," said Christopher with a grin. "I've

heard of that. I think it's something you get after about twenty years, when you finally catch up with everything you're expected to know. It's bad enough for us, and we don't have the first three weeks of term to catch up on. What with homework, extra training, and Hunts, the only *real* free time you get is at the weekends, and that's only after you've caught up with everything you didn't manage during the week. I think they're trying to keep us too busy to miss our computers."

"Computers? What about our phones?" Jennifer complained. She made a try for the last few bits of Shiro's food. Shiro pulled his plate away.

"Phones if you're you. The only mercy is they don't allow training on Sundays."

"Saturday mornings are fair game, though," Shiro added. He put his knife and fork down and rose. "Well, I'm off to meet Ze'ev."

Jennifer looked at him wide-eyed. "Ze'ev? You have made a will, haven't you?"

Shiro shrugged. "Good practice."

"Hey!" Ignis called. "What's a *neko*?"

"Some story from somewhere," Shiro said over his shoulder as he walked away.

Jennifer sighed as he vanished into the crowd. "He's gone. Another one lost to the bottomless pit of keen students. What is it about this place that turns perfectly normal people into workaholics? He hardly ever even talks."

Christopher grinned. "I think he was like that before he came here."

"You can't take the chance. The food's probably drugged." Before Christopher could react, Jennifer grabbed his tray. "I'll have to taste it for your own safety. Hmm." She chewed thoughtfully. "It tastes OK. Still, I'd better make sure."

By the time Christopher managed to get his meal back, half of it was gone.

Physical training was in the afternoons. Over lunch, Christopher had told Ignis and Allandra that the long buildings built over the stream were *dojo*s: training halls. They were used all year round, although occasionally, in good weather, classes were conducted in clearings in the forest.

"Finally!" Allandra exhaled as they approached the *dojo* with the rest of the first years. "We get to learn something useful!"

"You were the one who signed us up for this," Ignis pointed out.

"Well, this was why." Allandra's eyes were bright. Ignis looked at her dubiously. When Allandra had announced her grand plan to defeat their father and rescue Michael,

Ignis had assumed that his sister would have forgotten all about it in the morning. She seemed to be taking it more seriously than he'd expected.

The *dojo* was made out of wooden planks and a floor of some kind of rubbery material. Without being told, the students formed up in three lines, kneeling. Their teacher knelt in front of them and placed her hands together. The class bowed and said some words in Japanese. Not knowing what they meant yet, Ignis mumbled along with the rest. There was a brief warm-up and some stretches, then the class proper began.

The first class was gymnastics. Their teacher was called Yarnya, a compact woman with fair skin, dark blonde hair and an Eastern European accent. She was sharp with the students when they made mistakes, which was often. Their first task was learning breakfalls, and both Allandra and Ignis were set to practising, learning to turn the fall into an arc so that they went down smoothly. Each time Ignis froze up or forgot something, he hit the floor. Relax, Yarnya told Ignis again and again, but before long his back and legs were covered with bruises. Next, they were set to practising rolls.

"What's the point of this?" Ignis asked, annoyed.

"A roll turns a downwards motion into a sideways one." Yarnya's expression was stern. "It softens a fall. Until you learn to roll perfectly, you cannot be trusted to practise techniques. Now, try again. Lower your weight, place both hands on the ground, tuck your head in, and go down upon your shoulder. Your *shoulder*, Allandra."

Allandra had done a neat, symmetrical roll over her neck. "But that's how I was taught to do it," she protested.

"That is a gymnastics roll. Fine if you are on a mat, but it places too much weight on the back of your neck. You will hurt yourself if you do that on concrete. Your shoulder this time, and imagine you are curling yourself up into a ball. I'll check on you in ten minutes."

Yarnya strode on to the next group, leaving them to practise. Allandra, with her gymnastics training, started to pick it up before long, but Ignis couldn't even master the basic form by the time the bell rang for the end of the class.

The bell rang again. The next lesson was *taijutsu* – unarmed combat – taught by a quick-moving Japanese man who introduced himself as Mr Akamatsu. Punchbags were brought out, and they started practising strikes. Ignis had never thought that throwing a punch could be difficult, but he quickly found that a punch was only one of dozens of strikes he was expected to use. He was also expected to know how to hit with his middle knuckles, with his toes, with the ball of his foot, with the heel of his hand, and even with the tips of his fingers. Ignis's hands were aching after an hour, and at the end Mr Akamatsu called him aside, gave Ignis a sheet of paper with descriptions of the various striking techniques and their Japanese names, and told him to memorise it.

The next class was evasion, and the students were partnered off. One person would throw a punch, and the other would have to avoid it without backing away or using his hands. The teacher started off by showing them one way to move away from the attack, set the students to practise, then after a few minutes told them to stop and showed them a different movement. In between, he would walk around the sparring couples and give corrections and orders. Because Ignis was new, he was singled out for special attention. His partner, a stocky Japanese boy, showed no expression, pulling his blows whenever Ignis failed to get out of the way. Mr Akamatsu, however, seemed to be always looking over Ignis's shoulder, telling him to do a dozen things at once. His weight wasn't low enough. He needed to move more smoothly. "Punch through the target, not at it. Don't blink when the fist comes towards your face. Keep your head at the same level when you move. Slide, don't rise and fall."

Before long, Ignis's head was spinning. "This doesn't make any sense!" he snapped. "How am I supposed to do all these things at once?"

"With practice," Mr Akamatsu said cheerfully. "And report back here to the *dojo* after dinner. You need to learn stances."

Ignis stared, his jaw dropping, but Mr Akamatsu moved on to correct Allandra without waiting for a reply.

When the four o'clock bell finally rang, Ignis was staggering. He was too tired to even be annoyed at Jennifer's chatter as the short girl led Allandra away to the girls' washrooms. Ignis hit the showers and collapsed back in his room. He fell asleep over the sheet of striking names, and was only woken when Shiro arrived to take him up to dinner.

After dinner came the extra class in the *dojo*. There were fourteen basic *kamae* – stances – in ninjutsu, from the *shizen* position, standing with his arms by his sides, to the defensive *ichi mongi*, the more aggressive *jumonji*, and *seiza*, which was simply sitting on his ankles with his knees together. A dozen times Ignis was on the point of flaring up and storming out of the door, but his promise to Allandra held him. Mr Akamatsu remained in good humour no matter how many mistakes Ignis made. He finally let Ignis go when he could repeat the names of all fourteen stances and get them half right, but reminded Ignis as he left that if he couldn't do them well enough by tomorrow, he'd have to stay behind to do it again.

By the time Ignis got back to his and Shiro's room, he wanted nothing but to go to sleep. He persisted with the list of strikes for half an hour before throwing it across the room in frustration. He pulled off his *gi* and sank into bed.

When the bell woke him the next morning, Ignis groaned. His muscles were stiff and aching, the back of his neck hurt from rolling on it the day before, and he was spotted with bruises all over. Feeling Shiro's gaze on him, Ignis forced himself up and down the hill for the morning run, hoping that this day wouldn't be as bad as the last.

It was worse. He'd forgotten to do the English and Maths homework, so the teachers made him spend his lunch hour hammering away at algebra and poetry. The afternoon was hideous. Because he was stiff and clumsy, he made more mistakes in training, tore a muscle in gymnastics, and did the stances just as badly as the day before, with the result that Mr Akamatsu kept him behind after class a second time.

By the time the dinner bell rang, Ignis was tired, hurt, and out of patience. He'd taken this for as long as he was going to. Ignis stormed into his rooms to find Shiro. "OK, who's in charge of the first year?"

Shiro looked up from a book. "Mr Oakley."

"Where does he live?"

"Just past the fifth *dojo*, on the right side." Shiro's eyes travelled over Ignis. "Did you want something?"

"All I want is to leave."

Shiro nodded as though he hadn't expected anything else. "Goodbye."

Ignis felt a flash of anger, then turned on his heel. It wasn't worth the effort.

Yellow light glowed from the *dojo*s in the gathering dusk, and the sounds of people training came from the open doors. Ignis limped slightly as he crossed the bridge, the thin wooden logs rattling under his feet. Fortunately, Mr Oakley's room was on the lowest level; Ignis wouldn't have been able to manage a climb. He knocked and entered as a voice from inside called, "Come in."

Shelves covered the walls, packed with books, curios, ornaments, and yet more books. The books overflowed from the shelves onto the chairs, fighting with stacks of paper for space on the seats and the three heavily loaded tables. Mr Oakley was perched in an armchair, studying a yellowing document with a magnifying glass. "Oh – Ignis, isn't it? Pleased to see you. I've just found the most fascinating thing—"

Ignis cut in. "I'm going to leave."

Mr Oakley blinked and seemed to come awake. He picked up his glasses and adjusted them on his nose, scrutinising Ignis carefully. Ignis stared defiantly back.

"You want to leave?"

"I said I'm *going* to leave, whether you let me or not."

"Of course you can leave if you want to, dear boy. This isn't a prison." Mr Oakley looked mildly at Ignis. "Might I ask why?"

"Why? Because this place is insane!" Ignis paced up and down the study. "I'm working from dawn to dusk! I've never done half the stuff in the lessons, and I'm expected to be an expert at it; I get homework in every class even though this is supposed to be a martial arts school; my free time's a joke; and there's no TV! And if I say anything about it I get set more work!"

Mr Oakley regarded him quizzically. "Yes?"

"What do you mean, 'yes'? Why should I bother to do all this stuff? Instead of learning how to fight, I'm learning Maths and English! It's a waste of time. I don't want to do all this useless work, I want to do something fun! I want—"

"You want, you want, you want. You're learning something different here, Ignis. It's called discipline. The world won't always arrange itself to your desires, and the routine here is designed to teach you that." Mr Oakley studied him. "And as regards your desire to learn to fight, a ninja is not just a fighter. A true ninja is a warrior philosopher, an exemplar of the benevolent heart. *That* is the essence of what you are taught here, not how to hurt or maim. A man who knows only how to fight is not a warrior, he is a thug. What you are given here is a real education, not a programme to turn you into a killer."

Ignis laughed. "An education? I know what that's worth."

Mr Oakley's eyes hardened. "I very much doubt that you do. An education gives you the ability to think, to understand, and to benefit from the culture you live in. The Mathematics, English and History classes that you think so little of are the gateway to all of those things. What they teach you, you need to know – no matter how you choose to spend your life."

Ignis thought of his father, and his profession. "I already know what I need to."

Mr Oakley raised his eyebrows. "Really? Thirteen years old and you've already figured out everything that you need? What a remarkably knowledgeable child you must be."

Ignis scowled. "This isn't worth the trouble. Why should I do what all you teachers tell me? Anyway, it's too hard."

"It *is* hard." Mr Oakley sighed and pointed to one of the chairs. "Sit down. You can shift the books onto the floor. No, not that one. Put it on the shelf. Yes, there." Resentfully, Ignis did as he said, then glared at him, ready to leave at a moment's notice. Mr Oakley didn't seem to notice. He adjusted his glasses and leaned forward.

"Listen to me, Ignis. Contrary to what you seem to believe, the teachers here in Rokkaku are trying to help you, not hurt you. They are pushing you hard because they are trying to lift you to a very high standard. The goal we hold up for the students here is to match the strength and the skill of the ninja of feudal Japan, and the academic standards of a top-rank school. The work is hard because the goal is hard. The ancient ninja trained themselves to a level that we would find almost incredible nowadays. It wasn't for nothing that they acquired a reputation as invincible warriors. The standards we will hold you to are not nearly so high, but even so, if you stay, you will have to work harder than you ever have before. Most schools set their students less work in a week than we expect from you in two days. Not everyone can handle it. The drop-out rate for even the first year of this school runs to fifty per cent. For every ten boys and girls that put on the white belt, five of them leave before the summer. To stay through to the very end is a commitment few are capable of."

"What if I don't want to?" Ignis demanded.

Mr Oakley tilted his head. "Then leave." He picked up his magnifying glass again and held it over the document he had been studying. "If you are quite certain that you wish to go, come back here tomorrow morning. I'll arrange your trip home." Ignis stood and looked down at him, then abruptly turned and walked out.

Shiro didn't look up as Ignis walked through the shared room, and slammed the door to his own bedroom. Ignis dropped flat onto his bed and stared at the ceiling. His body already hurt from two days' training. The thought of an entire week of it made him shudder. And he was sick of the teachers telling him what to do. He and Allandra and Michael shouldn't have to be ordered around by anybody. He ought to go and find Allandra, get out of here, and—

And what?

That was the catch.

He and Allandra had nowhere to go except back home. That was what had always doomed their escape attempts to failure. Getting away from Vargas and Pete and Tav was one thing. Staying on the run, trying to dodge his father's men and the police and anyone who might report them missing, while still finding places to eat and sleep . . . that was all but impossible. They had got clean away from home half a dozen times in the past two years, and Vargas *always* found them, always tracked them down no matter where they went, because once they got away there was almost nothing they could do except wait for him to find them. Ignis wouldn't admit it, but he had never really believed that any of their escape plans would work. For Allandra, their escapes had been her hope for the future; she was the one who meticulously planned and prepared, when Ignis would have been ready to walk out of the door and take his chances. For Ignis, the escapes had always been more about getting back at his father than about getting away from him.

He rose and walked about his room, trying to decide what to do. The paper above the bed caught his eye and he looked closer. It read:

Ninjutsu Hiketsu Bun

The essay on the essence of Ninjutsu by Takamatsu Toshitsugu, 33rd Soke in Togakure Ryu Ninjutsu

The essence of all martial arts and military strategies is self-protection and the prevention of danger. Ninjutsu epitomises the fullest concept of self-protection through martial training in that the ninja art deals with the protection of not only the physical body, but the mind and spirit as well. The way of the ninja is the way of enduring, surviving, and prevailing over all that would destroy one. More than merely delivering strikes and slashes, and deeper in significance than the simple outwitting of an enemy; ninjutsu is the way of attaining that which we need while making the world a better place.

The skill of the ninja is the art of winning. In the beginning study of any combative art, proper motivation is crucial. Without the proper frame of mind, continuous exposure to fighting techniques

77

can lead to ruin instead of self-development. But this fact is not different from any other beneficial practice in life carried to extremes.

Medical science is dedicated to the betterment of health and the relief of suffering, and yet the misuse of drugs and the exaltation of the physician's skills can lead people to a state where an individual's health is no longer within his or her personal control. A nutritious, well-balanced diet works to keep a person alive, vital and healthy, but grossly over-eating, overdrinking or taking in too many chemicals is a sure way to poison the body.

Governments are established to oversee the harmonious inter-working of all parts of society, but when the rulers become greedy, hungry for power or lacking in wisdom, the country is subjected to needless wars, disorder or civil and economic chaos.

A religion, when based on faith developed through experience, a broad and questing mind and unflagging pursuit of universal understanding, is of inspiration and comfort to people. Once a religion loses its original focus, however, it becomes a deadly thing with which to deceive, control and tax the people through the manipulation of their beliefs and fears.

It is the same with the martial arts. The skills of self-protection, which should provide a feeling of inner peace and security for the martial artist, so often develop without a balance in the personality and lead the lesser martial artist into warped realms of unceasing conflict and competition which eventually consume him.

If an expert in the fighting arts sincerely pursues the essence of ninjutsu, devoid of the influence of the ego's desires, the student will progressively come to realise the ultimate secret for becoming invincible – the attainment of the "mind and eyes of God". The combatant who would win must be in harmony with the scheme of totality, and must be guided by an intuitive knowledge of the playing out of fate.

In tune with the providence of heaven and the impartial justice of nature, and following a clear and pure heart full of trust in the inevitable, the ninja captures the insight that will guide him successfully into battle: when he must conquer and conceal himself protectively from hostility; when he must acquiesce.

The vast universe, beautiful in its coldly impersonal totality, contains all that we call good or bad, all the answers for all the paradoxes we see around us. By opening his eyes and his mind, the ninja can responsively follow the subtle seasons and reasons of heaven, changing just as change is necessary, adapting always, so that in the end there is no such thing as a surprise for the ninja.

Ignis read the essay through. When he had finished, he frowned in puzzlement. It wasn't the sort of thing he was used to reading, and much of what it said was strange to him. He read it through a second time, more carefully. As he did, Ignis felt a strange feeling stir somewhere inside him, as though someone was trying to tell him something. He shook his head, turned away, and stared out of the window at the night valley.

He thought of the big house back in Hampstead and the grey dullness of his life there, living under the ever-present shadow of fear cast by Vargas's iron rule. Going back had always seemed inevitable. What if there was some way to stay away?

He opened the door and looked out at Shiro. "OK, I'm staying."

Shiro nodded.

"Just for one week. Then I'm leaving."

"Are you sure?"

"Yes. One week, then I'm gone. There's no way I'm staying any longer . . . What are you smiling at?"

Shiro smoothed his face. "Oh, nothing. Welcome to Rokkaku."

3

LIFE IN THE VALLEY

The one week became two weeks, and the two weeks became three. Ignis was too tired to think of leaving, and Allandra never mentioned it. Several times Ignis was on the point of bringing it up, but something always made him put it off further and further until he finally forgot about it.

Living with a roommate was a new experience for Ignis. It would have been less jarring had Shiro been like Allandra or Michael, talkative and familiar; but Shiro was neither. The tall, slim boy was a silent enigma. He never discussed his family or his background. When Ignis demanded to know anything, Shiro would simply act as though he hadn't heard, and neither demands, insults, nor shouting would stir him. Not only would Shiro not answer personal questions, he wouldn't ask them either. He made no queries about Ignis's family, or why they were even here – as though it were normal for students to be dropped off at a school unconscious and injured. Ignis knew that he ought to be pleased at Shiro's lack of curiosity – the less people asking questions about him and Allandra, the better

– but instead, he found Shiro's aloof reserve irritating. It was as though he thought himself better than everyone else. Once Ignis had a chance to see Shiro in class, his dislike grew stronger. Shiro excelled in all subjects, doing almost casually what Ignis couldn't manage no matter how many times he tried. If Shiro had boasted about it, it would have been easier to handle, but instead Shiro seemed to avoid drawing attention to himself, completing all the set tasks quickly and quietly. Somehow this lack of display infuriated Ignis all the more.

Allandra seemed to be getting on better with Jennifer and Christopher, from what Ignis could see. Jennifer was a ball of energy, always up to something and in trouble with the teachers more often than not. She and Christopher had been best friends for years, and the two of them were almost always together.

Afternoon classes were split between *taijutsu* – hand-to-hand fighting – and other skills. Gymnastics, taught by Yarnya, took up three hours a week. Once everyone had learned to breakfall, the focus of the class shifted to rolling. There were five basic rolls, and they had to master each and every one of them before they would be allowed to practise throwing and sweeping techniques. Swimming was conducted in the cold waters of Llyn Garedig, in a bay out of sight of the roads, and climbing class started with trees and moved on to the disused quarry in the northern woods. Then there was *tongyo*, or stealth, class. The teacher for this was Mr Morimoto, a small, soft-voiced man who hardly spoke. The class was always held outside, even when rain had made the grass slippery and footprints easy to follow. Half the class would be assigned as sentries, the other half as infiltrators. The infiltrators would have to slip through the ring of sentries to Mr Morimoto, standing in the centre of the clearing. Anyone who made it all the way through would be quietly congratulated, followed by a listing of every twig, leaf, or blade of grass they had rustled.

It was the *taijutsu* that was the focus of the teaching, however, and it was these lessons that were the most taxing. There were the fourteen *kamae*, and the sixteen strikes, and the five movements within *sanshin*. There was the trick of how to slide away from a punch without seeming to dodge, how to measure the reach of an opponent and stand just outside it, and how to move when striking so that the blow landed with the weight of all one's body instead of only the arm. Everything was practised over and over again. The teachers were exacting, refusing to let them go on to actual fighting techniques until they had perfected the basic movements.

Nearly everyone in the class, apart from Ignis and Allandra, seemed to have had some kind of martial arts training before coming to Rokkaku. Ichiro and his friends were especially good, and watching how fast they learned, Ignis felt slow and clumsy. On top of the strictness of the routine, it was one thing too many for Ignis to put up with. Finally he snapped.

It was after the last *taijutsu* class of the evening. The students were starting to drift away, with only half a dozen or so left in the *dojo*. Ichiro and one of his friends, a stocky boy called Hiroshi, were passing Ignis on their way to the door, talking in Japanese. Hiroshi said something to Ichiro, who laughed.

It was enough to push Ignis over the edge. He jumped to his feet. "What was that?"

Ichiro and Hiroshi turned to look at him. "Hello?" Hiroshi asked.

"What did you just say?"

Hiroshi glanced quickly at Ichiro, then looked back at Ignis. "A private conversation."

"Tell me what you just said, or . . ."

Hiroshi looked at Ignis in annoyance. "Or what?"

Ignis took a threatening step forward. For an instant Hiroshi stopped in surprise, then he stepped smoothly backwards into stance, his expression shifting as he watched Ignis closely. Ignis tensed, ready to leap.

"Stop where you are!"

Ignis and Hiroshi froze. Mr Oakley was striding through the doorway towards them, and this time the expression on

85

his face was neither vague nor good-natured. Ichiro and Hiroshi straightened and took a step back. The other students in the *dojo* faded quickly away.

Mr Oakley stopped in front of them, glaring at Hiroshi and Ignis. "Well? Explain yourselves."

Ignis hesitated. Then, unexpectedly, Hiroshi spoke up. "Training, *sensei*."

"What training?"

"We were practising the *Kihon Happo*, *sensei*."

Mr Oakley snapped his eyes to Ignis. "Really?"

"Uh – yes. I asked Hiroshi to show me one of the techniques. Sir," he added as an afterthought.

Mr Oakley studied both of them. His brown eyes were sharp. "Well," he announced after a pause. "And do you think you've mastered this . . . technique now, Ignis?"

"Um – yes, sir."

"Then you can leave the *dojo* free for others to use."

Ignis and Hiroshi nodded, and started to go. Mr Oakley held up a hand. "Ignis." He looked down at him, his eyes hard. "I do not want to see you performing any further out-of-class 'training'. Understand?"

Both Ignis and Hiroshi nodded. Mr Oakley pointed. "Out!"

Once they were outside the *dojo*, Ignis gave Hiroshi a curious look. "Why did you do that?"

Ichiro was already walking away. Hiroshi looked back

at Ignis for a moment before speaking. "Because I don't need the teachers' help to protect myself from you." He turned and followed Ichiro.

Ignis watched the two of them go, then shrugged and went back to his room.

Slowly and reluctantly, Ignis began to settle into Rokkaku's routine. He still wasn't willing to try as hard as Allandra, who was studying the *taijutsu* as though her life depended on it, but he followed most of the rules. The work was difficult, however, and he did only what was demanded, cutting corners whenever he thought the teachers wouldn't notice.

But if Ignis and Allandra were finding the routine difficult, others were finding it impossible. As the days passed, faces began to disappear from the morning runs, and students would be sent to tidy up rooms that were now unoccupied. The numbers in the class dwindled from thirty to twenty-five, and from twenty-five to twenty. Jennifer's roommate was one of the first to go. Her departure left Jennifer and Allandra as the only first-year girls, and Allandra was moved into Jennifer's room.

Like normal schools, Rokkaku had three terms: autumn, spring, and summer. Ignis and Allandra had arrived three weeks into the autumn term. Something called the "Hunt" was supposed to begin in the spring, but for now, as

September faded into October and the leaves turned brown on the trees, it was all Ignis could manage to try and catch up on what he and Allandra had missed. Unfortunately, new things kept being added on.

"So *where* are we supposed to be going?" Ignis asked Christopher as they walked in single file through the forest.

"Balance class," Christopher answered. "I thought Allandra told you?"

Ignis shrugged. The truth was, with the insane workload, practically the only time he saw Allandra was in class and at meals, and when he did she was usually talking with Jennifer, leaving Ignis with no one to talk to but Christopher. Christopher was one of the clever students, usually reading, and at the top of the class in Maths, History and most of the other subjects. He was also friendly, easy-going, and interested in everyone, which Ignis found odd. "Balancing what?"

"Balancing yourself, silly. What, were you planning to stay on the ground all year long?"

"I wish." They were walking up towards Dalarwen, a secondary peak to the northwest of Rokkaku, away from the lake. The gymnastics teacher, Yarnya, was leading them. Ignis glanced behind him towards Rokkaku, but saw nothing but trees. In the first week, Shiro had warned him not to go into the forest, since he would get lost. Ignis had laughed. But now that he was outside the valley for the first time, Ignis was secretly glad he'd never put Shiro's claim to the test. The buildings of Rokkaku had long since disappeared behind them, and the trail Yarnya was leading them on was so faint that if he had been on his own he would have walked past it without ever noticing.

Ignis glanced up at the line of white-belted students walking in front of them. "Hey, Chris, what's with the belts?"

"They're your rank," Christopher answered. "Ninjutsu ranks are measured in *kyu* grades up to black belt, then dan grades afterwards. White belts mean *mu-kyu* – no *kyu*. When you pass your first grading, you go to ninth *kyu*, which is a green belt. Ninth *kyu* through first *kyu* is all green belt. After green belt is black belt, and from then you count up in dan grades. Getting from first dan to second dan is supposed to be as hard as going from white to black. But that doesn't matter here, anyway."

"It doesn't?"

"Nope. Within the school, ranks are done by year. First years have white belts. Second through fifth years have green belts if they're boys, and red belts if they're girls. Sixth formers have black belts, as long as they've passed the test. So no matter how good someone is in the first year, they still wear white."

"Sounds complicated."

Christopher grinned. "Think of it this way. Anyone with a white belt is probably better than you, anyone with a green belt is definitely better than you, and anyone with a black belt is right out of your league."

Annoyed, Ignis swiped at Christopher, who ducked. Suddenly he realised that the boy in front of him was vanishing upwards. Before them was a tall pine tree with a ladder built into its side, and everyone in front of him had already climbed it. Christopher nudged him. "Go on, it's fine."

Dubious, Ignis tested the rungs. They held. With a sinking heart, he started climbing.

By the time he was ten metres up, the forest was feeling lighter. At fifteen metres, he emerged suddenly into sunlight. Built around the trunk of the pine tree and supported on three sides by its neighbours was a wide, wooden platform on which the class was now gathered. Ignis stepped off the ladder and walked a few paces to one side, looking at the view in amazement.

It felt as though they were standing on top of the world. The sky stretched all over and around them, bright blue with huge white masses of cloud floating in it like puffy islands, large as cities. Below, through the treetops which surrounded them, Ignis could see hills and mountains. To the east and north, the hills seemed to go on for ever, one range succeeding another, each one smaller and greyer until they were so faint that they couldn't be told apart from the distant clouds. To the south, Ignis could see a mountain range. And westwards, at the very edge of their vision, was a dark, flat line. Ignis studied it for a moment before his eyes went wide. "Is that . . .?"

"Yup," Christopher answered, climbing off the ladder. "The Irish Sea. If you bring binoculars, you can see the ships carrying cargo to Bristol."

As Ignis looked down, he realised that the platform they were on was only one of several. Another was built into another tree about seven metres away: beyond and below were two more. The only way to get across was strung ropes. Ignis's eyes went wide in disbelief. "We're supposed to *walk* on those?"

"Class, form a line!" Yarnya called out.

"Come on, we want to be at the front." Christopher led Ignis forward next to Jennifer. Ignis walked hesitantly to the edge and peered over. Leaves concealed the ground. They were at least fifteen metres up.

"OK, let's get started," Yarnya called. "One at a time across the ropes and do a full circuit. Across to the second flat, down to the third, across to the fourth, and back here by the branches. Remember, don't touch the ground. If you fall, go back to your starting platform and try again."

"*Try again?*" Ignis hissed at Christopher.

91

"Don't worry, you'll get it after a few tries."

"That won't be much help if I kill myself on the first one!"

Jennifer waved her hand airily. "Relax. It's harder if you tense up."

"This is nuts! Gymnastics is Ally's game, not mine!"

Jennifer grinned. "Watch and learn."

She stepped out onto the rope. As the rest of the class watched, she walked forward without touching the guide ropes, her hands by her sides. Halfway across, Jennifer stopped and raised both arms. Leaning forward, she placed her hands on the ropes, then vaulted up into a handstand. There was a gasp from somewhere behind Ignis. As the class watched in fascination, Jennifer held the pose for several seconds, balancing vertically on the rope. Then she scissored her legs down, coming up with her hands spread and a "ta-da!" expression on her face. There was a scattered burst of applause and Jennifer bowed, balancing above the drop.

"Very nice, Jennifer." Yarnya's voice was dry. "If you have the time to impress everyone, you can help with teaching. Go to the third flat and assist the rest of the class with the upward climb."

"Yes, miss," Jennifer said with a grin. She pivoted easily and walked quickly to the other side. Christopher gave Ignis a nudge. "You're next."

Ignis peered out over the drop. The leaves weren't anywhere near enough to break a fall. "This is crazy!"

Christopher grinned. "Scared?"

"Chris, I swear, if I die, I'll find some way to come back from the grave and get you for this!"

"Let's go, Ignis!" Yarnya called out from one side.

Ignis swallowed. He took hold of each of the waist-high ropes from either side and, very cautiously, stepped onto the tightrope. It swayed alarmingly underneath him. Step by step, he inched forward, sweat beading on his forehead. The swaying increased.

"How's the view?" Christopher called out from behind him.

"Shut up!"

"You could at least take your hands off the training ropes."

"I said," Ignis shouted, twisting his neck around, "shut—"

His foot slipped and Ignis dropped like a stone. The force of the fall ripped the ropes out of his hands. He had time for one terrified yell.

Something yielding caught him, and he bounced gently before coming to rest. Ignis looked in disbelief at the black mesh he was lying on. Some kind of wide, fine, safety net was woven through the branches and leaves like a huge spider's web. Its colour had made it invisible from above.

"That was a really great scream," Christopher called from above. Ignis looked up to see his grinning face. "I told you you'd be fine."

Ignis shook his fist, swearing. "You piece of . . .! I'm going to get you for this!" He tried to scramble to his feet, but lost his balance on the net. To one side was a rope ladder leading back up to the platform and Ignis grabbed at it.

"You'll have to get across first," Christopher called, stepping out onto the rope.

Two and a half hours later, Ignis and Christopher were sitting on one of the higher flats, watching the sun set. The breaks had come more and more frequently as the afternoon had worn on, and now they had been allowed to rest for the last twenty minutes. Almost out of sight on the furthest platform, Yarnya was helping a couple of slow learners, but otherwise only a few dedicated students were still on the ropes. The setting sun cast the students in red light, long shadows from the treetops stretching over the platforms.

One of the students stepped out from the adjoining platform, his hands off the training ropes. It was Shiro. Back straight and body vertical, he carefully walked forward along the tightrope, his arms by his sides.

"Doesn't that guy ever do anything except train?" Ignis

asked, yawning.

"Who, Shiro?" Christopher shrugged. "Yes. But he keeps to himself."

"More than keeps to himself," Ignis muttered. "He's a freak. He won't even say anything about where he comes from. It's really weird."

Christopher glanced at Ignis. "Not as weird as you might think."

"What are you talking about?"

"Well, it depends. How much do you know about the sort of kids who come to this school?"

Ignis shrugged. "Not much."

"Rokkaku is isolated." Christopher leaned back against the tree. "The students here have to come a long way, and they don't see much of their parents. That's a reason not to come, for most. The ones that do, though – sometimes it's because they don't *want* to be near their parents. Some are from foster homes, or don't have a family at all. Others do have a family, but there are . . . problems. For those ones, Rokkaku's a new start, a place where they can get away from whatever they're trying to leave behind. So a lot of the students here aren't too keen on talking about where they come from."

Ignis thought about it for a few seconds. "Why are so many kids here from overseas?"

"Rokkaku is a mixed sort of place. Part British and part

95

Japanese. So it suits children who are from mixed cultures as well. Like me. My father's German, and my mother's from Thailand. I grew up in London with Jennifer."

"Oh." It explained what Ignis had been wondering. He'd never seen anyone with Christopher's looks and skin colour before.

"Most of the Japanese students haven't grown up in England. They're here because their families have moved here. One of their parents gets an overseas job, the family relocates, and they end up in a new school. To you, Rokkaku feels Japanese, but to them, it feels British. That's why they mostly stick together."

Ignis shrugged. "Or maybe they just don't like anyone else."

Christopher sighed. "You know, if you and Jennifer would stop trying to annoy Ichiro and Hiroshi all the time, you'd find out that they're pretty decent guys. There's a reason all the Japanese first years do what Ichiro tells them. They know he's someone that they can count on. Kentaro and Yori might be bad news, but the rest of them aren't."

Ignis was silent. "How do you know all this?" he finally asked.

Christopher smiled. "I like knowing things."

Ignis looked sharply at Christopher. "If students here don't talk about where they're from, how come you just did?"

Christopher grinned. "Well, every rule's got an exception. I've got a very nice family. A mother and father, one brother and two sisters. And I like all of them."

"So why'd you come here?"

"Because Jennifer did. Anyway, school was too easy and I was bored. I wanted a more interesting life."

"Well, I'm so happy for you. You must have a lot of fun studying everybody else like this, going home to your stupid happy family whenever you want. Just born lucky, huh?"

Christopher looked at him, hurt. "What are you so angry about? I was just—"

"None of your business." Ignis jumped to his feet. Hiroshi and Ichiro were just coming off the ropes onto their platform. Ignis strode towards them. "Hey, Hiroshi!"

Hiroshi turned towards Ignis. "What?"

Ignis grinned. "I'm bored. Let's finish that 'training session'."

Wary, Hiroshi drew back into a fighting stance, but Ichiro made a sharp motion with his hand and Hiroshi stopped. Ichiro stepped forward, looking at Ignis.

Ignis laughed. "Want something, Itch?"

"You are a troublemaker." Ichiro was tall and strongly built. His face showed nothing. "If you have a problem with Hiroshi, you have a problem with me."

"Suits me. Let's party."

Ichiro stood, relaxed, hands by his sides. Ignis took a step forward. The evening air crackled with tension.

Then suddenly Shiro was between the two of them, appearing as though from thin air. "Stop it!"

"Get out of the way, Shiro," Ignis snapped.

Shiro rounded on Ignis, his eyes cold. "You're acting like a fool. Start a fight up here and one wrong step will take you off the edge. It's fourteen metres straight down. Are you trying to kill yourself?"

Ignis growled. Then Allandra was next to him, putting a hand to his arm. "Ig!" she whispered. "He's right. Back off!"

Ignis looked around; several other students were there too. He shook Allandra off. "Fine." He looked up at Ichiro. "See you later," he promised.

Ichiro's eyes were calm. "I'll be waiting." He turned and stepped out onto the rope, just brushing the safety ropes for balance. Hiroshi followed. The others dispersed. The glances they threw him made Ignis clench his fists. Jennifer started towards Allandra, but Christopher led her away, leaving brother and sister alone.

"What's wrong, Ig?" Allandra asked quietly.

"Those boys think they're so damn good. And what Christopher said made me . . ." Ignis let out a breath, shook his head. "Forget it. It's not like we should care about Vargas. We don't even live with him any more."

A shadow passed over Allandra's face. "But Michael does."

Ignis looked at her. His sister's eyes were clouded, and Ignis's anger dissolved suddenly. For all that Michael got on his nerves, he knew how much Allandra loved her twin. The two of them had always been together, Allandra guiding and supporting Michael. They had never been separated like this before. "He's probably OK. Anyway, there's nothing you can do. Don't worry about it."

Allandra opened her mouth to say something, but just then a whistle blew from the first platform. It was the signal that lessons were over for the day. Slowly, the class began to drift back towards where Yarnya was waiting. Allandra hesitated, letting herself fall behind, looking east, in the direction of London. The eastern sky was dark with the coming dusk, and between the clouds, the first stars were appearing. Somewhere in those shadows was Michael – and her father.

The big house in Hampstead was silent and still. A whisper of movement drifted occasionally from the hallway below, but the footsteps were furtive and hurried. The master of the house was angry, and no one wanted to risk his attention.

The creak of the gate woke Michael from an uneasy sleep. Rolling off the bed, he tiptoed across the room to the window. Outside, in the darkened street, the door of a police car shut with a bang, followed closely by the rumble of the engine starting. It nosed out of the parking space and purred away down the road, slipping in and out of the patches of orange light cast by the streetlamps. Michael watched it out of sight, then turned away.

And jumped. His father was standing in the room next to him.

"Sit down." Vargas's voice was flat. Michael obeyed quickly, hurrying to his bed. Once there, he watched out of the corner of his eye, his heart beating fast.

But Vargas wasn't looking at him. He stood over what had been Allandra's bed, staring down out of the window. A minute passed, five minutes, and Vargas didn't move. Michael was growing scared. His father never entered their room without something to say. This silence frightened him.

"Tell me what your plans were when you ran away."

"We – we didn't mean to really stay away." Michael swallowed. "We were going to come back. I think Ally just got lost, or confused, or—"

Vargas spoke evenly, without raising his voice. "I said tell me what your plans were."

"Ally said that we should – that we should split up if one of us was – if one of us was . . . She said we should all split up. It wasn't my idea, I wanted to stay together. I never

100

thought that it'd end up with . . ." He trailed off.

His father gave no sign of having heard. The silence stretched on. Michael waited, his nerves on edge.

"How long has it been since you went to Emery Road School?"

Michael blinked. "Uh – last year."

"For how long? Two weeks?"

"Three – then there was that thing, and we left . . . "

"You'll be going back. You'll join a class next week."

Michael closed his mouth just in time.

"It was a mistake to keep the three of you so isolated." Vargas turned to face his son, leaning back against the wall. "You'll start at Emery Road on Monday, and I'll expect you to do well. Then, once you've settled in, you'll start on the family business. Oh, stop looking like that, Michael. I'm not going to put you out on the street, but it's time that you started learning how this job works. You'll work with me and Pete in the warehouse, and Tav'll teach you some other things you need to know. After a while, I'm going to start putting you in charge of small things, but for now, you'll work under me."

Michael stared. "But . . ."

Vargas's eyes narrowed. "You'd better not be about to tell me that you don't want to, Michael, because what you want doesn't have anything to do with it."

Michael hesitated. "Do I have to?"

"Yes, you have to. I'm not going to have you sit around here for the rest of your life like a spoilt brat. You're twelve years old. It's time you started growing up."

"But what about Ally?" It was the only thing Michael could think of to say.

For just a moment, Michael thought his father's eyes flashed, but the next instant, they were calm again. "Allandra and Ignis aren't going to be back for a while. I've looked, and I'm going to keep on looking, but for now, you're going to have to get used to living without them."

"But . . . can't you find them?"

"Oh, yes, I'll find them all right." His father stared into the distance. "It may take a month, or a year, or five years. But I will find them, and I'll bring them back here."

"Will you?"

Vargas rose, looking down at Michael, and for the first time he smiled. "Yes. I will. Now, go to sleep. Tomorrow I'll see you get some textbooks so that you won't be too far behind when you go to school." He walked out of the door.

Michael was left with his head whirling. School . . . and working with Vargas. He'd only been to school twice in his life; and had never gone with his father on one of his business trips. The last time they'd gone to school, they'd managed fairly well to begin with, and he'd seen his father and Pete and Tav working enough in the basement . . .

. . . but back then, he'd had Allandra with him.

Michael climbed miserably back into bed. He didn't know what to do. As he lay in the dark, he felt tears come to his eyes. "Ally, please come back," he whispered into the darkness.

But Allandra didn't come. Michael cried quietly into the pillow, muffling his voice in case anyone should pass in the corridor. Finally he turned over and pulled the blankets over his head. Sleep was a long time in coming.

4

KENTARO

"*Ichi!*"

Wham!

Allandra's hand landed with a crack on the punch pad. She stepped back into the *doko* ready stance, one foot back and her fist behind her head. Christopher, holding the heavy foam cushion, gave her a thumbs-up. "Step through, remember."

Allandra nodded. From the other end of the *dojo*, the instructor called out "*Ni!*" and she hit the pad again.

"*San!*"

Wham!

"*Shi!*"

Wham!

"*Go!*"

Wham!

The strike they were practising was called *shitan ken*: striking with the middle three fingers of the hand, stiffened into a dagger. When she was first shown it, she'd thought of it as a jab, but she'd since realised that it wasn't: the power came from swinging the arm through like a pendulum. It was designed to be used against the stomach, armpit, or other small, vulnerable targets.

"*Roku!*"

Wham!

"*Shichi!*"

Allandra saw the *taijutsu* teacher, Mr Akamatsu, watching her and put all her weight behind this one. The sound as it landed was not *wham!* but *whump!* and Christopher was actually knocked back a step. "Hey, that was good!"

Mr Akamatsu's eyes swept over her and onto the next student. Allandra frowned.

"What is it?" asked Christopher.

"I thought I got it right that time, but he didn't say anything!"

"Well, he's not telling you that you're doing it wrong any more. That's an improvement, right?"

Allandra was spared from having to reply by the end-of-class bell. The class scattered, some students going to talk to the teacher, others flopping down to take a few minutes' rest on the benches. Christopher wandered with her to one of the benches. "You're not so bad now, you know."

Allandra smiled. "Thanks." She *was* getting better. It hadn't been easy, though. She had struggled desperately in the first part of the term, trying to adjust to the demanding

105

routine. Only now, now that she had caught up on what she had missed and that classes had been reshuffled to give space to tightrope walking, which she found easy, was she beginning to settle down.

Jennifer bounced over. Allandra gave her a wave. She had said nothing of it to Ignis, not wanting to give him any excuse for leaving, but the truth was, if it hadn't been for Jennifer, she didn't think she could have made it through that awful first week. The smaller girl was a livewire who never seemed to get depressed or discouraged, and with chatter, jokes, company and insults, she had managed to keep Allandra's spirits from flagging when she had been close to giving up.

"Hey, guys!" Jennifer announced. "Guess what?"

"Uh – we've finished class?" Allandra asked.

"Nope! Guess again."

"They're giving us tomorrow off?"

"Nope! Guess again. It's about what we're doing next week."

"We're going to hang you upside down from the trees till your batteries run out?" Christopher suggested.

"Nope! Guess again."

Christopher sighed. "Fine, we give up. What *are* we doing next week?"

"We're having our first night class!"

Ignis wandered up. "What's a night class?"

106

"It's like stealth class, but at night. It's like a rehearsal for the Hunt."

"So how are we supposed to see?" Allandra asked.

"You learn to be a cat, of course. Right, *Neko-kun*?"

"Stop calling me that," Ignis snapped. "What does it mean, anyway?"

Allandra pointed. "Hey, who's that?"

Mr Akamatsu was standing at the entrance to the *dojo*, talking with a short, bald-headed man. Allandra recognised him as the one who had been training at the *dojo* when she first awoke at Rokkaku. As they watched, Mr Akamatsu clapped the short man on the shoulder and walked out of the door. The short man turned towards them.

"Uh-oh," Christopher said quietly.

"That's Ze'ev?" Allandra murmured to Jennifer.

"Yup, that's Ze'ev. They say he used to be in the SAS."

"He's that tough?"

"Worse."

Christopher groaned. "I've still got bruises from his last lesson. And that was nearly a month ago!"

Ze'ev clapped his hands loudly. "Three lines in *seiza*!"

Allandra moved to the centre of the *dojo* along with the rest of the class. When everyone was ranked up, Ze'ev sat down in *seiza*, facing the picture of Masaaki Hatsumi, the grandmaster of ninjutsu, where it rested at the front of the *dojo*. He placed his hands palm to palm, rubbed them together, and sat silent for a second before calling out in a clear voice, "*Shikin Haramitsu Daikyomyo*."

"*Shikin Haramitsu Daikyomyo!*" the class echoed. Everyone clapped their hands twice, bowed, and clapped their hands again. Ze'ev turned to face them and bowed one last time.

With the ritual that began every training session completed, Ze'ev jumped to his feet. He couldn't have been much more than five and a half feet tall, his head was shiny bald, and he was glaring at the class with a pair of bright blue eyes. Allandra wasn't sure whether to laugh or be scared.

"Right," he barked. "Akamatsu claims you're starting to learn some *taijutsu*. We'll find out if he's right. You!"

Scared, Allandra decided.

He was pointing at Kentaro, one of the Japanese boys. Kentaro lumbered to his feet and approached.

"Let's start you off on the *ichi mongi* form of the *Kihon Happo*. All you have to do is block and *shuto* to the neck. That's the same thing you've been doing for a month, so even you might be able to manage it. Punch."

Kentaro looked at him suspiciously, then launched a blow at Ze'ev's chin.

Ze'ev's chin wasn't there. His left hand came up to catch Kentaro's punch as the heel of his right hand thumped into Kentaro's neck, knocking him off his feet and sending him down on his back with a crash.

"What the hell was that? Haven't you learned how to roll yet? Get up and have a proper try."

Kentaro pulled himself up. He was breathing heavily, but didn't complain. The second time he managed to stay up, only staggering back a few metres. The movement was so fast that Allandra hardly saw it the first two times. Only when Ze'ev slowed the action down and broke it into three separate parts could she follow. After the sixth repetition Ze'ev dismissed Kentaro and turned to face them. "Now, you lot try it. Remember, move away as well as blocking, otherwise if you miss you'll get a fist in the nose. You're aiming for the three *kyusho* points along the neck. Partner off and go."

Allandra looked left to see that Christopher and Jennifer were already partnered, as were Ignis and Shiro. Cautiously, she approached Kentaro. They found a space and began practising.

As the class trained, Ze'ev walked among them, pulling out anyone who didn't perform the technique to his satisfaction. Allandra did her best to avoid his attention as he worked his way around the room, but after only a few minutes she heard a growl behind her.

"No! Stop right there. Try it on me."

Allandra's heart jumped. Carefully, she faced Ze'ev.

"Take stance." Ze'ev waited impatiently as Allandra tried to find the right position. "No, no. *Ichi mongi*, not *doko*. Left hand eye level, right hand over your heart. And put more weight on your back leg. That's better. Now I attack."

The punch wasn't as fast as Allandra had expected, but even so, she fumbled the block, and had to jerk back to avoid being hit. Trying to regain her balance, she struck at his neck. Nothing happened.

"What are you trying to do, catch a butterfly? This isn't a karate chop. Step through with it. Again!"

She put her weight behind it. This time it landed with a thump, but it bounced right off his neck muscles. He shook his head impatiently. "No, no, no! Haven't you learned a thing in *taijutsu*? Strike with the body, not the arm. Go back and practise, and when I get back around I want you to be able to knock me off my feet." He moved on to the next pair.

Glowering, Allandra turned back to Kentaro. He motioned. "You attack."

"I thought it was my turn?"

"Now it's mine."

"I need to practise."

"You'll do what I tell you."

Allandra stared at him. "What?"

"Attack."

Allandra attacked and was hit twice more, then stopped. Kentaro gestured. "Again."

"I said, it's my turn!"

Kentaro smirked. "You won't be here long enough for it to matter. You're going to quit, like all the other *gaijin*."

Allandra stared at him. "As if! I'm not quitting, I'm learning this! Now let me practise!"

Kentaro stared down at her, then laughed. "You?" He called out something in Japanese to one of his friends, Yori, who was training nearby. Yori stopped, looked at Allandra and laughed, saying something back to Kentaro. He grinned and turned to her. "He says you ought to be working the streets in Tokyo, not trying to learn martial arts. They like schoolgirls there, especially blonde ones."

Allandra's eyes widened. "You . . ." Kentaro turned and said something else to Yori. There was more laughter, and she clenched her fists. "Get back here and attack, or I'll make you regret it!"

"You'll what? Oh, the schoolgirl's threatening me!" Kentaro laughed again. "Fine, I'll attack." He struck.

This time instead of the slow, controlled movements that they'd been doing before, Kentaro's fist streaked at her face. Allandra tried to block, but she wasn't fast enough. The blow snapped her head back. Stars flashed across her eyes, blinding her briefly. As her vision cleared, she saw Kentaro and Yori laughing at her.

Allandra lost her temper.

Kentaro took the attacking *doko* stance with a grin. "Ready?"

Allandra was ready for him. As he struck she slid to the right, letting the blow fly past her head. Kentaro's other arm was already rising, guarding his neck from the counterattack, but Allandra wasn't going for his neck. She drove in low, swinging her arm up with the three middle fingers extended in *shitan ken*, sinking them into the soft spot just underneath the ribcage.

Kentaro gagged, losing the air in his lungs, and dropped to his knees. The other two boys stopped laughing. "Oops," Allandra said sweetly. "Missed." Other students stopped to look at them.

"Hey! You're not here to talk!" Ze'ev shouted from across the room. "Kentaro, are you doing a floor inspection? Everybody change partners!"

Allandra moved away, catching a murderous glance from Kentaro as he pulled himself to his feet. This time her partner was Christopher, and she turned back to the *ichi mongi* technique.

The class was two hours long, but it felt like four. Ze'ev took them through five different techniques, making them practise each one over and over again before he would let them onto the next. Next class, he announced, they would study the last three techniques of the *Kihon Happo*, and he'd expect everyone to be able to remember the first five perfectly.

By the time the class ended with Ze'ev's final shout of "*Yame!*", Allandra was exhausted and covered in sweat. She went through the end-of-class bows, grabbed her bag from the side of the *dojo*, and headed for the showers. She let the hot water run over her body for a long time, enjoying the warmth, then wearily put on some clean clothes and walked outside.

Two big hands grabbed her and slammed her into the wall.

Kentaro stared down at her. "Hello, schoolgirl."

The other boy, Yori, was blocking the path. "You shouldn't have hit Ken back there."

Kentaro released her and stepped back. The showers were at the lowest part of the valley, with only empty buildings around them, and she could hear nothing from either above or below. They were alone on the path. Overhead, the sky was clouded and cold. Allandra swallowed, trying to keep her voice from trembling. "You're brave – with him there."

Kentaro grinned. "Oh, he's just to make sure you don't try to run. I want you all to myself." He beckoned. "Come on, schoolgirl. Time to play with the big boys."

Allandra was shaking, partly from fear, partly from a strange tension. She turned to face Kentaro as he walked slowly around her, his feet crunching on the path. He stopped and thrust out his chin. "Why don't you try to hit me, schoolgirl? See how tough you are."

Allandra glanced at the other boy: he was standing in front of the path back up the valley. She looked at Kentaro, towering above her, still grinning, still holding his chin out.

She hit.

Jennifer jumped up when Allandra pushed the door to their room open. "Ally! Chris was just about to come looking for—" She stopped dead as she saw her.

Allandra pushed past her into her bedroom. Their rooms were like her brother's: a larger room in front and a smaller one behind. Jennifer stared after her. "Ally? What happened to your face?"

"Nothing."

"But you're—"

Allandra whirled around. "I said, nothing happened! Leave me alone!" She slammed her door and flopped down on the bed. Her right eye was throbbing, and her back hurt terribly from where Kentaro had kicked it as she lay curled on the ground. She stared up at the ceiling, tears leaking from her eyes.

There was a gentle knock at the door. Allandra didn't answer.

The knock came again, louder. Allandra wiped her eyes. "Go away!" she shouted, trying to keep her voice from breaking.

The door creaked open. First Jennifer's head, then Christopher's, peeked in. Allandra turned towards the wall. Footsteps approached, and Jennifer's hand touched her shoulder. "Ally?"

"Go away," Allandra repeated dully.

"We brought you some food." It was Christopher, his voice encouraging. "From dinner. They said they weren't supposed to do take-out, but . . ."

"I'm not hungry."

"It's your favourite."

Allandra twisted to look at him. "I don't have a favourite."

"Well, yeah. But it sounds better than 'I brought rice and meatballs', doesn't it? Hey, you can try and guess the canteen mystery meat! Jennifer's already guessed people. I guessed dog food."

Allandra turned away again.

Jennifer spoke quietly. "It was Kentaro, wasn't it?"

For a long time Allandra lay still. Then, slowly, she nodded.

"Ally, what happened?"

"Outside the showers," Allandra whispered. "Him and Yori . . ."

115

"Yori? Him as well?" Christopher was outraged. "They ganged up on you?"

Allandra shook her head. "No. Just Kentaro. Yori . . . watched." She twisted to look up at Jennifer. "I tried, Jen. I did my best. He was just too strong."

"It's OK, Ally." Jennifer stroked her hair. "Just rest. We'll be here."

"It's not OK. It's not . . ." Allandra's voice broke and she turned back to the wall and started to cry. "Leave me alone. Just . . . leave me alone."

Christopher hesitated. Jennifer took his arm and led him firmly into the outer room, closing the door behind her. Pulling the pillow over her head, Allandra covered her ears and lost herself in misery.

The next day was a Saturday, for which Allandra was grateful: there would be no classes in which she'd have to face the other students. She got up late and walked out of her room to see Jennifer combing her hair and Christopher on the sofa.

"You stayed here all night?" Allandra demanded. Then she shook her head. "Never mind. I'm going out."

Christopher and Jennifer looked at each other. "Are you sure you're all right?" Christopher asked.

"I'm fine."

"Ally, we—" Jennifer began, her face filled with

concern. Allandra couldn't bear to look at it. She slammed the door.

Once she was out of her room, Allandra slowed, looking for other students. When she was sure nobody could see her, she scrambled quickly up a notched log to the next path, followed it along, then took a high bridge to the other side of the valley. With a final glance back, she vanished into the woods.

As soon as Allandra was out of sight, her head slumped and her path began to waver. She wandered aimlessly, picking her way between fallen branches and around the steep slopes of the lake side. It was a clear November day, with puffy white clouds floating in the sky and beams of sunlight slanting down through the branches. The leaves were starting to fall in earnest, and they crackled under Allandra's feet as she angled downwards towards the lake.

Finally she reached the shore. Llyn Garedig stretched out in front of her, the sun glinting white and yellow on the ripples. Allandra flopped down underneath an alder, just short of the lapping waves.

She stared out over the water. Schools of wavelets swept slowly across the lake's surface, the choppy patches following the gusts of the north wind as it blew southwards towards the dam.

What am I doing here? she thought.

I've been training for a month. I've learned the strikes and the stances, and I can't even beat the class bully. The first fight I ever have and I get beaten to pulp. I thought I was going to learn to be a ninja, but I'm never going to make it.

I should just give up and go home. At least there I only get hit for doing something wrong.

She was so lost in her thoughts that she didn't hear the footsteps until they were right behind her. Allandra spun round, fear leaping through her. Had Kentaro come back to finish the job?

But it wasn't Kentaro. It was Shiro.

"What are you doing here?" Allandra demanded. She was conscious of her black eye and bruised jaw, but she refused to turn away.

Shiro shrugged. Tall and slim, he looked comfortable amidst the trees. "Walking."

"You followed me, didn't you?"

Shiro shrugged again and sat down a little way to Allandra's side. Allandra sighed. "Oh, what the hell." She sat. The two of them stared out over the lake for a moment.

"Kentaro?" Shiro asked after a few minutes.

"Does *everyone* know?"

"A few. Ken was bragging."

Allandra put her head in her hands. As if it wasn't bad enough being proved a weakling. Now everyone in the class was going to hear about it.

"It's OK," Shiro said.

Allandra glared at him. "Do I look OK?"

"You lost a fight. It happens."

"I didn't just lose a fight!"

"Ken's been fighting for years. You can't expect to walk up to someone twice your size and knock him down first try."

"I didn't walk up to him! He went for me!"

"Doesn't matter much afterwards."

Allandra looked at Shiro, studying him closely. He wasn't Japanese: his skin was too pale, and he was too tall. But something about his manner, the way he looked away when he spoke . . . if he had sat in the middle of the Japanese boys, he wouldn't have looked the slightest bit out of place. He even sat in *fudoza* as they did, sitting on one folded leg with the foot braced against the opposite knee.

"Don't take it personally," Shiro said after a pause. "Kentaro's a bully. Normally, he'd pick on the smallest Japanese boy in the class, but Ichiro wouldn't let him get away with that here. So he's going for you instead."

"Why me?"

"You're a girl, and you're smaller than him."

"So you're saying I'm an easy target?"

"Pretty much."

119

"Oh, thanks. Now I feel a lot better. How come you're such an expert?"

"I knew a lot of people like Kentaro when I lived in Japan."

"How?"

Shiro looked away.

Allandra waited for an answer for a few seconds, then gave up. "OK, fine. What are you doing out here?"

"I like the woods."

"Why are you right *here*?"

Shiro turned back to look at her. "Maybe I wanted to help you."

"You're going to help me?" Allandra couldn't keep the sarcasm out of her voice. "Fine. Then tell me how to deal with a bully."

"There are lots of ways. You can stay away from him. You can run away from him. You can turn him into a friend. You can ignore him. You can trick him. You can make yourself so difficult to fight that he'll pick an easier target. You can get your friends to deal with him. Or you can beat him yourself."

Allandra stared at him. Shiro looked back at her, his eyes steady.

"Are you serious?"

Shiro didn't answer.

"Which one's the right one?"

"It depends. Staying away is the easiest."

"That doesn't work. I'm in his class. I can't see him wanting to be my friend, either."

"Then you could report him to the teachers. They'll help you, if you—"

Allandra shook her head. "It doesn't work. It's no good if someone else solves it all for me."

Shiro paused. "You don't have to do this all on your own."

"Yes I *do*." Allandra sighed. "Look, Shiro, it's nice of you to try and help. But that wasn't why I came here. My father . . ." She hesitated, wanting to tell Shiro the truth, knowing that she couldn't. "There's – someone I care about a lot. He needs my help. Some day soon I'm going to go back for him, and when I do, I need to be strong. If I can't even beat Kentaro . . . if I can't do this, I can't do anything."

Shiro was silent for a moment. "Then all that leaves is beating him yourself."

Allandra flopped back. "Easy for you to say. You're a boy, and you're tall. I'm not. And I've never learned any of this stuff! Everyone here knows ninjutsu already, I don't . . ." She stopped. Shiro was shaking his head.

"You don't 'know' ninjutsu. Or any other martial art. You just study it, and you keep on studying. The more you train, the better you get. Everyone here just got a head start on you, that's all."

"But they're so much better than me! What am I supposed to do?"

Shiro looked at her. "Well . . . there *is* one thing you could try."

Shiro's directions took Allandra to the top of Rokkaku valley, and she took a quick look around to check for any other first years before climbing down out of the trees to the lower buildings. The house she was looking for was low down near the stream, north of the *dojo*s. When she was sure she had the right one, she took a deep breath and knocked.

"Come!" a gruff voice called.

Allandra opened the door. Ze'ev glanced up from a chair. "What do you want?"

The room was sparsely furnished. Bookcases stuffed with hardbacks filled two of the walls. A framed photo hung on the third wall: it showed a group of men in white-and-grey army fatigues, kneeling on desert sand and grinning at the camera. Allandra took a deep breath. "I need your help. I need to learn how to fight."

Ze'ev grinned. "So that scuffle with Kentaro had some fallout, did it? Oh, don't look so surprised, girl, I'm not blind. And as for teaching you how to fight, you're learning that every day. Go to more classes if you're that eager."

"I – I want to train with you. Sir."

"Why me?"

"Because . . ." Allandra swallowed. "You're supposed to be . . . the others say you used to be in the SAS, and—"

She was cut off by a roar of laughter. "So that's what they say, is it? That's a good one. No, girl, not the SAS, a different army. But that's no use to you."

Allandra blinked. "But I thought—"

"That I'd teach you some kind of secret technique, and you'd go off and break Kentaro's neck? I could, but I won't. This is ninjutsù school, girl, not boot camp. You're here to learn how to defend yourself, not kill people."

Allandra stood, frowning.

"They never explained the difference to you, did they?" Ze'ev sighed. "I keep telling them they ought to teach you children a little more theory before they go into techniques. The adults here might be trying to achieve spiritual enlightenment, but the kids just want to be Neo from *The Matrix*. Well, then, listen. The martial arts as they're taught in the West have four focuses, not one. Combat, discipline, spirit, and sport. Combat is learning to break heads and survive. Most people think that that's what martial arts are all about, but they're wrong. They're also a discipline – mental and physical – that's both a tradition and an art form. The spiritual focus is about personal development and health, and it's something you only come to understand over a long time. Go and read the essay in your room if you want to get a glimmer of that. And sport is just for competition and fun. Now, every martial art and every teacher focuses on a different one of the four. Most forms of tai chi concentrate on the spiritual side. Karate and tae kwon do are mostly taught as sports in Britain, and so on.

"Ninjutsu is a mixture of the first three focuses. It's a combat art, a discipline, and a spiritual path. The only one it doesn't include at all is sport, since combat and sport don't mix unless you want the loser of a match leaving in an ambulance. It's better on the combat aspect than most, but its main purpose isn't to kill people.

"Now, what we learned in our training was pure combat. No frills. Just how to kill. And that's not the kind of thing I'll teach a twelve-year-old. No, girl. Stick with the regular classes. Akamatsu's a good teacher. Give him a year or two and you'll be good enough to stand up to Kentaro, if you work at it."

Allandra stood firm. "I'm going to the regular classes. But I want extra ones. If you won't teach me the special stuff, then teach me how to do the ninjutsu techniques better." She took a breath. "Please. I need to learn this."

Ze'ev frowned. "You're serious, aren't you?"

Allandra nodded.

"Why don't you just get help from your friends? Shiro

or your brother would take on Kentaro for you if you asked."

"I don't want anyone to fight my battles for me. I want to be able to take care of myself."

Ze'ev grunted. "Hm." He got to his feet and tossed the chair into the corner. "Start the *sanshin*."

Allandra hesitated. "Which side?"

"Both. Come on, girl, I haven't got all day."

Allandra stepped back into the earth – or *chi* – form of *sanshin*. She finished it, started the water form, and Ze'ev spoke. "Stop. Run through the strikes."

Allandra struck at an imaginary target, focusing to the best of her ability, going through all sixteen one after another. Ze'ev walked around her as she struck and pulled back and struck again. Finally he held up a hand. "That's enough. How long did you study gymnastics for?"

"A few years." Allandra hesitated. "Um, how did you know I—"

"Because that's how you move. Good balance, but no power. You've a gymnast's build, too. Quick and light." Ze'ev heaved a sigh. "I don't suppose there's any chance of you giving up on martial arts and becoming an ice skater or something, is there? You'd make both our lives a lot easier."

Allandra's eyes flashed. "That's not funny."

Ze'ev grinned. "Wasn't meant to be. Very well, little

one, you're on. Let's find a *dojo*. Your first lesson starts now."

By the time she got back to her room, Allandra was exhausted and aching – but satisfied. Jennifer jumped up from her bed as she walked in. "Ally, where'd you go? I was looking for you all day!"

"Oh, around." Allandra yawned. "Can I use the bathroom? I'm tired."

"In a sec. Ally, can we talk?"

"What?"

"Look, me and Christopher were talking about Kentaro, and I came up with this plan. You know how Kentaro shares a room with Yori? Well, they're usually out of it in the afternoons, and I—"

"No!" Allandra stopped dead. "Jennifer, don't you *dare*!"

"Why not? After what he did? Look, I even managed to get Chris to agree, and you know how stick-in-the-mud he is about jokes."

"I don't care. Jennifer, I mean it. Don't even go *near* Kentaro or Yori. I'm not having the two of you dragged into this as well. This is my fight, stay out of it!"

Jennifer stared stubbornly at her. Allandra sighed and lowered her voice. "Look, Jennifer, if you try and do some kind of revenge stunt, you'll just make things worse. I'm

126

going to handle this my way. Let me fight my own battles, OK?"

"But we want to help! OK, what if we went to the teachers? Mr Oakley would—"

"No! If you want to help, stay out of it!" Allandra looked at her. "I'm serious, Jen. Don't get involved in this."

Jennifer sighed and nodded reluctantly. "You'd better know what you're doing."

"I do." *At least, I hope so*, Allandra added to herself. She opened the door. "I'll be back in a minute."

She circled up the slope to Shiro and Ignis's room. She knocked softly and Shiro opened the door. "Hello, Allandra."

"Hi, Shiro." Allandra slipped in. "Is Ignis around?"

"No, he's not back yet. Did Ze'ev . . ."

Allandra nodded. "He said yes. I'm going to stick with it. Listen, Shiro, can I ask a favour? Make sure Ignis doesn't know about me and Kentaro."

Shiro's eyebrows rose. "Are you sure?"

Allandra sighed. "You don't know my brother. If he sees what I look like now, God only knows what he'll do. Could you just make sure he . . ." Allandra paused. Shiro was looking over her shoulder. "What is it?"

"Too late," Shiro said quietly. The door opened behind Allandra.

Allandra jumped and spun around. Ignis strode in, took one look at her and stopped dead, his eyes wide.

"Ignis!" Allandra thought fast. "I'm fine. It's just . . ."

Ignis strode forward, staring at Allandra's face. "Who did this?"

"Nobody. I mean, it wasn't someone you know."

"It was one of those kids, wasn't it? I'll kill them!" He jumped for the door.

"No, Ignis! Don't—" The door slammed behind him. Allandra sank down on the bed with a groan. "Oh, hell."

Ignis stormed up through Rokkaku, fury filling him. Who had done this? His eyes flicked over the students, looking for someone to take his rage out on. The students walking in the afternoon valley, crossing the bridges and talking in twos and threes, all wore green or black belts. But below him was the fifth *dojo*, free for first years to practise in. Ignis swung towards it.

Inside was Ichiro. The Japanese boy was running through some kind of complex form. "You!" Ignis snarled.

"What?" Ichiro didn't look up. He pulled back onto one leg, raising the other for a kick.

Ignis walked forward and grabbed for it. Ichiro leaped away, coming down to look at Ignis with narrowed eyes. "What do you think—"

"You know what happened to Allandra. Either you did

128

it or you ordered it."

"I have no idea what you are talking about," Ichiro replied coldly.

Fury boiled up within Ignis. "You'll tell me everything or . . ."

Ichiro's eyes glittered. "Don't mistake me for some two-bit bully, Ignis. You have no idea who you are dealing with."

Ignis lunged. Ichiro dodged left and came up in a fighting stance. Ignis spun to face him.

Ichiro was as tall as Ignis and a little heavier. He stood with one hand forward and the other over his heart, fingers together. His eyes watched Ignis unblinkingly.

Ignis was too angry to think of being subtle. He swung a punch at Ichiro's face. Ichiro leaned aside and struck into Ignis's ribcage. As Ignis grunted and dropped his shoulder, Ichiro slammed the heel of his other hand down into the side of Ignis's neck. The blow landed like a hammer, knocking Ignis to the ground, stunned.

Pain clouded Ignis's brain as he knelt on the floor, shaking his head. His vision cleared and he saw Ichiro standing in front of him, in the same stance, waiting. Ignis came to his feet with a snarl and charged.

He caught one blow on his cheek and another on his shoulder on the way in, but this time he managed to get a grip on Ichiro's left arm. Ignis yanked on it, aiming to

129

smash a punch at Ichiro. As he began to strike, Ichiro moved forward and to Ignis's side, disappearing from his sight. Suddenly Ignis's elbow was swung up into the air and his back leg was kicked out from under him. Completely off balance, he fell flat on his back, landing with a slam that knocked the breath from him in a gasp. Before he could rise Ichiro dropped to one knee and punched down, his fist striking the spot just below the centre of Ignis's ribcage.

Ignis couldn't breathe. His lungs were frozen in pain and he felt as though he was suffocating. He rolled over, trying to get air. His vision swam with grey sparks.

Dimly, he was aware of Ichiro rising to his feet and walking away. At the door Ichiro paused and turned back. His voice was calm. "For your information, I have not seen your sister since yesterday's classes. But I will not allow anyone to insult me in that way." Then he was gone.

Ignis stayed on his hands and knees, gasping. The floor beneath him wavered and spun. Gradually, his breath began to return as the blow that had briefly paralysed his diaphragm wore off. The floor steadied.

Ignis rose, staggering slightly. He knew what he was going to do.

The storerooms were at the top of the valley, beyond the canteen, and were forbidden to first years. Ignis pushed open

130

the door of the one Christopher had pointed out again a week ago. Training weapons lined the walls: staffs and swords, daggers, scythes and clubs. All were made of wood – the edged and spiked weapons were elsewhere. Ignis walked in and picked up a *hanbo*. It was a cylinder of Japanese red oak, one metre long and four centimetres wide. Ignis gripped it like a baseball bat and took an experimental swing, then another. He imagined it striking into a body and smiled.

"What are you doing?"

Ignis spun. It was Shiro. "None of your business," Ignis answered.

Shiro was standing in the doorway, the afternoon light shining through behind him. His eyes measured Ignis. "Going after someone to try and beat him up with your bare hands means that you're so angry you can't think. Or that you want to prove you're stronger. Going after some-one with a weapon – that means something different. That means that you're trying to cripple him. Or kill him."

Ignis smiled coldly. "Good guess."

"Do something like that and you're finished here, Ignis. The teachers might overlook a fight, but if you think they'll allow one student to try to seriously injure another, you're a fool. That's if you even survive trying to use it."

"It's not me you should be worrying about."

Shiro's voice was quiet. "Try and use that on Ichiro and he'll do a lot worse than just knock you down."

131

"Screw Ichiro!" Ignis snarled. "Do you know what he just did to me?"

Shiro studied him. "And he attacked you first, did he?"

"Get out of my way." Ignis walked towards the door, pushing past Shiro.

Shiro slid sideways, and the *hanbo* came out of Ignis's hands. Ignis spun, furious, to see Shiro two metres away, holding the *hanbo* in front of him, hands spaced along its length.

"Walk away, Ignis," Shiro said softly.

Ignis lunged with a snarl. The *hanbo* snapped up. Ignis was thrown backwards, crashing into a stack of *bokken*s leaning against the wall to tumble to the floor.

His vision blurring, Ignis struggled to his feet. He could feel the wetness of blood on his head where the blow had landed. Pain pulsed and stabbed through his body.

Shiro was standing in the same stance. He seemed not to have moved. Shiro watched steadily as Ignis staggered and recovered himself.

"I will not let you leave here with a weapon," Shiro said. A drop of Ignis's blood beaded the end of the *hanbo*.

Ignis turned and ran, and kept on running. Rokkaku's buildings flashed past and vanished behind him as Ignis kept going upstream, tears of rage and pain blurring his sight. The paths faded away as Rokkaku began to recede behind him. Ignis kept on going, uphill, away from the school, north and west towards Dalarwen. When he came to the ladder in the trees he started climbing, hand over hand as fast as he could go until he was on the platform they used for tightrope practice.

Standing on the empty wooden platform – the red-tinted sky of the early evening glowing above him, the treetops all around, alone in the vastness of nature except for the birds singing in the trees – Ignis threw back his head and screamed, a wild wordless shriek of helpless fury, echoing out all around into the still evening.

The sound died away into stillness. The birds all around had fallen silent. With a sob, Ignis fell back against the tree. He lay motionless as the sun slowly set and the forest faded into darkness.

5

CHOICES

When Allandra didn't see Ignis on the Sunday, she assumed that he had stayed in his room with Shiro. She had been afraid of some sort of explosion between her brother and Kentaro. When nothing happened she relaxed.

Monday brought new problems, however. Kentaro seemed to be everywhere she looked, gloating during morning lessons and laughing with his friends in the dining hall. He kept up his taunts, jokes and sly asides until Allandra finally exploded and went for him. In the fight that followed Allandra used a trick Ze'ev had taught her, and gave Kentaro a bloody nose.

Kentaro beat her so badly she had to miss the afternoon's classes.

She was called to Mr Oakley's room to explain her absence. "Well?" he demanded sternly from behind his desk.

Allandra had to speak from around the swollen side of her mouth. "I fell off one of the bridges, sir."

"Really? And the ground hit you on both sides of your

face at once, did it? You've been fighting."

Allandra said nothing.

"Who was it with? Kentaro's been causing trouble all day. Was it him?"

Allandra still said nothing.

"Just because we study fighting doesn't mean that this place is lawless, Allandra. There are rules here as much as any other school, and beating up other students is against them. So is bullying. I want you to tell me what happened."

Silence.

Mr Oakley drummed his fingers on the desk. "You're not helping me here, Allandra."

"Sorry, sir."

He sighed. "Do this again and I'll put you on kitchen chores for a month. The same for whoever you're fighting. And I *will* find them. Go."

Allandra turned to leave.

"Allandra?"

She looked back.

"Whatever you're planning to do about this – please try not to get yourself seriously hurt. Or anybody else."

Allandra smiled. "Yes, sir."

"Good. One last thing. Do you know where your brother is?"

The smile vanished from Allandra's face. "No, I – hasn't anyone seen him?"

"Not that I'm aware of. Well, I expect he'll turn up soon enough. Go to Dr Furuta and get yourself looked at."

Ignis sat cross-legged on the high platform, looking out over the forest. It was an overcast day, the layer of cloud overhead glowing white from the light of the sun above.

He had stayed up in the treetops for the past two days, only descending to drink from the stream. Up here, the only sounds were the wind, the birds in the trees and the occasional hum of a car from over the hills that hid the lake. The tightropes hung silently in the air, mocking him – he had never managed to walk one, so he couldn't cross to the other platforms. There was nothing to do except sit and think.

It had taken only an hour on the Saturday evening for the rage and humiliation to fade away. Ignis's outbursts always left him tired, but this time he felt only a kind of impossible frustration. He didn't want to go back to Rokkaku. Nor did he want to go anywhere else. So he sat, and looked at the forest.

Time passed slowly. He hadn't had his watch with him when he'd run, but from the sky, it looked to be five o'clock or so. The school day should be over.

Steps sounded on the platform behind him. Ignis glanced back, and his eyes went flat. It was Shiro. Ignis looked away.

136

Shiro walked up next to him and sat in *fudoza*. Ignis didn't react.

"It took me a long time to find you."

Ignis gazed out over the forest. "Come back for a rematch?"

"If I hadn't stopped you, you would have been thrown out of Rokkaku. You know that."

"It would have been worth it."

"Don't!"

Ignis turned in surprise. Shiro's face showed open anger. Ignis began to answer, but Shiro cut him off.

"Don't give me that I-don't-care attitude. It would *not* have been worth it. If you'd attacked Ichiro with that *hanbo*, either Ichiro would have taken it away from you and you would have been expelled, or Ichiro would have taken it away from you, broken a few of your bones, and *then* you would have been expelled. And for what? Ichiro didn't do anything to you or to Allandra."

"How do you know?"

"Because I asked him. And trust me, neither of us enjoyed that very much." Shiro paused, then continued, his dark eyes watching Ignis closely. "It was Kentaro who beat up your sister, and not on Ichiro's orders, either. So you attacked Ichiro without a reason. And when he defended himself, you used that as an excuse to try and attack him again. Not exactly behaviour to be proud of."

137

"He acts like he's better than me," Ignis muttered.

"That's because he *is* better than you."

Ignis glared at Shiro. "How do—"

"What did you expect?" Shiro snapped. "That you could just walk in here and be the best in the class without even *trying*? Ichiro's studied martial arts for years, and he's used to fighting boys twice your strength. Of *course* he wiped the floor with you. The students here work *hard*, Ignis. If you want to keep up with them you have to work hard as well. Not take a short cut. Going for a weapon like you did – that's a short cut. It's the same as admitting that you can't match up to the other boy in a straight fight, but you want to beat him anyway. If you were fighting for your life, then that would be one thing – but you weren't. You were doing it just because he hurt your pride."

"So maybe that's all I've got."

"So maybe you need to get something else."

Ignis narrowed his eyes. "Got all the answers, haven't you?"

Shiro's eyes were steady. "When someone proves that they're better than you, you have two choices. Either you try to pull them down to your level. Or you try to lift yourself up to theirs."

Ignis slumped down. "It never works."

"What doesn't?"

"My whole life. My father and his men would always

push me around, trying to tell me what to do. When I didn't, they'd get angry. And if I did what they said, *I'd* get angry. When I went to school, the other kids would say things and I'd fight them, and after that they'd hate me. The teachers didn't like me. And my father's the worst of all. Always trying to tell me what to do. Ever since our mother disappeared . . . He wouldn't let me go, but only because he thinks I'm his property. Not even his most valuable property. Just his property. And no one else even cares if I live or die."

"Your sister does."

Ignis shrugged.

Shiro let out a breath in exasperation. "So *that's* what you've been doing up here? Feeling sorry for yourself? Telling yourself what a hard life you lead and how no one loves you?"

Ignis jumped to his feet and looked down at Shiro, eyes blazing. "What gives you the right to judge me like that? You've no idea what I've been through. Everything's easy for you. If your life is so great, go back to it and leave me alone!"

Shiro looked up steadily at Ignis. "You think my life's easy?"

"How would I know? It's not like you ever say anything about it. You just sit there without showing a damn thing, like you don't need anyone around you."

Ignis glared down at Shiro. Then Shiro looked away, out over the forest, and sighed softly. "I suppose you're right. It's an old habit. It's not that I don't care about any of you . . . just that I'm used to not showing weakness."

Shiro didn't move. After a while, Ignis sat. Eventually, Shiro began to talk.

"I don't remember my parents very well. I moved to Japan when I was five years old, staying with a foster family. They were OK. The neighbourhood wasn't. The school I went to was a bad one. I stood out – that made me a target. So the boys there started beating me up.

"I had the same choice you did. I didn't have anyone to go to for help. Finally, I joined the local ninjutsu *dojo*, and trained every hour I had.

"It still wasn't enough. After a while, I could beat any one or two of them, but I still wouldn't have a chance against them all. So I learned to guard myself. I didn't show anything that could be used against me. I didn't rely upon anybody but myself. I was trying to make myself so difficult a target that they'd give up and find someone easier. And eventually they did. I didn't relax, though – I thought that if they had come once, they could come again. And by the time I realised that they weren't coming back, that no one would even think of trying something like that on me any more, it had become a habit. Not showing anything on the outside."

Ignis looked at Shiro in silence for a few seconds. "You never even told me you lived in Japan."

"Like I said, habit. Anyway, you were very pushy when you came to Rokkaku. I didn't feel like talking about it."

"Hmph. Well, I'm not in Rokkaku any more."

"Don't be so sure. A lot of students vanish in their first term. Runaways. Usually, the teachers write them out of the class as having gone back home. But I went to Ze'ev and told him that you hadn't run away, that you were staying on. He told me that if you wanted to stay, you should come to the last *dojo* this evening at eight o'clock. Show up, and they'll keep your name on the class roll."

Ignis scowled. "Why do you care what happens to me?"

Shiro sighed. "Because, hard as you might find it to believe, I don't like to see anyone get hurt. And I know what it's like to be on your own in a place you don't under-stand." Shiro rose to his feet. "I'll be back in our room."

"Say I do go back. What about Ichiro?"

"Ichiro didn't tell the teachers about what you did."

"I thought fighting was against the rules."

"I told Ichiro that. He said that a fight wasn't the same thing as an execution."

Ignis stared at Shiro, then gave a short laugh. Shiro smiled slightly, then he turned and was gone. Ignis was left sitting alone on the platform.

He stared out at the distant mountains. Idly, he

strummed the tightrope stretching out in front of him. The mountains beckoned. Go, or stay?

Ignis got up and walked around the platform. Even thinking about the fight with Ichiro made anger rise up inside him again, and he pushed the memory away roughly. *Fighting for pride* . . . He stepped out onto the rope and began walking, his thoughts elsewhere. Was that really all it was? Was Shiro right?

His foot came down on wood. Ignis stopped and looked down. He was on a different platform. He looked back at the tightrope and realised that he'd crossed it.

He stared at the rope for a long moment. "Huh."

Ignis stayed up on the platform until the sun set, watching the ball of yellow and red sink down below the horizon. Finally, after the clouds overhead had turned black with the coming night, he stood and headed for the ladder. One way or another, he was going to settle this.

The globes between the houses cast Rokkaku in soft light as Ignis walked back down to the *dojo*s. The light was on in the one at the end.

"You're late," Ze'ev said without opening his eyes as Ignis walked in. The teacher was sitting in the middle of the *dojo*, legs crossed.

"Sue me."

"Going to tell me why you went missing for two days in

142

the middle of term?"

Ignis folded his arms. "None of your business."

Ze'ev opened his eyes and grinned suddenly. "About what I expected." He jumped to his feet. Ze'ev was barely taller than Ignis, but his stocky build made him look larger than he was. "Well, then. Know why you're here?"

Ignis said nothing.

Ze'ev turned aside and began strolling across the *dojo*. "Mr Ignis Havelock," he recited. "Arrived in Rokkaku early this term. Since then, you've started fights, shirked in class, avoided homework and generally made a sufficient nuisance of yourself that one might almost think you were trying to get yourself noticed by the teachers." Ze'ev raised his eyebrows. "Well, here I am. Now you've done all this work to get my attention, what d'you have to say?"

"I've done the work I had to," Ignis replied sullenly.

"You've done the bare minimum. No extra classes, and any homework you do is as short as possible. When you're in lessons, your attitude is 'You can't make me'. When you're not working, you provoke the other students. Essentially, boy, you've tried to live in Rokkaku without adapting to it in the slightest."

"So? I do what you tell me."

Ze'ev sighed in exasperation. "Everything except the most important part. Stop treating this as though it's a legal contract. We're trying to teach you something here. The essence of ninjutsu is survival and persistence: that's what *ninpo* means. Do you understand the concept of discipline?"

Ignis sneered. "What? Beating somebody up?"

"I meant self-discipline."

"Beating *yourself* up?"

There was a flicker of movement, and Ignis's jaw stung and jerked to the side. Ignis held the side of his face, staring at Ze'ev. The slap had been so fast he hadn't seen it. Disbelief turned to fury. Ignis lunged.

Ze'ev leaned aside and Ignis went flying past. Something tripped him. Instinctively Ignis went into a roll, bringing his hands down and tucking in his head as he'd been forced to practise in gymnastics class. He came to his feet.

Ze'ev was standing a couple of metres away, his hands clasped behind his back. "Self-discipline is the ability to school and direct your feelings." His voice was friendly. "Because you lack it, all of that fire within you amounts to nothing at all. Strength is feeling paired with discipline. You can hammer a rock for days without breaking it, but one sharp strike from the point of a chisel will split it in two. Feeling without discipline is like a hammer without a chisel. A lot of noise, but not much use."

"You think you can push me around like this?" Ignis snarled. "I'm not your lapdog!"

Ze'ev's eyes narrowed. "What you are is a waste of my time, boy. Now, I'm getting tired of your mindless rebellion. Shape up or ship out."

Ignis tensed, ready to spring. Ze'ev was standing at ease, watching Ignis calmly.

Then suddenly, as Ignis stood looking at the teacher, he recognised what he was seeing. Ze'ev was facing Ignis in the same way that Ichiro and Shiro had in the moment before Ignis had attacked them. When Ignis had seen the posture the first two times he had taken it for contempt. Now he realised that it was something else; Ze'ev simply knew that there was no possible way Ignis could be a threat to him.

In that instant Ignis knew that what Shiro had told him was true. The people of Rokkaku *were* better than he was. He took a step back.

Ze'ev stood waiting for several seconds more, then when Ignis did nothing, he spoke. "You remember the *sanshin* forms, Ignis?"

Ignis answered, his voice flat. "Earth, water, fire, air, void."

"Your sister is air with a touch of fire. But you're fire all the way through. Passion and aggression and intensity, all burning together. You know, most people's lives can go a lot of different ways. They have lots of little challenges, many decisions to make, and each one makes things a touch better or a touch worse. But you, boy – you're not like that. There are only two ways your life can turn out. You can learn to control your fire, discipline yourself. If you can focus it, learn to use it for others apart from yourself, you might amount to something."

"Or?" Ignis asked.

"Or you carry on as you're going. You fight everyone you run up against. You burn away your energy accomplishing nothing. And eventually you destroy yourself. I've seen it happen enough times. There were plenty like you in my unit. Wild spirits, daredevils. The ones who could control themselves made the best soldiers in the regiment. The others kept on spiralling, getting more and more dangerous to everyone around them. They'd be discharged, and from then on the method they'd use would vary. Brawls. Drugs. Crime. But the end result was always the same. They died. And usually, they'd take one or two people with them. Friends, or neighbours. Brothers." Ze'ev cocked his head. "Or sisters."

Ignis's head snapped up.

Ze'ev's eyes were calm. "Decision time, boy. Learn, adapt, and grow. Or die." He turned and walked to the exit, speaking over his shoulder. "Lesson's over. Go away and make your decision. I'll be waiting here tomorrow at the same time. You show up, I'll teach you what you need to learn. You don't . . ." Ze'ev shrugged. "Close the door on your way out."

Ignis stared at the empty doorway for a long time after Ze'ev had gone. Finally, with slow steps, he walked home.

Shiro looked up as Ignis walked in. He gave Ignis a nod, then returned to his reading.

Ignis opened the door to his bedroom. Allandra sat up on his bed, her face lighting up. "Ignis!"

"Yeah, I'm back." Ignis accepted a hug.

Allandra leaned away, her hands around Ignis's neck. "Where were you?"

Ignis looked down at his sister's concerned face, and remembered Ze'ev's words, thought of her hurt or dead. He shook his head, pushing the images away. "Just thinking. Ow, careful!"

"Oh, sorry." Allandra took her hands away, then looked with concern at him. The marks from his abortive fights with Ichiro and Shiro were still on him. "What happened to you?"

Ignis looked down at Allandra's black eye and bruised cheek. "Me? What happened to *you*?"

"Kentaro." Allandra's eyes were determined. "You have to promise me you won't try and do anything this time. I'm going to settle this myself."

Ignis sighed. "The way I've been doing the last few days, you'd be better off without me."

"Don't say that. I'll never be better off without you. You're my brother."

Ignis looked at her, then dropped his head and nodded. Suddenly he laughed. "God, we're a sorry pair, aren't we? We look like we've been through a war."

"Well, you do, anyway. Did someone hit you with a club?"

"Me? You're the one with the black eye!"

Allandra laughed as well, then was suddenly serious. "Maybe. But if this is a war, we're going to win it. I'm not giving up."

Ignis studied his sister, then nodded. "Neither am I."

The next morning, Vargas strode into the living room in Hampstead.

Pete looked up from where he was reading the *Sun*. "What's up, boss?"

"Pack the Land Rover, and get Tav. We're going hunting."

6
TRIALS

Ignis did go back to Ze'ev the next day, and the next day,
and the next. Ze'ev took Ignis back through the basic
principles of *taijutsu* that he had only half learned the first
time around, making sure that his movement was perfect.
He also taught rolls, evasion, or anything else that he
thought Ignis wasn't doing well enough – which was most
things. After that first night, Ze'ev discussed nothing
beyond individual techniques, but instinctively Ignis knew
that the lessons weren't just remedial *taijutsu*: they were a
test. Ignis stuck with it, working hard not only at Ze'ev's
lessons but also in the classroom and *dojo* during the day.
To begin with it was almost unbearable, and only sheer
willpower drove him to each class and piece of work. But
gradually, Ignis's determination began to grow. He *would*
succeed and become strong. He would prove to Ze'ev and
to everyone else that he was someone to be reckoned with.

For Allandra, on the other hand, Ze'ev was simply a
teacher, if a harder one than she was used to. Ze'ev wasn't

149

cruel, but he was ruthless, giving her no slack or second chances. He would show a technique once, and then expect her to be able to use it against him. If she got it wrong, she'd get hit. The only way not to get hit was to do it right. Allandra learned quickly never to drop her guard, since Ze'ev's way of showing her an opening in her defences was to go through it. Again and again Allandra was floored. "What are you doing!" she snapped one day, glaring up at Ze'ev from where she was lying rubbing her leg. "I was practising wrist locks! Why'd you kick me?"

"You left your front leg exposed. You think your enemy'll just sit there while you try something on him?"

"You could have just told me. Or tapped me!"

Ze'ev grinned. "That *was* a tap."

After that, Allandra stopped complaining. The lessons seemed endless, however. Finally, after half an hour struggling through a throwing technique one day, Allandra threw up her hands. "I can't do this! Haven't we done enough drills yet?"

Ze'ev looked quizzically at her, then shrugged. "Fair enough. Let's spar."

"Seriously?"

"You've been learning techniques against straight attacks. Let's see if you can use 'em."

It was midday, and they were alone in the *dojo*. Allandra took up a position three metres from Ze'ev. Ze'ev bowed, and Allandra returned it. Then she fell back into the *ichi mongi* receiving stance, alight with excitement, waiting for Ze'ev.

He came in without subtleties, punching at her face. Allandra jumped back out of range. A second blow came in, then a third. Allandra dodged, then when she felt she had his measure, grabbed the arm as it whistled past her ear, trying for a wrist lock.

The wrist didn't move. Ze'ev yanked her in and struck her under the ribcage with the other arm. Allandra sank to the ground, gasping for breath.

When she had recovered, Ze'ev was standing in front of her, waiting. She scrambled to her feet and nodded.

This time he moved in with both hands, trying for a grab. Allandra let him get a grip of her jacket with one arm but pulled away with her body as she did, trying to jerk him off balance. Ze'ev didn't budge an inch. He spun her around, tripped her as she staggered past, and pinned her to the floor with her arm twisted up behind her back.

The third time, Allandra kept her distance, striking at his body, but Ze'ev kept on closing in until Allandra was backed into a corner. Allandra struck, feinted, then finally charged, trying to break past. Ze'ev simply grabbed her around the waist and lifted her up, slamming her against the wall and holding her there. Then he reached up and placed the edge of his hand against her throat. Allandra's

151

arms were shorter: she couldn't reach past Ze'ev's grip. It took her a moment to realise that he'd stopped. "Keep going!"

"Fight's over, little one."

"No it's not!"

"If I'd struck with this hand," he moved the one against her throat, "you'd be choking on the floor right now."

Allandra glared at him. Ze'ev lowered her to the ground. "Want to keep trying?"

"I know you're better than I am! This isn't proving anything. I—"

"I wasn't using any skill at all, girl. The way I came at you was the same way a brawler would. The way a bully would. And you lost."

Allandra sagged, her resolve crumbling. "I – I just –" She looked up. "What am I doing wrong?"

Ze'ev looked at her and sighed. "Come on outside."

It was an overcast day, the thick clouds above them sweeping from east to west. Dead leaves drifted down from the trees, spinning and rising on the autumn winds before falling to lie in thick drifts on the valley paths. The *dojo*s on either side shielded them from the wind's full force, but odd side draughts blew through the gap, sending Allandra's hair streaming out behind her. At their feet ran the stream, flowing under the steps and under the next *dojo* on its bustling progress down to the lake. Ze'ev lowered himself down onto the *dojo* steps and Allandra sat next to him. They sat in silence for a few minutes.

Finally Ze'ev spoke. "What you're doing wrong is that you're not a boy."

Allandra just stared at him.

"Look, Allandra, every girl has to face this some time in her life, so you might as well learn it early. Men are just better fighters than women. Stronger, faster, more aggressive – all ways. You're not a bad student. You're fast and you have a feel for the fighting arts – if you were a boy, you'd already be better than Kentaro. But you're not."

"So what?" Allandra demanded angrily. "Are you saying I can't win? I should just give up?"

"Easy, girl. I haven't finished. You're still doing what most students do for their first ten years – trying to fight with strength. That's why you lost to Kentaro, and why you're losing to me now. Back in that hall, you were trying to pull me over, hit me harder than I could hit you. If you fight like that, you've lost your battle before you've started. You have to move with your opponent, not against him. Move around his attacks, take his balance, stay out of range, but never let the battle be strength against strength. If you don't fight your opponent head on, it doesn't matter how much muscle he has. The real masters hardly use their muscles at all. They just move in such a way that their enemy defeats himself."

153

"But they're sixty years old! What am I supposed to do?"

Ze'ev grinned. "I didn't say you had to be perfect. You just have to be better than your enemy. Come on, I'll show you how to do those locks you were trying for properly. Remember, use your body weight, not your muscles. Do it right and it should feel relaxed."

"Yeah, yeah," Allandra muttered as they got up. "I'd feel more relaxed if I didn't have to worry about you hitting me whenever I made a mistake."

"Relaxing stops blows hurting so much. See? I'm doing you a favour. Let's go."

The days became colder as autumn started its change into winter and the Christmas holidays approached. Ignis, Allandra, Christopher, Jennifer and Shiro began to form a loose group. They spent most of their time together, talking about the new tricks they were studying in *taijutsu*, which teachers they liked the most and the least, what was going to happen over Christmas. The one subject Allandra avoided bringing up was Kentaro, and every time Ignis or one of the others mentioned him, Allandra changed the subject. In classes she would do her best to ignore Kentaro's insults, and she carefully avoided letting herself be caught alone outside of lessons, sticking close to one of the other four. To anyone who didn't look too closely, it was as if she'd forgotten about him. In the meantime, she carried on training with Ze'ev, adding his lessons to the main classes that were already tiring her. Bit by bit, Allandra came to understand what he was trying to teach her – to move with her body and balance, redirecting an opponent's attack instead of trying to meet it head on. Most times now she could actually throw Ze'ev when he attacked her, instead of struggling for a hold which never came. Lessons and her friends formed a comfortable frame that Allandra settled into as the days went by. If it wasn't for thoughts of Michael, she could almost feel at home.

"Now where?"

Vargas traced his finger down the map. "We've tried both banks of the Tawi. I don't see how they could have got further downstream than Llangweision. Not without someone seeing them."

"What if someone's hiding them?"

Vargas snorted. "In a village? Someone sneezes too loud in a place like that and everybody knows about it by the next day. A boy and a girl being washed up on the riverbank could never be kept quiet. Someone would have come for the reward."

Tav frowned in thought, then pointed. "What about there?"

" 'Mynydd Garn-goch'. It's a moor. Deserted."

"What about down there, the place with the red marks? That looks empty."

"That's because it's an artillery range, Tav."

"Ah."

The two of them were standing over an Ordnance Survey map laid out across the living-room table in Tawelfan. Vargas laid both hands on the table and stared out of the window, drumming his fingers.

After a few minutes of silence, Tav cleared his throat. "Vargas, are you sure they're still here? You know the girl's not stupid. Probably the first thing they did was hitch a lift. They could be the other side of the country by now."

"If that's so, why hasn't anybody caught a trace of them?" Vargas stared into the distance, eyes narrowed. "Ten weeks is a long time. A very long time to stay on the run. You have to pass a lot of people to travel across this country, and the descriptions have been sent everywhere. A reward of fifty thousand's enough to make anybody sit up and take notice, no matter how little attention they usually pay kids. Then there's the police and the Missing Persons, and my own searchers. By now I should have got a lead of some kind. An overnight stay, a bus ride, a sighting on a street corner, anything. Instead I've had nothing but hustlers on the make and an old lady who says she saw Allandra in a train carriage with Elvis."

Tav didn't answer. Six foot one and smartly dressed,

with Latin good looks, he had the face of a lady-killer rather than a professional criminal, but appearances were deceptive. Tav was a tough, competent man, who had risen to the position of second-in-command in Vargas's organisation through ambition, ruthlessness and knowing when to shut up. This was one of those times.

"So why hasn't there been a trace?" Vargas asked after a pause, then answered his own question. "Because they're not moving. They're holed up somewhere. And if you wanted to hole up somewhere, this would be the place to do it. This part of Wales is one of the wildest and most deserted spots left in Britain. They could be hidden here, and nobody would know." Vargas straightened. "We've been trying south and west for too long. We'll go north. Maybe to . . ." His finger traced along the map, tapped it. "This lake, Llyn Garedig. We'll check it out tomorrow."

Saturday morning. Climbing practice.

Perched on the rockface, Allandra reached up and slipped her fingers into a crack in the stone, testing it for strength. Once she was sure it would hold her weight, she pulled herself up around the overhang. The hill she was climbing had been a quarry once, but the miners had gone away a long time ago. The old road that had once been used to cart away slate had been swallowed up by the forest, and the quarry was surrounded by trees. It was a beautiful morning, the sun shining bright off the tree-tops.

Allandra loved climbing. It was the one subject where she was at the top of the class. Here on the cliffs, her light weight became an advantage, and she could scramble easily up ledges that the bigger boys struggled with.

A noise from below made her look down. "Come on, slowcoach!"

Three metres below her, Ignis muttered something inaudible before painstakingly pulling himself up another few centimetres. Allandra and Ignis, along with the better half of the class, were on one of the "intermediate" climbs, on the east face of the hill. The rest of the first years and the climbing teacher were on the "beginner" slopes on the north face. Allandra had had to cajole her brother to get him to join her on the harder climb; for all his love of heights, Ignis didn't seem to like climbing much. Allandra put it down to laziness.

She hooked her arm around a protruding rock and shook her hair back, enjoying the sun. "You know," she called down to Ignis, "there's a wonderful view from up here."

Ignis didn't answer and Allandra grinned mischievously. "You can see nearly the whole lake. It's a beautiful day, isn't it? Do you want to sit here for a while?"

"Shut *up*."

"Catch me and I will."

Ignis pulled himself up, aiming for her. Allandra scampered quickly up a chimney. There was a ledge half-way and she perched herself on it, looking down. Ignis was still struggling with the chimney. The bushes that marked the top of the quarry were only a minute's climb away.

"The view's even *better* now," she called down.

"You're going to pay for this."

"Oh, like you could get close enough."

Ignis grabbed at her leg. Allandra swung it out of range easily and climbed to the top of the chimney, grinning as she watched her brother try to keep his balance on the steep crevices.

There was a flash of movement at the edge of Allandra's vision. She ducked and a stone struck the rockface where her head had been an instant ago, bouncing off to spin earthwards. For a second she couldn't figure out what had happened, then she saw the pair of figures laughing at the bottom of the quarry. She was too high to see their faces, but she recognised the one on the right.

Kentaro.

For an instant Allandra was almost blinded by rage. If that rock had hit her, he could have killed her. In that instant, she made her decision. Allandra jumped back-wards off the rock, sliding down her safety line. A second stone clattered above her as she abseiled down, bouncing three times off the quarry face before landing with a thump, her knees bent to absorb the impact. She detached the line and started towards Kentaro.

Ignis came down behind her and caught her arm. "Ally!"

Allandra shook him off. "No."

Ignis's eyes were frustrated. "Let me—"

Allandra's eyes flashed. "No. Don't you *dare*, Ig. What do you think I've been training for? If you want to help, make sure no one interferes."

Ignis let out a breath. "I hope you know what you're doing." He let go of her arm.

So do I, Allandra said silently. She stalked towards Kentaro. He grinned at her. "Ooh, looks like someone's—"

"This ends, Kentaro. Right now. I'm challenging you."

"You?" Kentaro laughed. "What are you going to do, slap me?"

"I'm going to take you apart, Kentaro. You're so stupid that you're a class behind everyone else your age, so the most you can do is try and beat up everyone younger than you. Even then you're such a coward you don't have the guts to fight someone your own size. You have to pick a girl who's so small that even you couldn't manage to lose, as if you hadn't proven you were weak enough already. You—"

"Shut up!" screamed Kentaro. "I'll break your neck!"

"Come and try." She and Kentaro were in a circle of

students now, with more and more gathering round. Allandra saw Ignis, Christopher, Jennifer, Ichiro, Shiro. She had less than five minutes before the teacher noticed the disturbance and came to investigate. "That is, if you can even work up the guts to fight on your own. I've never seen you without at least one friend to pull your butt out of trouble."

"I don't need anyone to beat you!"

Yori was standing apart from Kentaro, in the circle with the others. Allandra was relieved. It was the first time she'd ever really tried to provoke someone, and the insults hadn't come naturally to her. Now that Kentaro was alone, she could do what she'd been longing to. "Then prove it." She hit Kentaro as hard as she could and jumped back.

Kentaro lunged at her. Allandra sidestepped, catching Kentaro in the gut with her elbow. She hit without force, but with Kentaro's charge, it was as if he'd run into a tree branch. Kentaro doubled over, losing all the breath in his lungs in a gasp. As he staggered Allandra punched him in the head and the side. The third blow whistled through the air as Kentaro backed away, out of range. He circled, crouching, with murder in his eyes. Allandra circled with him, wary, watching for the shift in weight that would tell her he was about to attack.

From behind Allandra, Yori watched with a frown. This wasn't what was supposed to happen. Kentaro should have already put the girl on the ground by now. She shouldn't be able to actually hurt him.

So when Allandra's back was to him, he took a step forward, intending to trip her. Once she was down, Kentaro should be able to beat her easily. On the other side of the circle, Ignis saw the movement and tensed, ready to charge in to help his sister.

Someone took Yori's wrist and twisted it sharply. Pain shot through his arm and suddenly Yori was standing on tiptoe, holding his back very straight and feeling as though his arm was about to be wrenched out of its socket. With a gasp he looked back over his shoulder.

Shiro smiled at him. "Ah, ah. No interfering."

Kentaro feinted once, then again. Allandra didn't react. Watch the body, Ze'ev had told her again and again. Movement comes from the body.

Kentaro's body moved. Allandra jumped back, sliding away from his blows. Students behind her dodged out of the way as the two of them backed past. One of Kentaro's blows went wild, and Allandra slid into the gap, slamming a *shikanken* strike into his ribcage. Kentaro punched Allandra, making her stagger, and before she could get away he had a grip on her coat. This was the situation Allandra had always dreaded: body to body, where her lesser weight and strength became deadly.

But Kentaro's punches didn't have the accuracy of

Ze'ev's. One blow glanced off Allandra's cheek and another off her forehead as she stumbled, trying to regain her balance. As the third blow came in, Allandra found her footing. Sliding her left foot across in a sidestep, Allandra twisted, pressing her right elbow down on top of Kentaro's left, aiming for the pressure point just above the joint. Suddenly Kentaro was lunging into empty space. Allandra stepped sideways and back, spinning him down into the ground with a crash. Before he could recover Allandra straightened his arm, resting the wrist on her shoulder and pressing down with both hands on the back of his elbow. Kentaro was helpless.

"Give up?" she asked quietly.

Kentaro didn't move for a second, then nodded.

As Allandra released him and straightened she saw Kentaro's shoulders shift. Kentaro came up swinging to meet the heel of Allandra's hand in his throat. He doubled over, gagging. He curled up into a ball, shaking. Allandra stood ready in *ichi mongi*, but after a second she realised that he wasn't shaking in anger. He was crying.

Allandra turned and walked away. Christopher and Jennifer were waiting for her; they slapped her back, punched the air in triumph.

"You did it!"

"Yeah!"

"You rule, Ally!"

"Kicked him into orbit!"

Shiro and Ignis ran up. Ignis was grinning with delight. "Damn, that was good! Where'd you learn to do *that*?"

A high, wavering scream sounded from behind her. "*Allandra!*"

She turned. Kentaro was on his feet, his eyes wild, his face streaked with blood and tears. "You'll die for this! You hear me? *You'll die!*"

"Only if she ever has to see your ugly face again, Kentaro!" Jennifer shouted back.

Then the shakes finally started for Allandra. Ignis noticed and put an arm around his sister. "Let's go."

The sun was beginning to dip in the western sky when Allandra climbed to the peak of the northwestern hill and flopped down on the scrubby grass. The trees here were sparse and the sun beamed down on Allandra's back as she lay, her head supported by her hands, staring out at the road which wound across the far side of the lake.

A whisper of movement behind her made her turn. Ignis was climbing the hill towards her. He raised a hand. "Hey, Ally."

Allandra didn't answer. Ignis walked over to her and lay down, leaning on an elbow. "Chris and Jennifer are back in your room with Shiro. I think they want to celebrate."

Allandra looked out over the lake.

164

"Not going?" Ignis asked.

"I'll go back in a bit," Allandra finally replied.

"What's up?"

Allandra let out a breath. "What happened with Kentaro. I never . . ."

"You've never had to do something like this before." Ignis shrugged. "I know. It's always me who gets into trouble. You've never had a real fight before, have you?"

Allandra shook her head.

"Well, you did a good job. That last strike was a beauty. Finished him in one hit."

Allandra didn't answer. Ignis cocked his head to see her face; she turned away. "What's wrong? I know you're not happy about fighting—"

"No!"

"Then what is it?"

Allandra took a deep breath. "It wasn't that I didn't want to. I wanted to too much." She looked into Ignis's eyes, searching. "I enjoyed it. When I was in the middle of that fight, it felt like I— What the hell are you laughing about! You think this is *funny*?"

Ignis grinned. "Yes, it's funny. It's funny that you think that's so bad you have to creep off and feel guilty."

"Listen to me, you idiot! I enjoyed the fight. It felt like I was alive, really alive, for the first time ever. And when he was on the ground that last time . . . I didn't want to stop.

I wanted to drag him up and keep hitting him, keep fighting until there was nothing left of him. Don't you get it?"

Ignis looked seriously at her. "Of course I get it. It's you that doesn't. Enjoying a fight doesn't mean there's something wrong with you, Ally."

"But I *wanted* to hurt him! In the middle of that fight, if we'd had weapons – I think I could have killed him." She looked up at Ignis. "How does that make me any different from him?"

Ignis shrugged. "I would have done a lot worse to him if you'd let me."

"You were just trying to help me, though."

"You were trying to help yourself."

"But I *enjoyed* it."

"That was why you could win. Look, Ally, if you couldn't enjoy fighting, you wouldn't be any good at it. If you really hated fighting, you never would have trained to fight Kentaro in the first place. You would have let me handle him for you."

"I know. And I didn't want you to. It's just . . ." Allandra sighed. "I like martial arts. But I'm not sure how much I like using them for real."

Ignis shrugged. "So you can just do it for fun, after you've given up on your crazy plan to go back and rescue Michael."

Allandra glared at him. "It is *not* a crazy plan! And I will!"

Ignis grinned. "Now you're back to normal."

Allandra swiped at Ignis. He ducked and Allandra laughed. The two of them lay back on the grass in the sun, and for the first time that day, Allandra felt as though the world was in its right place.

"You know," she said after a pause, looking up at the sky, "I think we could make this work. We really could stay here."

Ignis gazed into the distance, and nodded. "Maybe we could."

On the other side of the lake, two hills down, a Land Rover was climbing the gradient, its engine growling as it clawed its way upwards in second gear.

"How much further?"

Tav turned the map left, then right. "Next hill, should be. Or maybe the one after. Look, I'm not a bloody bird-watcher!"

"Shut up and tell me when we're over the lake."

"There!" Tav pointed left where a dip in the road offered a brief glimpse of shining water. "That's it, over this hill."

"So what happens now?"

The afternoon sun beamed down on them as they looked

167

out over the lake. The rays passed over their heads and reflected away off the water, illuminating the western hills. Dying bracken glowed brown amidst the green of the grass. A pair of wild ponies grazed below the road.

Ignis rolled over onto his chest. "Well, Chris told me that Mr Oakley was looking for you. Both you and Kentaro are going to get in trouble."

"I can deal with that."

"Are you going to keep training with Ze'ev?"

Allandra yawned. "I don't know. I guess I probably should." She thought about it. "Maybe less often. How about you?"

Ignis nodded slowly. "I'll stick with it."

The hum of a distant engine rose from the other side of the lake, and a car emerged from around one of the hills. It crawled slowly from right to left across the slopes, following the twists and turns of the road. It looked almost, Allandra thought lazily, like their father's Land Rover.

"See anything?"

Tav squinted. The sun was setting over the hills across the lake, and the reflection off the water was dazzling him. All he could see was forest, and shadows under the trees.

The car turned away out of sight to the north, the hum fading into the distance. Allandra yawned once more and rolled over. "Come on, then. Let's get back." The two of them walked back down the slope, squirrels racing away through the branches above them.

Vargas braked the car, coming to a stop. "Anything?"

"No. There's nothing here, boss. We're the only people for miles."

Vargas drummed his fingers on the wheel for several long seconds, then shook his head. "This is a waste of time. They can't be this far north. Let's get out of here." The Land Rover spun in a U-turn and pulled away southwards.

7

WINTER AND SPRING

Allandra did get into trouble. Mr Oakley gave her a long lecture and put her on kitchen chores for the rest of the term. The lecture bothered her more than the chores. Allandra had grown to like Mr Oakley more and more, and she didn't like being in his bad books. Still, she didn't see what else she could have done.

Kitchen chores meant peeling potatoes, cooking rice, gathering firewood and carrying water from the lake to the purifying tanks at the top of the valley, where the grit in the lake water was allowed to settle out before it was used for cooking. Allandra kept a wary eye out for the first few days. To fetch water she had to take the path down the valley and through the dozen long-stemmed wind generators placed between the alder trees at the mouth of the stream. The area was deserted in the evenings, and the thrum of the generators drowned out the sound of footsteps – the perfect place for Kentaro or his friends to ambush her. But although Kentaro still came to lessons, gave her vicious glances from behind his plastered nose and muttered sentences to Yori in which Allandra caught her name a few times, he came no closer. After two weeks, Allandra began to relax.

The Christmas holidays came, and snow arrived overnight in Rokkaku, covering the trees' leafless branches with white and turning the valley bright and still. Christopher and Jennifer went home, but Shiro and enough of the other students stayed for Allandra and Ignis not to be too lonely. They cut a small pine sapling from the forest and set it up in Allandra's room for a Christmas tree. Most of the other students in Rokkaku were surprised that Allandra and Ignis were so cheerful at being away from home for Christmas. The two of them laughed over it in private.

More frustrating to Allandra was the restriction on going outside the valley. As part of her punishment, she had to stay in Rokkaku, while Ignis and Shiro could take trips up into the winter forest whenever they wanted. With nothing else to do, she started borrowing books from Mr Oakley. After a while he got her a catalogue from a nearby library, and agreed to take out books for her on his Sunday trips. He also brought her books that she hadn't asked for. Allandra's library at home had mostly been early readers, mixed with a few novels from school English classes like *Stig of the Dump* and *A Wrinkle in Time*. The books Mr Oakley picked out for her were older stories, by Charles

Dickens, Rudyard Kipling, and Richard Adams. Some Allandra found too strange or slow, but others fascinated her: *Watership Down* was her favourite, and she pestered Mr Oakley until he gave her a copy of her own. As the long winter nights brought snow and frost to Rokkaku, Allandra could be found more often than not curled up in her bed, reading over and over the story of the escape from Efrafa, and Bigwig's last stand against General Woundwort.

For Ignis, the days came to focus more and more around his lessons with Ze'ev. For his own reasons the teacher had chosen to stay in Rokkaku over the winter, and with nothing else to do, Ignis trained with him every day.

When classes started again in January, Ignis found to his surprise that he had not only caught up, but was ahead of the other boys. Ze'ev's lessons had accumulated without him noticing, and Ignis found himself being praised by the teachers. Being approved of by teachers – or any adults, for that matter – was a new experience for him, and he wasn't sure what to make of it. Rumours started to circulate in the class about the 'Hunt', an event that would occur in the middle of the term, and as the date drew nearer, excitement mounted.

It was a Sunday late in February. Allandra was lying across the sofa in Jennifer's room, reading. Her own room was quieter, but she liked having the light through the windows. Jennifer was on her bed with a sheet of Maths problems and an exercise book. For the last few minutes she'd been staring into space, her pen tapping absently on the half-completed equations.

"Hey, Ally?"

The steady *shhhhh* of falling rain pattered on the windows. The past few days had been so wet that morning runs had been cancelled in favour of work-outs in the gym. Everything else had been moved into the *dojo*s.

"Hey, Ally!"

Allandra flipped a page. "Hmm?"

"Where do the staff keep the flour?"

"In the top storehouses."

"Where do they keep the glue?"

"In the— Why do you want to know?"

"Oh, it's for History class."

Allandra went back to her book. The room was quiet but for the raindrops on the window.

"Want to go out?" Jennifer broke the silence.

"Not really."

"Let's."

"I want to finish my book."

"What is it?"

"*The Jungle Book*."

"C'mon, you've read that one already!"

"I like it. Anyway, it's raining."

"We could go practise in the gym."

"We did that yesterday."

"But the first Hunt's on Friday! Don't you want to train?"

Allandra shrugged. Although she *was* a little nervous about the rumoured 'Hunt', she didn't see how she could train for something when she didn't know what it was.

Jennifer stared out of the window. "Do you think the kitchens would have any feathers?"

Allandra sighed. "Who is it this time?"

"What do you mean?"

"Jen, that innocent look only works on the teachers."

Jennifer kept up her expression of wide-eyed surprise for a few more seconds, then giggled. "Oops. I'd better practise it."

"You'd better. The next time everything blows up, I don't think the teachers are going to believe me when I tell them you were sitting quietly in your room. When you told me you were going to give Yori a pet squirrel, I thought you meant in a box, not inside his—"

"Blah, blah, blah. I don't know how you ever manage to do anything, you always find so many things wrong with an idea."

"Hey, back in London, *I* was the one who came up with all the dangerous plans. Next to you, *anyone* would look like a stick-in-the-mud."

"Then you should be more like me!" Jennifer rolled sideways and hung her head off the end of the bed. "Turn to the chaotic side of the force, Luke, it is your *des*tinyyy . . . "

"*Your* destiny is to fail the Maths test, more like."

Jennifer reached down to the floor, then kicked off the bed into a handstand. She held it for a few seconds, then let herself fall back, twisting as she did to roll back into a *seiza* stance. Allandra returned to her book.

"Hey, Ally?"

"Yes, I noticed how good a gymnast you are. Go impress Christopher."

"Ally, who brought you to Rokkaku?"

Allandra blinked. "What did you say?"

"You know, the person who pulled you and Ig out of the river, and brought you to Rokkaku. Did you ever find out who it was?"

"No. I thought it was one of the teachers. Or one of the older students, out on patrol. They go down as far as the Tawi, don't they?"

"Yeah, but how did they know your names?"

"Because—" Allandra stopped dead.

Jennifer looked at her.

"They couldn't have known our names," Allandra said slowly. "Ignis wasn't awake either. But when I woke up in Rokkaku, the teachers already knew who we were. They said it was in a letter . . . "

"A teacher wouldn't have left a letter. He would have just said it."

"But . . ." Allandra stopped. "That doesn't make sense. It *must* have been someone from Rokkaku. Who else could have been there?"

Jennifer shrugged. "I don't know. But there's the money, too."

"What money?"

"Well, you know Rokkaku charges fees, right? There's a scholarship thing, but if they haven't asked you about it, that means someone must be paying for you."

"How much does it cost?"

"A lot."

"Oh." Allandra shook her head. "I can't believe I didn't think of this before. Thanks, Jen. Where do you know all this from? Did you come here on a scholarship?"

Jennifer looked away. "Yeah." She got up. "I'm going to the gym. See you later." Jennifer grabbed her raincoat and slid out of the door, sending a brief gust of cold air through the room.

Allandra looked after her in surprise. *Was it something I said?* Then she frowned, looking out of the window into the pouring rain as she mulled over plans in her mind. After half an hour, she got up, marked her place in the book, and found her coat.

Mr Oakley was reading in his study. He greeted Allandra in his usual warm but absent-minded fashion as she shut the door against the rush of cold air. The tea was in its usual place. While it brewed, Allandra looked over Mr Oakley's shoulder. The book he was reading was written in Greek.

"Oh, thank you, Allandra," Mr Oakley said as she gave him his usual mug.

"Who's paying our tuition fees?" Allandra asked, sitting down.

Mr Oakley blinked and looked up. "Didn't I ever tell you?"

"No."

He shook his head. "Dear me, that was forgetful of me. Well, it was all in the letter that was left with you and your brother when you were first brought here. All it said was that the two of you were to be placed in the first-year class of Rokkaku, and, providing that you agreed to stay, it left details of a bank account from which the fees for your schooling will be transferred each term."

"Who wrote the letter? Whose is the bank account?"

"The letter was unsigned. And the holder of the bank account is anonymous."

Allandra dropped back into her chair in disgust. "It's so frustrating. This guy pulls us out of the river, brings us here, and sets this up, all in secret. Why doesn't he just tell us what's going on? I don't even know his name."

"Are you so sure it's a he?" Mr Oakley murmured.

Allandra looked up. "What did you say?"

"Never mind. Let me put it another way, Allandra. This unknown person has so far gone to a considerable amount of trouble to place you and Ignis here in Rokkaku, and also to ensure that you and your brother remain unaware of your helper's identity. To the best of my knowledge, your stay at Rokkaku has been greatly to the benefit of you both. So, since this person's actions in bringing you here seem to have been in your interest, why not assume that the secrecy might be in your interest also? This anonymous benefactor could easily have communicated with you before now. Since this has not been done, it suggests that there is some pressing reason that necessitates secrecy."

"But I want to know what's going on. And I won't be in Rokkaku for ever. I need to . . ." Allandra checked herself. "Look, could you write a letter for me? If you can get money from the bank, there must be some way to pass a message through. Just say that I want to meet him."

Mr Oakley sighed. "Allandra, what you lack in wisdom, you make up for in persistence. Very well, I will make sure your message is passed on. But please don't get impatient when you don't get an instant answer. You'll probably have to wait a while for a reply."

"Great! Thanks!" Allandra jumped to her feet. "Oh, are you going to be busy tonight? I'd like to play chess again."

"I should be available. Drop by at eight o'clock or so, and I'll make sure I have some biscuits so you don't start devouring my books while I'm contemplating my next move."

Allandra laughed and walked out, ducking her head against the falling rain. The door shut behind her.

Mr Oakley did not return to his copy of Homer. Instead, he sat in his chair, his head resting in one hand, looking thoughtfully after Allandra. He sat quietly for fifteen minutes, thinking. Then he rose and walked to his desk. Digging through the stacks of books and manuscripts, he found some notepaper and an old, battered fountain pen. Filling it with ink, he began to write a letter.

For Ignis, the week seemed to drag slower and slower as the date of the first Hunt approached. But Friday dawned clear and dry, and the anticipation in the class heightened with the coming evening.

They had been told to assemble at the third bridge at eight o'clock. Ignis and Allandra were there fifteen minutes early, with Shiro, Christopher and Jennifer. In the twilight, they could see the last members of the class arriving. Mr Oakley, Mr Morimoto and Dr Furuta appeared at five minutes to eight, walking down the valley carrying kit bags.

A register was called, then the teachers led them out into

179

the woods, up the north hill. The sun had set, and evening turned into dusk as they wound their way through the forest. Finally, light bloomed ahead of them.

The class stepped out into a clearing lit by a ring of dimly glowing lamps. The teachers were in the centre, the bags piled beside them. Mr Oakley held up his hand for silence as the students formed a semicircle around him.

"This is the Rokkaku Hunt," he stated quietly. The glow of the lights cast the students' faces in pale yellow; images of nervousness and excitement as they fell silent to listen. "The Hunt is a test of stealth, strength and skill, held at the middle and end of every term. The area you will be competing in is the woods around Rokkaku valley. The school itself is not out of bounds, but the area outside of the forest is. The duration of the Hunt is two hours. If you haven't been eliminated by then, return to this clearing. Now, your gear. Christopher, come here, please."

Christopher stepped forward, looking a little nervous. Mr Oakley motioned for him to turn around, then pushed a thin wire ring into the fabric at the back of Christopher's collar. It glowed a very faint fluorescent green. He clipped it shut, then gave Christopher a wristband with a glint of metal hanging off it.

"The ring is your lifeline. To break it, use the cutters on your wristband. If your lifeline is broken, you're dead: return here. The cutters are designed to only work on the rings. Your other two pieces of equipment are a flashlight and a whistle. The flashlight," he held up something that looked like a small Mag-Lite, "has an adjustable lens, so it can be masked. The whistle is to be used if someone is injured. The signal is three short blasts, repeated every minute. Once you have your equipment, split up and head to your assigned sectors.

"Now, the rules. The objective of the game is to eliminate all other students while staying alive yourself. This lasts until the Hunt is over or until you are killed, whichever comes first. But remember these three things. First, once you have been killed, return here to this clearing immediately. Failing to do so, or worse, continuing to fight, will result in being suspended from Hunts for the rest of the year. Second, weapons of any kind are forbidden. Third, while attacks to subdue other players are permissible, deliberate injuries of any kind are not. Anyone who breaks either of the last two rules will be expelled from the school immediately." Mr Oakley paused to let his words sink in.

"Finally, once you have been killed or it reaches eleven o'clock, return to this clearing to report to Mr Morimoto and hand in your equipment. Then go home. Scores will be posted tomorrow morning. Now form a line."

"This is so cool!" Ignis whispered to Allandra as they edged closer to the teachers.

"This is so *crazy*! How are we supposed to fight in the dark?"

Ignis grinned. "Let's find out."

"Here you go, Ignis." Ignis waited as Mr Oakley clipped the green ring around the back of his collar. The band wrapped around his right wrist with Velcro, and the whistle and flashlight fitted easily into his inner pockets. Mr Oakley gave Ignis a pat on the back. "Your starting sector is from Dalarwen to the northeast point. Good luck."

Ignis looked back at the edge of the clearing. Christopher and Shiro had gone already. As he watched, Allandra was sent off in a different direction. Ignis waved. Allandra waved back, then vanished out of the radius of the lights. Ignis took a deep breath, then set off into the darkness.

The sounds of chatter and movement behind Ignis quickly faded away as he headed northwards, leaving him alone with the crunching of his footsteps on the dead bracken. He was tracing a route not far removed from the one to the tightrope platforms, but in the dark it was hard to tell exactly how far away they were. No landmarks appeared, and eventually Ignis judged he'd gone far enough. He switched off his flashlight and waited.

Nothing is quite as uniquely menacing as a forest at night. In the sun's light, a forest can be peaceful and inviting, but when darkness falls, it becomes a strange, alien place. As Ignis stood under the tree, his night vision slowly adapting to show him the shapes of trees and bushes, standing still and silent around him, it felt as though he'd stepped back a million years into the feral times.

The trees around, so safe and unnoticed during the day, suddenly seemed strange and dangerous, concealing tiny rustles of movement. Ignis felt watched by invisible eyes. *We do not need you*, the forest seemed to say. *We existed before your time and we will cover the earth long after you are gone.* Ignis felt his excitement build. The wildness of the night called to something deep inside him.

A whisper of movement made him hold his breath. Was someone near?

The faint shrill of a whistle drifted up from the south. The Hunt had begun.

The attack came from his right. Ignis had barely time to turn before the other boy was on him, rushing him off his feet. Both of them fell, sliding and rolling down the slope, dead leaves crackling as the other boy landed on top of him with a thud. Fingers fumbled at Ignis's neck, reaching for the ring. Moving instinctively, Ignis twisted and hit up hard, striking with hands and knees. Ignis heard a grunt, then the weight was off him. He sprang to his feet, moving in for the kill.

His hand clutched on thin air. He swept left and right through the shadows, feeling nothing. The other student was gone. Carefully, Ignis backed up against a tree, then stumbled into it as a wave of dizziness hit him. It had happened so fast!

How did he get so close? Ignis thought, his head spinning. He stood in the darkness with his heart racing, trying to look in every direction at once. As his breathing began to slow down, Ignis realised. *He must have followed me from the clearing. I had my flashlight on, it would have been easy. Then he just sat and waited for the nine o'clock whistle.* Ignis let out a long breath. He'd just learned an important lesson, and didn't intend to forget it.

When he had recovered, Ignis started to pick his way south, more cautiously this time. Twice as he crept through the woods he heard shouts and crashes from ahead. The second time a yell drifted up that sounded like a girl's voice. Allandra? Ignis changed direction towards it.

The call had come from inside Rokkaku valley. The lights had been dimmed, but even so they seemed painfully bright as Ignis slipped down through the trees. On one of the high paths in front of him, a figure was slipping through the shadows. Ignis's eyes widened as he recognised the boy's face. He stepped out onto the path.

"Kentaro," Ignis grinned. "You know, I was kind of hoping I'd run into you."

Kentaro scowled at him, his face barely visible in the darkness. "You're that girl's brother."

"Bingo." Ignis flexed his shoulders and began to walk forward.

Kentaro didn't back away, or look afraid. Instead he waited, a grin growing on his face. Some instinct made Ignis look over his shoulder. Yori was creeping up behind him. As Ignis saw him, Yori lunged.

Ignis ducked aside, giving Yori a push that sent him stumbling into Kentaro, then grabbed one of the swing ropes and kicked off the platform. For one exhilarating moment the lights of the *dojo*s blurred underneath him as he soared through the night air, then he landed with a thump on the far side of the valley. Kentaro and Yori were running for the next set of ropes. As they swung across after him, Ignis looked around quickly. Running was no good; they would bracket him quickly, unless . . . Ignis grabbed a ladder and started climbing, pulling himself up to one of the tree houses. From its base a high rope ran for five metres to a platform built into a tall birch tree in the middle of the valley.

Ignis looked at the tightrope. It was shorter than the practice ones – but this time, there was no safety net to check the eight-metre fall to the stream. Footsteps sounded on the ladder behind him. Ignis focused, took a breath, then emptied his mind. He stepped out onto the rope and walked quickly and calmly across, alighting on the platform on the other side. He turned.

From their platform, Kentaro and Yori were staring at him open-mouthed. "You can't do that!" Kentaro shouted.

Ignis grinned and spread his hands. "Just did."

Kentaro stared, then nudged Yori. "Go and get him."

Yori turned, frowning. "Me? Why not you?"

"You get across and grab him. I'll go behind you."

Yori looked at the thin rope and hesitated. He muttered something, then carefully stepped out onto the rope, his eyes fixed on his feet.

Ignis watched with curiosity as the heavy-set boy took a wobbling step, then another. He waited for him to get halfway across, then spoke. "Yori, you're really not the sharpest tool in the box, are you?"

Yori looked up in confusion. "Huh?"

Ignis gave the rope a swift kick.

With a yell Yori lost his balance and toppled. He caught the rope as he fell, lost his grip, and tumbled into the branches of the tree below, where he hung, swinging.

Kentaro stared down in disbelief. Ignis clasped his hands behind his back. "Well, Kentaro? Coming? Oh, don't worry, I won't kick you off the rope. I've been wanting to meet you one-on-one for ages." Ignis grinned. "So what about it? Feel like matching up against someone your own size? Or is picking on girls smaller than you more your style?"

Kentaro glared across at Ignis. His gaze was pure, undisguised hatred. Then, silently, he turned and clambered away, down into the darkness.

With a laugh, Ignis turned, walked across another rope, then jumped down to land with a thump on the roof of the house below. The light came on in the window and a sixth-former stuck his head out as Ignis jumped off again to slide down a rope. "Hey!" he shouted. "Hunt quietly, I'm trying to sleep!"

"Sorry!" Ignis called back as he ran up and out of the valley again. Fading away behind him, he could hear Yori yelling to Kentaro to get him down. Ignis paused and turned at the valley peak to look back.

Something pushed him sideways. Ignis staggered left and a hand caught his neck. There was a snip and the grip released.

Ignis spun to see Ichiro, barely visible in the dim light, looking at him. He tossed the broken ring at Ignis's feet and motioned to Hiroshi, standing nearby. They faded into the night, leaving Ignis staring in disbelief. He felt the back of his neck. His lifeline was gone.

That was it?

Ignis stood there for a full minute, his nerves and muscles keyed up with energy. He took a step forward, burning to run after Ichiro and Hiroshi, tear into them –

and stopped, remembering the rules, and Ze'ev. He couldn't.

Damn!

With a noise of frustration, Ignis turned away north. The clearing was only a few minutes' walk. He handed in his wristband, flashlight and whistle, and trailed dispiritedly back to the bottom of the valley. He walked into Allandra's room.

Both Allandra and Jennifer were already there. Allandra was lying on the sofa, her head cupped in her hands. "You, too?" she asked as she saw him.

"I didn't even get anybody," Ignis muttered.

Allandra sighed. "Me neither. I guess we'll see how we did when they post the scores tomorrow."

"Well, this sucks," Ignis announced.

It was Saturday morning outside the *dojo*, and they were sitting in a circle on the grass by the stream. The rest of the class were scattered around, talking animatedly about the night's battle.

The five of them had done dismally. Ignis, Allandra, Jennifer and Christopher had all been eliminated in the first hour of the competition without getting a single kill between them. Even Shiro had been taken down in the final hour by Ichiro without managing to make a hit in response. The scoreboard was completely one-sided.

Ichiro led, predictably, with three kills.

"Yeesh." Jennifer stretched. "We really are bad."

"No, we're not." Christopher looked annoyed. "It was the pairs. They were working together, we were on our own. That was why we were beaten so easily. I can't believe I didn't think of it."

Laughter sounded from behind them. Ignis turned to see Ichiro and two of his group, chattering and joking together. Ichiro was miming a cutting motion, reliving one of his kills. Kentaro and Yori were all grins, glancing at Ignis and Allandra with a smirk. Ignis turned away sharply.

"So did Ichiro plan it all out?" Allandra asked.

Shiro shook his head. "No. Someone told him about the rules in advance. Hiroshi's got a brother in the fifth year: that's how they would have known."

"Who cares how they know?" Jennifer demanded. "They all paired up before we even knew anything was going on. Then when the Hunt started, we were sitting ducks!"

"But they couldn't have." Ignis shook his head in annoyance. "We were all split up. Everyone went to different sectors. That was the whole point, so that we'd be on our own from the start."

Christopher shook his head. "No. They didn't plan the pairs out."

"What makes you so sure?" Ignis demanded.

"Because they didn't have to. Look." Christopher started placing sticks on the grass, sketching out a map. "After I got home I couldn't sleep, so I worked it all out. The sectors the teachers assigned were big ones. My one was all the way from Dalarwen to the top of Nant Garedig. There wouldn't have been room for more than four of those, five counting the school as well."

"So?"

"So there are nineteen in the class. Nineteen among five is four to each, and one with three. So Ichiro and the rest could just hang back once they left the clearing, and watch who else was headed their way. If it was someone they knew, they'd meet up with them and go to their sector together. Four to each would mean three others in their sector. If all ten of them cooperated, the probability that at least eight of them would get paired up is over fifty per cent."

The other four looked at each other. Shiro nodded. "He's right."

"This has to be against the rules," Jennifer said.

Shiro shook his head. "No. There's nothing that forbids working together. It's probably a tradition here."

"OK, so we do the same from now on!" Jennifer declared. "Let's see how they like a dose of their own medicine!"

"No," Christopher answered. "There are only five of us. For a start, we're an odd number. Now, the chances of us

190

all ending up in different sectors are less than one in twenty-five, but the most likely distribution that leaves is two or three of us together and the others on their own. Even if we get lucky and get two pairs, that'll be two of ours against four of theirs."

Ignis, Allandra, Shiro and Jennifer stared at him.

"Could you say that in English?" Ignis finally asked.

Christopher sighed. "It won't work because we'll all end up in different places."

"Oh." Ignis shrugged. "So do you have a better idea?"

Christopher grinned. "Actually, I do. Come a bit closer." He glanced around, then lowered his voice.

"OK, here's the plan. Before the next Hunt, we agree on a meeting point near Rokkaku. It has to be easy to find in the dark, and close enough to the valley that we can reach it quickly from all five sectors. When the Hunt starts, we sneak to it and meet up. Then, we work together and hunt them down. It'll be five on two each time. If we do it quietly we could take down the whole class before they know what's hit them."

The four of them shared a long look. "We'd have to practise working in the dark," Shiro said after a pause, thoughtful. "And we'd need some kind of signal system."

"We could use Morse code," Christopher said. "Or birdcalls."

"It'd be a lot of work," Ignis said.

Christopher raised his eyebrows. "Is there something you'd rather be doing?"

Ignis and Allandra looked at each other, and grinned.

The six weeks that followed were busy ones for Ignis and Allandra. They had to learn to work together in total silence, identify each other by the system of birdcalls that Christopher invented, and be able to fight together without mistakenly picking each other as targets. Most difficult of all was doing it without any of the other students noticing. Shiro directed them all, organising night expeditions into the forest where they could practise without fear of being spotted.

But for all the activity, Allandra began to find her thoughts drifting towards home. Sometimes, as she lay in her bed with the moonlight filtering through the open door, she would think of bringing Michael here. Getting into her father's house wouldn't be too hard. If she could just bring Michael to Rokkaku, there would be no way Vargas could find them. All three of them would be safe together.

She knew it was a crazy plan. Even if she could make it out of the Hampstead house, they'd still face a two-hundred-mile journey back to Wales, dodging the police and her father's men at every turn. Yet no matter how many times she pushed the idea away, it came floating back. As the end of the spring term and their second Hunt drew near, she found herself wondering just how quickly she could make it to London without being spotted.

"Wristband, flashlight, whistle. Your starting sector's the southern bend of the forestry path. Good luck!" Mr Oakley clapped Ignis on the back and he ran into the darkness.

This time he didn't use his flashlight. After Ignis had run for thirty seconds, he stopped dead, waiting for his eyes to adjust to the darkness. There was no sound of pursuit, but he still counted to thirty before setting off again. He wasn't going to be caught napping twice.

The forestry path snaked around the edge of the headland that hid Rokkaku from the southern part of the dam and the reservoir, winding fifteen metres or so above the level of the lake. Ignis crossed it, then found himself a hiding place in the middle of a pine copse. The dead needles carpeting the ground would make it nearly impossible for anyone to sneak up on him without being heard. He settled down and waited.

The whistle shrilled faintly in the distance. Ignis listened silently for two minutes. When no other sound came, he set off northeast.

It was a cold and clear April night, the stars glittering in the sky and a half moon shining over the trees. Winds swayed the pines overhead, but down in the valleys only the faintest of breezes reached the ground. The forestry path was smooth, but Ignis kept well away from it: anyone using it would be painted clearly in the moonlight. When he finally had to cross, he did so quickly before moving up the slopes of the eastern hill near the top of the valley.

A massive oak rose up into the night ahead of him. Ignis's heart beat faster; were there friends or enemies waiting in its shadow? Wetting his lips, he made a shaky owl call.

For a moment there was silence, then a *tu whoo, tu whooooo* came from ahead. Ignis grinned; he recognised that owl's voice. He advanced.

Christopher and Shiro stepped out to meet him. "OK, you're the last," Christopher whispered.

"Hello, *Neko*," Jennifer said in a soft giggle.

"Stop calling me that," Ignis whispered. "Ally?"

"Here," Allandra whispered. "We're going to take the Dalarwen sector first, then sweep east. OK, Jen, ready to be bait?"

"Lovely. You and Chris had better have me covered, or you'll pay for it tomorrow."

Ignis could feel Allandra smile in the darkness. "Quit complaining and do your job."

The five of them spread out in a triangle. At the front was Jennifer, walking in the open. Behind, hidden more carefully, came Ignis and Allandra on the left flank, and Christopher and Shiro on the right.

Jennifer picked a path along the morning run route, clearly visible in the moonlight. As they moved eastwards, Allandra grabbed Ignis's arm in warning. Two dark shapes detached themselves from the darkness and moved in behind Jennifer as she walked on, oblivious.

"There," Shiro whispered. "On three. One, two – *now*!"

The two figures spun in surprise. Shiro was on the first before he could react, catching his arm and stepping through to send him sprawling on the ground. Then Ignis moved in, grabbing and reaching for the back of his neck. There was a *snip* and the lifeline came away in his hand. The second boy turned to run, but went flying: Jennifer had moved in from behind and swept his legs out from under him. Christopher and Allandra pounced and in a tangle of arms and legs took him down.

"*Nani?*" The first boy stared up at Ignis furiously, feeling the back of his neck. "What are you doing?"

"Sucks to be you, guys!" Jennifer called as they backed away, leaving two furious students behind them.

"That was so cool!" Allandra whispered. "I want to be bait!"

Ignis grinned. "Having fun?"

Allandra laughed. They reformed and began to curve in towards Rokkaku.

As they grew close, Ignis began to tense up. This was where Ichiro had been waiting last time. Allandra's gold hair glowed faintly in the moonlight as she moved ahead of them. Suddenly two shadows came between them.

Ignis crept forward, eyes alight. The boy in front of him closed in on Allandra, oblivious. Ignis was almost within touching distance when something made the other boy look around. Ichiro looked back at the four of them in astonishment.

"*Now!*"

Hiroshi was sent flying as Christopher charged into him from behind. Ichiro jumped away from Ignis's lunge, then turned to face Shiro.

Shiro struck lightning-fast: Ichiro blocked and hit out at Shiro's head. Ignis paused for a moment, watching in fascination. Hands and feet blurred in the moonlight as Shiro and Ichiro swayed back and forth, striking and blocking in movements too fast for him to follow.

Then Ignis moved in, flanking Shiro. Ichiro jumped back, trying to keep both of them in his sights, his guard up as he retreated – straight towards Allandra.

Allandra didn't even have to move. She just reached out and snipped Ichiro's lifeline. He spun and stared incredulously at her.

Ignis grinned. "What goes around comes around, Ichiro."

Ichiro's face was contorted. "*Baka!*" He took a step towards Ignis, hands balled into fists.

"Ichiro." Shiro's voice was soft. Ichiro turned. For a long moment they locked eyes, then Ichiro straightened, his face suddenly expressionless. He turned and vanished into the darkness.

Christopher and Jennifer appeared from downslope. "We got Hiroshi."

Shiro shook his head. "That's probably it for this sector. Let's try the south side, then we'll cut back into Rokkaku."

The Hunt passed in a series of quick, fierce battles in the darkness. Allandra and Ignis were both knocked down in the confusion, but each time, one of the others was able to get to them before they lost their lifelines. By the time the final whistle blew, they had swept three of the five sectors, killing everyone they'd met with no losses.

The five of them trooped back to the clearing to hand in their equipment, then walked back to Rokkaku, laughing and joking. Jennifer was doing an imitation of Ichiro's outrage that had everyone in stitches. They split up at Willowherb Row, heading for the showers. Ignis waved Allandra goodbye. "Nice going, Ally."

Allandra grinned. "Let's see what they think about this. Night, Ignis."

As Allandra showered, her energy quickly bled away, leaving her yawning. By the time she reached her room, she was exhausted and feeling every one of the bruises she'd collected in the battles in the dark. Still, she was happy. She'd got her first kill – and not just anybody, but Ichiro, the top student in the class. She felt good.

As Allandra opened the door to her and Jennifer's room, a piece of paper fluttered at her feet. She blinked and bent to read it. Suddenly her weariness vanished.

> *Allandra, meet me at the old cabin south of the headland. I'll be waiting from midnight.*
> *– Your friend from Junction Pool.*

When Jennifer arrived a minute later, the room was empty.

The moon was shining high in the sky as Allandra made her way along the forestry path. The lake winds had dropped away with the coming night, and the woods were silent but for the whisper of rustling leaves. When Allandra saw the track, she turned right uphill.

The cabin had been built decades ago, intended for loggers to live in through the seasons as they cleared the forest around them. The dam road had been widened and resurfaced, ready for the heavy vehicles that would tear down and take away the trees. But in the end the loggers did not come, and now all that was left was a square pattern of mouldering stones in the middle of the clearing, overgrown with moss and bindweed. Moonlight shone down on the grass. There was nothing to be seen. Allandra looked left and right, then stepped out into the open.

A voice spoke softly. "Allandra."

Allandra moved forwards. She could see nothing but darkness. "Who is it?"

"A friend."

"Come out where I can see you."

"It's better that you don't know who I am." The voice was soft and steady, an adult's. Allandra searched through her memories. The fall into the river. Being dashed against the rocks as she was thrown down the valley with Ignis. A figure pulling her out, and saying something . . . That voice . . .

"It's you, isn't it?" Allandra asked. "You were the one who pulled us out of the river, that day at Junction Pool." A tiny movement caught Allandra's eye. There was a shadow between two ash trees on the far side of the clearing.

The voice remained soft. "Yes."

"And then you took us to Rokkaku? And left us there with that letter?"

"Yes, I did."

"Why?"

"Because you asked me to."

Allandra paused, trying hard to remember. She had been freezing cold, her clothes soaked through with icy water.

Her eyesight had been fading: all she had seen against the sun was a dark silhouette and a pair of eyes. They had said . . . what had they said? For her to lie still. That she'd be . . . Allandra looked up. "You said Vargas would be coming to find me."

"And you told me not to let him. To take you somewhere safe." The voice spoke softly. "So I took you both to the only place I knew where Vargas could never find you."

Allandra's eyes narrowed. "How did you know about it? Rokkaku's supposed to be a secret school. Who are you?" She took another step forward.

"Stop! Please!" Urgency, now. "Allandra, I've kept myself secret from you for your protection, and for mine. Even talking to you like this, I'm taking a risk. I wouldn't have answered your letter if I didn't need to warn you."

Something in the voice was nagging at Allandra's memory. She'd heard it before, a long, long time ago. If she could just keep him talking . . . "Warn me about what?"

"Don't try to rescue Michael. I know you've been thinking about it, trying to figure out how you could get him away from London. Don't do it. Don't even go near your father until you come of age. Stay in Rokkaku where you'll be safe."

"Why not?" Allandra folded her arms. "I've got away

200

from him before. I can do it again."

"You *can't*." The shadow leaned forward. "You don't know how dangerous Vargas really is, Allandra. He's your father, and that's how you've known him."

"He's not my father."

"He is, no matter what you say. Allandra, what you don't understand is that as his daughter you've seen Vargas's *softer* side. No matter how frightening he might be as a father, it's nothing to what he is as a man. Have you any idea what Vargas had to do to set up his business in London? Why he doesn't have any competitors? How it is that no dealer in the city will think about stepping into his territory? You think the stories Pete and Tav used to tell each other over the dinner table, that you used to listen to from up on the landing, were bad? They don't talk about the really heavy stuff. They don't need to. Vargas hasn't taken your escape attempts seriously in the past, but he's taking them seriously now. Things have gone beyond escapes and spankings. If he catches you . . . You're not ready to face your father, Allandra. Stay away from him."

"How do you *know* all this?"

"It doesn't matter. What matters is that you stay here, stay safe, and— No! Don't!"

Allandra had been edging forwards, and as the figure took a step backwards she lunged. The shape seemed to melt into the shadows as she rushed into it. Allandra cast back and forth. A crackle of leaves from upslope sent her running, dodging around trees and bushes until the forest fell away and she was at the top of the hill. She came to a halt and looked around.

On all sides, the trees rose silent. To her left, the moonlight glittered on the waters of Llyn Garedig and the pale grey of the dam. To her right, the trees followed the slope downhill, rolling up and down until they faded away into the western fields. There was no sound. Allandra searched around the hill for another hour, but there was no one there.

8

BATTLES AND BRIDGES

Allandra slept badly, troubled by thoughts of her strange visitor. When she woke she didn't rush to the scoreboard like everyone else. Instead she went to see Mr Oakley, to ask whether any outside guests had visited the school yesterday. When she was told no, she went to see how they'd done.

The scores were enough to cheer her up. The five of them between them had taken down eight other students: three pairs, and two unlucky loners who hadn't had much time to be surprised at running into five opponents at once. Shiro had three kills, Ignis two, and Christopher, Jennifer and Allandra one each.

"Heads up," said Ignis as they finished congratulating each other. Allandra turned to see Ichiro coming towards them, flanked by Hiroshi and three other boys. Ignis and Allandra shared a grin. *This should be fun.*

"Hi, Ichiro!" said Jennifer before he could speak. "Did you have a good game?"

"You!" snarled Ichiro, pointing straight at Allandra. "What do you think you were doing?"

"Us?" Allandra looked innocent. "We were just talking about the scores."

"You cannot do this! The Hunt is pairs and singles only. You cheated!"

Jennifer laughed. "We learned from the best."

"Fighting in teams is against the rules. You will not be allowed to do this. You—"

Suddenly Allandra had had enough. "There's nothing about teams in the rules," she said curtly. "As you should know, since you set up those pairs to make sure you'd win last time. You ganged up on us, now we're ganging up on you. How's it feel?"

Ichiro stood dead still, staring at Allandra for a long moment. Then he turned on his heel and marched away. His group followed. As Ichiro passed Kentaro, he tapped his shoulder, then vanished behind the *dojo*.

"You shouldn't have done that," Shiro said quietly.

"Oh, he deserved it," Allandra replied, annoyed. "We went off on that first Hunt on our own. Then they pair up to make sure we don't have a chance, and now *they* say we're cheating?"

"You did cheat, by their standards."

"Who cares?"

"Allandra." Shiro looked levelly at her. Allandra opened her mouth to retort, but something in Shiro's eyes made her stop. Shiro waited for a second, then went on.

"Ichiro's playing by a different set of rules from you. He learned that the upper years hunt in pairs and not in bigger teams, so that means that pairs are established and teams aren't. So the way Ichiro sees it, by doing something that *wasn't* established, what we did was cheating. And he must have been very angry, or he wouldn't have confronted us like that."

"But what we did wasn't against the rules."

"Yes. And Ichiro'll realise that, once he cools off. But you pointed out his mistake in front of everyone else, and that means he's lost face in the eyes of his group, and that's something he *won't* forget. Now he's going to have to do something to prove that we haven't beaten him."

Christopher looked alarmed. "Wait a minute. You mean he'll try and attack us?"

Shiro shook his head. "No. That's against the rules, remember?"

Ignis gave Shiro a curious look. "How do you know so much about him?"

"So what *will* they do?" Jennifer asked.

"He won't go outside the rules. That doesn't mean he won't be ruthless within them. And now we've shown him a new way to organise, there's nothing to stop him copying us." Shiro pointed. Kentaro and the rest of the Japanese first years were gone.

The four of them stood silent for a minute. Christopher

was the first to put it together. His eyes widened. "Uh-oh."

"What?"

"They could do the same thing we did, except worse. Get all ten of the Japanese boys together. Then *we'd* be the ones being swarmed."

Allandra looked at Shiro. "Could Ichiro do that?"

Shiro nodded.

"Arrrgh!" Jennifer stamped her foot. "Now we're back to square one! What do we do now, run and hide?"

"No," Allandra said slowly. "We don't have to."

"Then what?"

Allandra pointed. The last four members of the class were just drifting away from the scoreboard. The five of them looked at each other.

"If they can get reinforcements," Christopher said slowly, "we could too, couldn't we?"

"Do you think they'd do it?" Jennifer asked.

Allandra looked after the disappearing students with a smile. "Oh, I think I could convince them."

Convincing them proved easier than expected. Once the rest of the class figured out that not agreeing meant being overwhelmed by one or other of the larger groups, they reluctantly agreed to join up with Allandra's team in the next Hunt. However, two days later the spring term ended, and further plans were put off until the coming summer.

206

Rokkaku broke up for the Easter holidays.

It was a windy April day. Waves were sweeping across Llyn Garedig and in the sky above Rokkaku, puffy white clouds were soaring. Allandra and Ignis stood in the shelter of one of the *dojo*s, looking up at the empty ropes. The valley, usually so full of movement and energy, felt a little empty in the holidays.

"So who are we supposed to be waiting for?" Ignis asked.

"I don't know. The note from Mr Morimoto just said to be here at eleven o'clock."

Ignis looked around. "Here comes someone."

Both Ignis and Allandra straightened up to face the boy approaching them. He was Japanese, seventeen years or so old, and powerfully built, standing several centimetres taller than Ignis. The black belt around his *gi* marked him as one of the sixth formers, and one who had passed the first-dan grading at that. "Hello there. You two are Allandra and Ignis?"

Allandra nodded. "Yes, *sempai*."

"No need for that. My name's Kazuki. Come along and we'll get started."

"What are we doing?" Ignis asked as Kazuki led them up out of the valley. The buildings of Rokkaku vanished behind them and they turned southwards.

"I'm here to show you the patrol routes. Normally you

wouldn't start patrol duty until the summer, but Mr Morimoto thought that since the two of you are staying in Rokkaku this Easter, you could help out. We're always short-handed during the holidays."

Ignis and Allandra looked at each other and shrugged. They didn't have much to do, with everyone else gone. "OK."

"Right. Watch yourself, we're coming onto the road."

They had passed the old cabin and arrived at the forestry path. Between the woods and the path was a hollow in the ground, blocked by a thick sprawl of brambles. Kazuki walked straight into it. As he stepped in, Ignis saw that there was a thin path around the edge of the hollow, where the brambles were replaced by bracken. Kazuki led them through the bracken and out onto the road. Ignis turned to look back. From the outside, the path they had just walked through looked like an impenetrable tangle of thorns.

"Not bad, is it?" Kazuki asked. "It took me forever to get the placement just right."

Ignis blinked in surprise. "You did that?"

"I planted those when I was fifteen. Of course, by then I'd had a lot of practice. Gardening work starts in the second year."

"We're going to learn *gardening*?" Allandra asked, taken aback.

"Of course. If you want to hide a school in the middle of

a forest, you have to spend a lot of time making sure the two blend in with each other. Haven't you noticed the way Rokkaku just seems to vanish into the trees as soon as you get any distance away from the buildings? That's not an accident, you know."

"That's how Rokkaku stays secret?" Allandra asked, sceptical. "Gardening?"

Kazuki shook his head. "Rokkaku has many protections. The defences are arranged in layers; get past one, and you come to another. Some of the layers are passive, like the camouflage you've just seen. And others are active, like the patrols."

Kazuki started walking south along the forestry path. The road ran along the curve of the hill, staying at roughly the same height. Through the trees to their left, fifteen metres below, they could see the waves on the lake. "The patrol areas for Rokkaku are arranged in concentric circles, with the school in the middle. The inner circle is the home ring: that's everything up to a half-mile around Rokkaku. That area is very closely watched. Nothing gets through there without being seen. The spotter ring is everything from a half-mile to a mile away from Rokkaku. That's where we have our outposts. We don't watch the whole of that area, only the roads. And everything from one to five miles away is the wide ring. We don't have anything permanent out there at all, but that's where the Wide Patrols do their ranging."

"So where are we now?" Allandra asked.

"Just leaving the home ring." Kazuki pointed. "See that stunted pine? That's the boundary. Beyond that you'll be in the spotter ring."

"So what do we do?" Allandra asked, interested.

Kazuki grinned. "Nothing just yet. You won't start patrols proper until tomorrow – this is just to show you around in advance. When you do start, you'll be in the spotter ring. The third and fourth years do the Wide Patrols, and the fifth and sixth years are in charge of the home ring. The first and second years man the outposts. That means that you watch from them, and report anyone you see on the road through your radios."

"That's it?"

"Apart from one thing. Don't get seen. If you do, Mr Morimoto won't be happy. He takes patrols very seriously. If he thinks your stealth skills are so bad that even a tourist can spot you, he'll load you with extra *tongyo* classes until he's sure you won't do it again. Oh, and sometimes he and the sixth formers play little games to make sure you're paying attention." Kazuki stopped. "Well, that's about it. How about you go up the road and check out South Point? That's our south road outpost. You'll probably be spending a lot of time there once your patrol duties start. Look for a dead tree and some ferns up the slope on the right. Don't worry, the road's clear. There's a Wide Patrol

210

doing a sweep down on the south side of the lake."

"Thanks," Ignis said.

Allandra hesitated. "Kazuki? Why do we go to all this trouble to keep Rokkaku secret?"

"You ask a lot of questions, don't you?" Kazuki laughed. "I'll give you a hint. It's something to do with why this school's here in the first place."

Allandra and Ignis looked at each other. "Why *is* the school here?"

"Sorry. Can't tell you. Not until you've been here a bit longer."

Allandra made a face. "Why not?"

Kazuki looked at them both, suddenly serious. "Because it's important, and having it spread around would do a lot of harm. Anyway, I'll see you back at the school. Make sure you return before the Wide Patrol gets in." He walked away.

"What do you think he meant?" Allandra asked as she and Ignis carried on walking south.

"Never mind." Ignis had been thinking about the Hunt during Kazuki's instructions. "Look, I don't like this plan."

"Which plan? Making one big team for the Hunt?"

"Yeah."

Allandra shrugged. "What else are we going to do? Anyway, it's not like the teachers told us not to."

"It's not like they told us we could, either."

Allandra laughed. "I never thought *you'd* be the cautious one. I thought you hated Ichiro? What's changed your mind?"

Ignis let out a breath. "A lot of things. Look, I tried getting into a war with Ichiro and his friends once. I learned my lesson."

"Oh, they started it. Hey, look." Allandra pointed to a group of ferns shielding a log. "That must be South Point. C'mon, I'll race you to the top."

April became May, and the summer term began. Ignis and Allandra's practices for the Hunts continued, but with the extra people their group had become cumbersome. Neither Jennifer nor Christopher really got on with the new boys, and they proved to be less willing to follow Shiro's orders. Ichiro and his group were practising too. Ichiro and Hiroshi were trying to conceal it, but their secretiveness and some not-very-subtle gloating from Kentaro was enough to tip Allandra off. The class began to drift almost imperceptibly into two groups: the Japanese boys on one side, and Allandra's mixed crew on the other. A slowly widening gulf began to appear in classes, the two groups training on different sides of the *dojo*. Although Allandra did her best, working with the other eight, she began to grow uneasy.

June came, and with it the midsummer Hunt, their second to last of the year. Allandra had a bad feeling as their group slowly and clumsily formed up at the oak tree. Once they were ready they began to sweep around towards Dalarwen.

They met Ichiro's pack halfway. Allandra heard a shout from up ahead, and saw Ignis struggling with two boys. She ran to help, and then everything dissolved into chaos. Their battle plans were forgotten as the night turned into a wild brawl of fists, feet and noise, with no room for technique or strategy. Allandra managed to tear one other boy's lifeline before being pulled down herself. Then some of the boys carried on fighting after being killed, their "dead" opponents joined in to stop them, and things started to get really ugly.

By the time Shiro and Ichiro had managed to restore order, everyone on both sides was hurt, marked as dead, or both. Allandra found Ignis, and together they slipped away, limping back to the home clearing while the argument raged behind them.

Allandra woke up the next morning feeling terrible. She didn't want to check the scores, and she especially didn't want to face Mr Oakley once he learned what had happened. Instead she headed away to the top of the valley, nursing a limp where someone had fallen heavily on her ankle.

Ignis met her as she skirted the teachers' houses. His eyes travelled down to her leg. "Did you see Dr Furuta?"

Allandra shook her head. "No. I don't want the teachers to find out about what happened."

"You are both a little late for that."

Allandra and Ignis turned with a jump. Allandra's heart leaped in her throat. Headmaster Nishiyama was standing beside them, watching them both with grey eyes. Awkwardly, Allandra bowed. "N-Nishiyama-*sensei*?"

"Walk with me a little way, if you would."

Ignis and Allandra traded an *Uh-oh* look. Nishiyama began walking at a leisurely pace upstream, and Ignis scrambled after him. Allandra followed, trembling. She'd expected trouble, but she'd never imagined it would be bad enough for the headmaster to get involved.

Nishiyama taught the sixth form and private classes, but rarely came into contact with the lower years. Occasionally Allandra and Ignis had seen him walking in the valley, often talking to one of the teachers or older students, but nothing more. Now he was strolling beside them.

They passed the storehouses and the small pool that marked the end of the settled part of Rokkaku. Nishiyama remained silent as he led them past it, up a winding path that ran alongside the stream into the woods. A small building appeared through the trees. Unlike the other buildings in Rokkaku, it was made of rough stone, with a roof upon which flowers were growing. The door and windows were open holes. Ivy covered the walls.

Nishiyama bowed at the door, stepped inside, and sat in *fudoza*. Ignis and Allandra copied him uncertainly, looking around. A low table against the far wall was covered with a cloth. On it were three boxes, herbs Allandra didn't recognise, and a burner from which the smell of incense was rising. The far wall was covered in a mural. It pictured snow-capped mountains lined with forests, with the smoke of villages rising into the sky. Between the mountain peaks two strange creatures fought with swords. They were ugly-looking things with long noses, the wizened faces of old men and black feathered wings that sprouted from their backs. In their clawed hands they grasped swords.

"*Tengu*," Nishiyama said, and Allandra jumped. "Mountain goblins, a mix of man and crow. In some stories they are helpful, in others malicious. All the stories agree on two things, though. They were mischievous, and masters of swordwork and battle. Legends say the first ninja learned their skills from them."

"Nishiyama?" Ignis hesitated. "Um, I mean Nishiyama-*sensei*. What is this place?"

"This is the Rokkaku shrine. One of the areas in which we have broken with tradition. Our ninja ancestors had no shrines, as far as we know. They revered nature, and their

215

temples were the mountains, forests and lakes. Still, it is right that a school should have a place set away to meditate in." Nishiyama rose, stretched, and backed out of the door. "Have you ever thought about the nature of Rokkaku, Allandra?"

Allandra blinked. "*Sensei?*"

"Rokkaku is a place of exchange. A Japanese tradition in a British forest, a mixture of two different cultures. Each year, the new students we take in are usually half from Japan, and half from Britain. It is natural for a certain amount of friction to result from this. In every year there are tensions, rivalries between the two groups. Usually, it fades with time. By the summer term, the students have started to mix. On the other hand," Nishiyama turned to look down at Allandra, "usually, there are not children such as yourselves busily organising the class into two armed camps.

"In your attempts to build yourselves an army here, there is something you apparently did not notice, Allandra." Suddenly, Nishiyama's voice was steel. "The purpose of this school is to teach ninjutsu and to educate its students. Not to host a race war. In dividing the class into two armed camps, you have both caused discord within the year and harmed Rokkaku as a whole."

Suddenly, the forest seemed very empty and quiet, and Nishiyama's eyes very hard.

"I'm sorry," Allandra whispered.

"I hope so, since it will not happen again. To make sure of this, the rules of the Hunt will be changed for your year until further notice. You will henceforth be sent out to compete in pairs. The two members of each will work together, but any kind of cooperation with another pair is strictly forbidden. You will train together in your free time. Ignis, your partner will be Hiroshi. Allandra, yours will be Ichiro."

"*What?*" Allandra yelped.

"That's not fair!" Ignis exclaimed. "They started it! All we did—" Ignis stopped. Nishiyama was looking at him.

"Did you have something to say regarding my orders, Ignis?" There was a dangerous look in Nishiyama's eyes.

"I . . ." Ignis paused.

"Well?"

Ignis scowled. "No."

"No, what?"

"No, *sensei*."

"Correct. One last thing. Until the summer term, all four of you are assigned to kitchen chores. You'll be on duty for the same hours as your new partners, so you should have plenty of time to work out your differences. Is there anything else you wanted to discuss?"

Allandra swallowed. "Um, no, *sensei*."

"Good. Now go and see Dr Furuta about that limp."

Nishiyama turned away, leaving Allandra and Ignis looking at each other in dismay.

Allandra showed up at the kitchens that evening with mixed feelings. She didn't have to compete with Ichiro any more – she had to work with him. She wasn't sure which was worse.

Ichiro arrived exactly on time. He marched past without seeming to notice her. Allandra looked at his retreating back and followed.

The main kitchen was a hubbub of noise and activity, filled with steam, shouts and the sound of clattering pans. The air was hot enough to make sweat bead on Allandra's skin as she stepped through the open door. Megan, the tough, heavy-set woman who managed the kitchens, was giving directions to one of the cooks. "Serve a hundred and twenty this time, not a hundred. And peel an extra half-sack of potatoes, the roast ran out at the second serving this lunch. You can take Eric off the beans to help, we always have more of those than we need." Megan glanced up. "Oh, it's you two. We need half a tank of water for the potatoes – take those buckets and fill her up. From the lake, mind. If I catch you using the stream you'll regret it. Look sharp!" Ichiro picked up a yoke and two buckets without comment. Allandra followed suit.

As they walked down the path and under the wind

generators, Allandra studied Ichiro from the corner of her eye. He was a little over average height, although his stocky build made him seem taller. His mouth was turned down at the corners, and there was a humourless set to his jaw. Now that Allandra thought about it, she'd hardly ever seen Ichiro smile.

Carrying water was exhausting work. The yoke, a wooden pole with a curve in the middle that allowed it to be laid over the neck and shoulders, spread the weight a little, but it didn't do anything about the effort of carrying the stuff uphill, or the strain of keeping one's balance on Rokkaku's winding paths. Ichiro didn't say a word throughout their trips, nor when the tank had been filled and they were set to peeling potatoes. *Fine*, Allandra thought. *Be that way.*

The evening went by. When their two hours were up, Ichiro left without a word. A second day passed in the same way, then a third. Ignis was complaining bitterly about having to work with Hiroshi, but at least they seemed to be talking. On the fourth day of silence, as Allandra and Ichiro were walking down to fetch water for what felt like the thousandth time, Allandra finally gave up. She was never going to outwait Ichiro. "OK, fine," she announced. "What is it?"

Ichiro didn't turn round. "What is what?"

"What are you so angry about?"

"I am not angry."

"Then why won't you talk?"

"There is nothing to say."

They filled their buckets. They carried the buckets back up the valley. They went down to fill the buckets again.

"You're still mad about the team thing, aren't you?" Allandra said eventually.

Ichiro said nothing.

"Look, we were just trying to even things up."

Silence.

"We never would have done it if you guys hadn't paired off to begin with, you know."

"We did not assemble in teams."

"No, but you assembled in pairs."

"The Hunt is conducted in pairs or alone. Not in teams."

"Well, why didn't you tell us that to begin with?"

Ichiro stopped. He looked back at Allandra.

"If you'd just told us from the beginning that you were going to pair up and compete that way, then we would have done the same and there wouldn't have been a problem. The only reason we got so angry was because we thought you were ganging up on us to make sure we'd lose."

"We did not gang up on you. Hiroshi and I fought against Kentaro and Yori, and against Isamu and Makoto."

220

"Really?" Allandra paused. "Oh. Well, if you'd just said that, there wouldn't have been a problem. We thought you were starting an us-against-them thing."

"We did not start that. You did."

"Yes, but only because we thought you were doing it first. See?"

Ichiro turned away and started walking again. Allandra hurried to catch up.

"Well anyway, we're not doing it any more," Allandra suggested as they walked under the slowly beating wind generators. "It's pairs only from now on – the way you wanted it from the start, right?"

Silence.

Allandra sighed. Subtlety had never been her strong suit, anyway. "Look, I'm supposed to be your partner, in case you've forgotten. Are we ever going to practise together, or are you going to keep marching up and down this stupid path pretending I don't exist?"

Ichiro gave her a brief glance. "Very well."

"Very well, what?"

"Very well, we shall train together."

"Tomorrow afternoon in the *dojo*?"

"Very well."

Allandra withdrew, satisfied. The remainder of their chores passed in silence.

Training with Ichiro was an interesting experience.

"You are off balance," he stated after they'd only been practising for five minutes.

"What's wrong with my balance?"

"Your weight is too far forward. When you are in *ichi mongi*, seven-tenths of your weight should be on the back leg. Turn your foot outwards."

Allandra was annoyed, but did as he said.

Five minutes later, Ichiro stopped. "You are still off balance."

"Now what?"

"Shift your weight back."

"We're supposed to be practising *omote gyaku*, not footwork. Who cares?"

He frowned at her. "*Kamae* must always be exact."

"Not if— Oh, fine." Allandra shifted her weight. "Better?"

Ichiro moved back to a defensive stance. Allandra punched. Ichiro took her wrist, pivoted, and locked it, forcing Allandra down. She rolled and came up again, then it was her turn to be *tori*. Ichiro began his punch, then stopped again and pointed at her feet. "Shift your weight back."

Allandra lost her patience. "Why does it matter where my weight is? You're not a teacher – stop telling me what to do!"

"You are off balance!"

"I don't care!"

"Then practise alone until you do!" Ichiro snapped. He turned on his heel and left, leaving an exasperated Allandra on her own in the *dojo*. She stormed off to Ze'ev to vent her feelings.

"Hmmm," he said after she was finished.

"Hmm, what?"

"Take *ichi mongi*. Now," he assumed an attacking stance in front of her, "defend." He struck. Allandra blocked and tried an uprooting trip. Ze'ev stepped back.

"He's right."

"What do you mean? I'm sure my stance was right."

"Yes, your stance was right. But as soon as you started to fight, you tensed up, which makes you lean forward. A lot of fighters do it."

"Isn't leaning forward better?"

"No. You feel as if you're hitting harder, but you're actually weaker. It means you're off balance, and that makes you more vulnerable. Remember, if you want to make someone fall, it's a lot simpler to mess up their footwork when they're off balance than try anything fancy."

Allandra sighed. "Great. Can you start teaching me again? It'd really help."

"Should be able to manage it, as long as you and your

brother don't come at the same time." Ze'ev looked at her keenly. "No more teams?"

"No more teams."

Ze'ev grinned. "You're learning."

Allandra showed up at the *dojo* at the same time next day, but no one was there. With a sinking feeling, she realised that she was going to have to apologise. Resignedly, she set off to find Ichiro.

But finding him proved more difficult than she had expected. Hiroshi, Ichiro's roommate, told her that he wasn't home. Yes, he was around. No, he didn't know where. No, he didn't know when he would be back. Allandra tried two more boys and got the same stone-faced reaction. Frustrated, she finally went to Ignis's room, but no one was there. Allandra climbed up and out, enjoying the summer breeze as she walked along the ridge into the forest. She found Shiro up in one of the clearings they used for weapons training. He was standing in the bumpy grass, practising.

Shiro was working through *sanshin no kata*, the five forms that had been the first real techniques the class had been taught. Each was styled after one of the elements: earth, water, fire, air and void. Like all basic ninjutsu techniques, they were defensive – *sente*, or striking the first blow, was not allowed. Fire was the most aggressive, blocking hard and striking in at the attacker's neck. Water struck at the same target, but through a more circular, evasive route. The earth form was the same *shitanken* strike Allandra had used against Kentaro, while air was a response to a low punch, sweeping it aside and striking with the thumb and knuckle of the forefinger for the joint line between the opponent's leg and pelvis. Void stepped aside from a kick to come in with a distracting strike at the face and a kick to the body. Shiro was working through all five, on both left and right sides. He moved slowly, looking relaxed as he flowed from one to another, and his feet seemed to slide rather than step as he moved. Although the movements looked casual, his feet and hands finished in exactly the same places every time. Something about the precision of Shiro's movements reminded Allandra of Ichiro. Mr Akamatsu had once told them that everything there was in ninjutsu was to be found in *sanshin* and the *Kihon Happo* – it seemed Shiro took him seriously.

Shiro caught sight of Allandra out of the corner of his eye and paused. "Allandra?"

"Hey, Shiro. Ignis around?"

Shiro shook his head. "Training with Hiroshi, I think." He quirked his mouth in what Allandra had come to recognise as a smile. "Assuming they haven't killed each other yet."

Allandra sighed. "Great. Look, maybe you can help me.

I'm supposed to be working with Ichiro and I think I've pissed him off." Allandra explained what had happened. "What's worst is that we're running out of time. There's barely two weeks to the next Hunt. We have to start practising soon."

Shiro was quiet. Allandra grew restless. "Shiro? Did you hear?"

"Yes . . ." Shiro paused. "Allandra, maybe there's something you should know."

"What?"

"It might not be you Ichiro's angry at. Yes, he's annoyed that you aren't doing the forms right, but that wouldn't be enough to make him walk out, not when he'd been ordered to partner you."

"So who is he angry at?" Allandra said with a laugh. "You?"

Shiro didn't smile. "That's right."

"Why?"

"I'm his foster brother."

"*What?*"

Shiro sighed. "You know that I was sent to Tokyo when I was five. Well, it was Ichiro's family I was living with, the Yoshimatsus. They were good people, especially his mother, but it was a big family and they didn't have that much time for me. There were three sons and a daughter, and they all ate together. That was how I got my name.

226

Shiro just means 'fourth son'. Somebody started calling me that over dinner, and it stuck. Eventually it became less trouble to use than an English name, so when I started school that was the name I gave.

"Ichiro and I didn't get on from the start: he was the eldest and he didn't want me to get in his way. When things turned nasty at school I found the local ninjutsu *dojo* and started training. Towards the end of that, I finally arranged a challenge with the boy who'd been picking on me the most, someone called Susumu. I won.

"I thought that was the end of it, but back then I hadn't understood how things worked. Susumu went to Ichiro for help. It turned out that Susumu's father worked under Ichiro's, and Ichiro had a *sempai-kohai* relationship with Susumu – sort of like an older brother. So Ichiro was obligated to help. I don't think Ichiro wanted to fight, but I wouldn't back down."

Allandra was fascinated. "What happened?"

"Ichiro was the judo champion of the year back then, and dozens of people showed up to watch. It was over in a few seconds. Ichiro was good, but I'd spent months training with judo people already. I took him down on the third move. The crowd wasn't happy, believe me. They'd come to see their champion stomp the *gaijin*, not the other way around. Ichiro lost a lot of face.

"Anyway, that was the end of it, but for one thing. Two

months after that, Ichiro turned up at the ninjutsu *dojo* as well. He's been studying it ever since. But since then, he's never spoken to me except when he has to."

"Wow." Allandra thought for a second. "So what, because I'm friends with you, Ichiro doesn't want to talk to me either?"

"Yes. He probably thinks that I organised the teams just as a way of getting at him, and that you and Ignis were following my orders."

"And that was why no one would tell me where he was?"

Shiro nodded. "Ichiro's a leader. He tries to look after his friends, and they look out for him in turn. If he doesn't want to see you, they won't take you to him. You can catch him in class easily enough, but I'm not sure how you can get him to listen. Maybe if I asked Hiroshi . . ."

Allandra grinned. "Don't worry about it. I think I know how." She jumped up. "Thanks, Shiro! I'll see you later."

Allandra ran back down into the valley. Shiro returned to his *kata* for a few minutes, but found it hard to concentrate. Finally he sat, looking down at the forest into which Allandra had disappeared.

Allandra waited for Ichiro after *tongyo* class the next day. He walked past without seeming to notice her. Allandra pushed herself off the tree she had been leaning against and fell into step beside him.

"Well, I checked out what you were saying about my stance," she began. "You were right. I'll do it properly this time."

"You checked it out?" Ichiro scowled at her. "You doubted what I told you?"

Oops. Allandra thought fast. "Oh, it wasn't that. I wasn't sure if I'd learned it right the first time around. It's easier to have it taught again by one of the teachers, don't you think?"

Ichiro grunted.

"So, do you want to start practice again?"

"I have a lot to do in the next—"

"Oh, that's OK. I knew after that first practice I was asking too much."

Ichiro frowned. "Asking too much?"

"Well, I really do try, but I'm just not as good as you guys. And you know what the black belts are always saying about how difficult teaching is, especially if the student's a slow learner. I mean, you have to be *really* good to teach ninjutsu properly. It's a lot to ask. So I thought I could find someone who wouldn't mind. Ignis said I ought to go and ask Shiro."

Ichiro stopped. "Shiro!"

"Yeah, Shiro. Someone was saying that he's probably

the best in the year, and so I was thinking that maybe he could teach me. Don't worry, I'll clear it with the teachers first. I know they wouldn't want a partnership that just doesn't work . . ."

"No! *Kancho* Nishiyama ordered that we would be partners and no one else. You will not change this!"

"But I have to learn this stuff from *some*where . . ." Allandra looked away.

"I am perfectly capable of teaching you," Ichiro answered stiffly. "I am, of course, not a qualified instructor, but I have assisted teachers for many years in the Tokyo *dojo*."

"Are you sure you wouldn't mind?"

"If you are to be my partner, then we must practise. We had better use the *dojo* while we can. The High Hunt is very soon." Ichiro turned off the path and began cutting down towards the end *dojo*. Allandra followed, hiding a grin.

Over the next two weeks, Allandra began to see that Ichiro's insistence on form might have something in it, after all. When he carried through a technique, his movements were always precise, always controlled. It made his balance more difficult to take than that of anyone else in the class, since he never overextended or took poor stance, even for an instant. Annoying though it could be, it was also good practice, and

230

Allandra lived with having most of her moves fail in exchange for learning how to do them properly.

Putting up with Ichiro, on the other hand, didn't get much easier. He was as demanding as Ze'ev, but he didn't have Ze'ev's sense of humour, nor his skill in showing Allandra how to do it better. Allandra finally got her revenge after a week of training. They were practising hip throws, a straightforward move where the defender slipped a punch, placed one arm over the attacker's neck and shoulders and a leg behind his stance, and threw him by twisting at the hips. As Ichiro performed the move on Allandra, she grabbed onto the side of his jacket. She went down, but the same movement that threw her also flipped him. Ichiro stumbled, tripped over Allandra, and went head over heels, rolling. He came up staring at her. "What was that?"

"Huh?"

"That technique. What school is it from?"

"Oh. It's from . . ." Allandra improvised. "*Shinden Fudo ryu*. A response to a throw."

Ichiro grunted, looking puzzled. Allandra had to bite back a smile. When she'd asked Ze'ev the same question, he'd replied that it came from the "aaargh!" school: moves that had been invented in desperation, by someone one second away from disaster. From then on, Ichiro was less overbearing, and even started to treat her with a tiny bit of

231

respect. From what Allandra saw of Ignis, he was getting on better with Hiroshi, too.

Christopher and Jennifer were doing well. And best of all, Kentaro seemed to have dropped off the radar. Allandra saw him from time to time, but whenever she did, he would only give her a scowl and turn away. Allandra had no idea why he had suddenly decided to cease his taunts, but she wasn't complaining. With the approach of the last Hunt of the year and summer holidays, everyone began slowly to wind down, and the final two weeks of term took on a relaxed, lazy feel.

9

SHADOWS

"Five flips."

"That's too easy. Four flips and two cartwheels."

"Three flips, two cartwheels and a handspring."

"No problem."

"With the handspring at the end? No way!"

Jennifer grinned. "Just watch me."

The gym was crowded on Friday afternoons. Jennifer and Allandra had the runway to themselves, though: thirteen metres of open mat, with foam wedges as obstacles. Normally the class would rotate between pieces of equipment, but the two girls were far enough ahead of the rest of the class in gymnastics that Yarnya would usually let them have one piece to themselves for the last fifteen minutes. The game was one Jennifer had started in the spring term: see who could put together the most difficult string of acrobatics. So far Allandra had only managed to beat her twice. She stepped back to give Jennifer a clear run. "You're never going to make this one."

233

Jennifer closed her eyes. "I can't heeeaar you . . ."

"You'll miss the last spring," Allandra predicted. "Just wait and see."

Jennifer walked back to the wall, turned, took a deep breath, let it out, then started her run. As she reached the mat she spun into one cartwheel, then a second. She twisted to land backwards, backflipped over the first wedge, backflipped over the second, spun again at the end of the third backflip and cleared the last wedge with a handspring, landing on both feet. She lifted her arms in the finishing Y, pivoting to give Allandra a big grin.

Allandra stared. "You lucky, *lucky* little . . ."

Jennifer bowed. "Thank you, thank you. Thank you – no, please, sit down! Thank you! No, really, it was nothing . . ."

Allandra sighed and walked to the wall. She turned, took a breath, and ran. Cartwheel, cartwheel, twist to flip the first wedge, flip the second, flip and spin – and she lost her balance. She went tumbling into the foam barrier, sending it rocking, to fall with a slap onto the mat.

Jennifer was doubled over with laughter. "Oh, shut up," Allandra said ruefully, rolling back to her feet.

"And Jennifer Cass once again defends her title! The crowd goes wild!"

Allandra couldn't help smiling. It was impossible to be annoyed with Jennifer for long. "So you win again. I'll

234

get you next time."

"Bring it on, shorty."

The bell rang. Laughing and talking, the class streamed out for the last lesson of the afternoon. Allandra yawned as they walked out together. "How did you get to be so good? I was pretty good at school but I don't think the best girls there were as good as you."

Jennifer shrugged. "I just practised a lot. It's nothing special."

"Yes it is. You should enter competitions or something. Did your parents teach you?" As soon as the words were out of her mouth Allandra bit her tongue. Jennifer never talked about her family.

Jennifer looked away. "No. I taught myself." There was a brief, awkward pause, then Jennifer's face cleared. "Hey, did you hear about what's happening this Hunt?"

"No, what is it?"

"It's called a High Hunt. The whole school competes at once. The first years, the second years, the sixth form, everyone."

"You're kidding. Won't the sixth form wipe out everyone else?"

Jennifer grinned. "Maybe not. I heard that the teachers join in as well. Someone told me that sometimes even Nishiyama goes out to see just how good his students are."

Allandra laughed. "That I'd like to see. Ooh, Ichiro is going to be even more obsessive about practising now."

"How's that going, anyway?"

"Actually, really well. He's never rude or anything. I just wish he'd smile occasionally." Allandra brightened. "Hey, if you and Makoto are around this weekend, we could train together. I don't think they'd complain."

Jennifer shook her head. "Sorry. I'm going to be gone."

"You are? Where?"

"Family."

"Oh."

Jennifer looked up at the blue sky. "It's – difficult." She turned towards Allandra and gave her a half-smile. "Look, Ally, I'll tell you about it some time, I promise. Just – not right now, OK?"

Allandra waved her hand in a don't-worry-about-it gesture. "Oh, sure. It's no problem." Inside, she felt a little guilty. She'd never told Jennifer anything about Vargas or Michael, even though she'd badly wanted to, and Jennifer had never pushed her about it. "When are you leaving?"

"Just after the last class. Coming?"

"No, I've got patrol with Shiro. I'll see you when you get back?"

Jennifer grinned. "No, I was going to turn invisible. See you Monday!"

"Bye, Jen!" Allandra waved and turned towards the

south hill.

Shiro and Ignis were waiting at the top of the path. "So, are you sure Hiroshi's not going to get me as soon as my back's turned?" Ignis was saying.

"Yes," Shiro said, patient. "No matter how much good reason you might have given him in the past."

Ignis gave Shiro a stubborn look. "He deserved it."

"I should have hit you harder that time in the storeroom."

Ignis glared, then laughed suddenly. Walking up, Allandra gave him a curious look. "What time?"

"Oh, nothing. See you guys later." Ignis ran back down to the *dojo*.

Allandra looked after him, then rolled her eyes and joined Shiro. He tossed aside a blade of grass he'd been peeling, and they set off.

Allandra had come to enjoy patrols. With the long, hot summer, tourists and hikers had started coming to the lake, but most turned back before they got all the way round the long, winding road that followed the lake's shore. The few persistent ones who made it right into the neighbourhood of Rokkaku would usually stick to the road, walking straight past the hidden pathways into the valley itself and leaving Allandra and her partner no task but reporting them in. She'd heard older boys complaining about patrols in the winter or in the rain, but on warm summer days like this one, patrol duty was as good as a holiday.

South Point was half an hour's walk away from Rokkaku, in the middle of the spotter ring. The fallen tree was placed well up on the hillside above the lakeside path, the foxgloves and fronds of bracken making it almost invisible from the path below. There was no equipment in the outpost, and the radios were taken away every night. If any especially curious tourist were to climb up the slope to get a closer look, it would look like nothing more than a dead tree amidst a patch of overgrowth.

Allandra and Shiro relieved the two second years already in the outpost, unpacked their suppers and settled down, keeping a casual eye on the path below. They talked as they ate, about who was friends with whom, who was going to come top in the High Hunt, which teachers they liked and which ones they'd like to be able to trade with another year. It was safe, comfortable chat, about small things, the kind you can only have when there are no problems to worry about. The setting sun was shining through the leaves, and as Allandra sat, safe and warm, the dappled sunlight shifting on her clothes and with Shiro nearby, she felt happy and at peace.

"Oh, looks like we've got someone." Shiro glanced down at the hill and lifted their radio. "Central, this is South Point. We've got two people passing us going north.

A woman and a little boy. They're not moving fast, I doubt they'll reach the valley before sunset."

"Copy that, Shiro," the radio answered, its sound muffled. "One of the wide patrols reported them an hour ago."

Below them a woman was leading a boy of six or seven along the path. She was pointing out across the lake as she spoke down to him. Allandra murmured as the woman pointed, "Yes, babykins. *This* is the lake, and *there's* the dam, and behind *there* is the secret ninja school." Shiro laughed.

"It'll be fun once we get into the sixth form," Allandra thought aloud, as the figures below passed by. "Then we get to do interception. I wonder how they handle it?"

"I think the logging story's the usual one. They put up a barrier, show up in forester clothes, and tell them that the area's being cleared and they can't go in for safety reasons." Shiro grinned. "Although I did hear that once a couple of sixth formers convinced some tourists that Area 51 was behind the hill and if they tried to go any further they'd be shot by soldiers."

Allandra laughed. "No way. The teachers would have killed them."

"Only if they found out." Shiro tucked the radio away again. "You haven't said anything about Kentaro for a while."

"Yeah, it's weird. He hardly even tries to insult me any more. Maybe he's coming down with something."

Shiro shook his head. "It's because you're Ichiro's partner. If Kentaro were to try anything now, it'd be a direct challenge to Ichiro, and Kentaro knows that Ichiro wouldn't tolerate that. If he came near you, Ichiro would smack him down hard."

Allandra laughed. "You make it sound like I'm his girlfriend."

Shiro looked away. "Training partner. Close enough."

They talked into the evening. As the sun began to set, Shiro yawned. "Well, that's it until next week." He glanced down. "Oh, wait a second, there's two more of them." Allandra looked downslope and froze.

Beneath them, on the lakeside path, were her father and Michael.

Time seemed to slow to a crawl. Allandra could pick out every detail of the figures walking below as though they were beside her. Vargas's measured, smooth stride; Michael's brown hair, messy at the back where he always forgot to comb it; the tilt of her brother's head as he listened to Vargas's words. Then they were gone, disappearing beyond the curve of the hillside.

"Central, this is South Point. Two people just passed us heading south, a man and a boy . . . Ally, what's wrong?

Why are you shaking?"

"Shiro – I –" Allandra couldn't speak. The world faded, narrowing inwards in a cloud of flickering grey.

"Ally! *Ally!*"

Shiro was kneeling over her. Allandra realised she was lying down, her back against the tree.

"Ally! Are you all right?"

Allandra shook her head.

Shiro picked up the radio. "Central—"

"No!" Allandra grabbed his wrist. "Don't. Just . . ."

Shiro looked at her. "Go back? Do you want me to take you back?" Allandra nodded wordlessly. "OK. Up you get."

Allandra was pulled to her feet. She looked downslope, her heart leaping, but the path was empty.

The walk back to Rokkaku was one of the longest in Allandra's life. Every sound made her jump. Every movement in the leaves made her freeze. Several times she would have stopped dead if Shiro hadn't been there to encourage her. He led her down through the valley, and into her own room.

"Who were they?" Shiro asked, closing the door behind her.

Allandra just shook her head.

"Are you OK?"

She nodded.

241

Shiro asked some more questions. Allandra answered vaguely, without hearing a word he said. Eventually, he left.

Allandra stared at the wall for ten minutes. *Vargas is here*, she thought.

He's looking for us. It was the only reason he could be near Rokkaku. Fright made Allandra's heart jump. He was looking, and sooner or later he would find them . . .

No. Calm down. You've done this before. Allandra took a deep breath, and then another. The paralysing fear began to loosen its grip, and she could think again. *He can't know where we are – if he did he would have come here already. We're safe here. Rokkaku is safe. The patrols would spot him if he tried to get in.*

But how could Vargas be here? He must be close. Maybe he was staying nearby, at— Allandra sat bolt upright.

The house in Rhosmaen.

It's only two miles away. I could go and get Michael!

Get to the Rhosmaen house under the cover of darkness. Sneak in, get Michael out the same way they'd left last year, and take him to Rokkaku. They'd be back before anyone had noticed she was gone. It was so easy she almost couldn't believe it.

Energy rushed through Allandra and she jumped to her feet. She looked through the window to see the trees at the top of the valley painted in the golden light of the setting sun. If she didn't leave soon she'd have to find her way in the dark. She would have to do this now. And she'd need tools.

Allandra kept a wary eye open for her friends as she walked up the valley. She knew exactly what Ignis would say if he found out what she was planning, and he might well try to stop her. The casual glances of the students she passed suddenly took on a new meaning, and Allandra breathed a sigh of relief as she slipped into the top storeroom. She took what she needed quickly and stepped to the open door. Only then did the magnitude of what she was doing hit her.

Below her, Rokkaku valley spread downwards into the trees. The globe lights were being lit one by one, each a dim glow in the evening shadows. The air was lazy with the fading light, and students relaxed and talked in ones and twos on the paths, their day's work done. The wind had dropped off, and the only sound was the murmur of voices from downvalley, and the quiet chuckle of the stream. A boy walked across a tightrope between two tree platforms, the light of the sunset turning him into a red-gold painting against the hills behind as he returned to his treetop home.

For a long moment Allandra stood looking down. When she had first suggested to Ignis that they stay in Rokkaku, she had thought of it as a place to train, a structure from which they could take what they wanted. But in the nine months that she and Ignis had lived here, the valley had become her home. For a moment, Allandra had the strange feeling that her place was *here*, not outside the valley in search of her brother.

She shook it off. Then something caught her eye: the path upvalley, winding into the trees. Slowly, she followed it.

The shrine was silent and empty, the ivy reflecting the last rays of the setting sun. Allandra stepped inside and knelt in *seiza*. Minutes passed in silence.

"I don't really know who I'm talking to," she finally said, hesitantly. "I don't pray or anything. I don't even know if I believe in God or not." The eyes of the *tengu* looked down at her, inscrutable. "But if anyone can hear me . . ." Allandra swallowed. "Please let me rescue Michael. It's all I've ever wanted. For the three of us to be safe together, to not have to be afraid of my father any more. It's why I've worked so hard, all this time in Rokkaku. I'll never ask for anything ever again. Only, please . . ."

The trail of smoke from the incense swirled silently in the still air. Allandra got to her feet and backed to the door. Hesitantly, she bowed towards the front of the shrine, and left. Once outside, she took a last look back into the valley, and turned south.

Allandra could feel the eyes of the watchers on her as she went out. To them, she knew, she would just be another student going off into the woods. Still, she only relaxed once she had left the home ring and passed out of sight. Skirting the outposts, she came down onto the lake path and started walking around the edge of Llyn Garedig.

By the time she reached the dam, darkness was falling. The path along the top of the dam ran for nearly a quarter-mile, bordering the lake. To the left was Llyn Garedig. To the right, the back slope of the dam plunged down at an angle of forty-five degrees. At the very bottom, far below, jets of white water from the pumping station sprayed nearly twenty metres into the air, leaving a faint mist of water behind them. That same water, further down the slate-edged valley, became the rapids into which she and her brother had fallen so long ago. Two-thirds of the way along the dam was a wide concrete spillway. Over the spillway was a bridge. The car park at the end of the dam was empty, for which Allandra was glad.

As she began the slow climb down the Tawi valley, Allandra grew tense, watching for cars. But the sun had set, and the valley was almost deserted. The road was a long one. By the time Allandra reached Rhosmaen, it was close to midnight.

Once into the village, Allandra became more cautious,

slipping from shadow to shadow. The vicarage passed on her right, then two more buildings, and suddenly Tawelfan was looming up in front of her.

Allandra hid behind a hedge for ten minutes, watching. The driveway was empty but for the black Land Rover. Behind it, all the windows in the house were dark. Allandra crossed the road at a quick run. She hid behind the tree at the base of the driveway, searching the shadows in the front of the house for the shape of a guard.

Five minutes, ten minutes, nothing. Slowly Allandra circled the house, moving towards the back. Once there, she scanned the lawn. Still nothing. Allandra frowned. The three of them had made one escape from this house less than a year ago. Why was there no guard, no security?

She circled around to the front and slipped on her climbing claws. *Shuko*, as they were called, were sets of three finger-length, hooked steel claws, mounted on a padded metal band that fitted around the palm. They were best for climbing trees, but worked almost as well on stone and brick. They were also lethal weapons, but that was not the use Allandra had in mind for them tonight.

She hooked one claw into a crack in the wall, got a grip on the drainpipe with the other hand, and swarmed up onto the roof. Once on it she paused again, listening for a sign that someone had woken. When no sound came, she crawled up the tiles. Allandra had brought tools to deal with the window catch, but it was unlocked. She slid it open, took a deep breath, and entered.

Even before Allandra's eyes had adjusted to the dark, she recognised the breathing coming from the bed against the far wall. Her heart leaped. Silently she moved next to the bed and placed a hand over the one lying on top of the covers.

There was a gasp and a movement. Two eyes opened. "What? Who—"

Allandra covered Michael's mouth with the back of her hand. "Sssshhh!"

Michael nodded, eyes wide. Allandra took her hand away. He sat up, staring. "Ally?"

"It's me." Allandra hugged him, hard. She had to blink back tears. "It's me."

Michael leaned back, disbelief in his eyes. "Where – I don't . . . How did you get here?"

"It doesn't matter." Allandra laughed, muted it just in time, and shook her head. "It doesn't matter. Not now that you're here. Come on, we've got to go."

"Go where?"

"I'll tell you on the way. It's a long story – oh God, there's so much I have to tell you!" Allandra giggled softly. "But there'll be time later. We have to get out."

"But Ally, wait. Why are you here?"

"To rescue you, silly!"

"But . . ." Michael shook his head.

"What's wrong? Look, I promise, we'll make it this time. I know a place where he'll never find us, any of us. We'll be safe."

"But there's a meeting tomorrow."

"A what?"

"A meeting. With one of his supply contacts. He always wants me around for setting up when that happens."

Allandra stared in disbelief. "And since when do you do what he tells you? Come on, Michael! We're trying to get away! Remember? The escaping thing, where we don't stick around and become good little drug dealers ourselves? We have to get *out* of here!"

Michael shook his head. "No. You get away. I'm staying here."

"*What?*"

"I can't leave. Anyway, I'd slow you down. You go."

"Like hell! You're coming with me!"

"Ow! Let go!"

"Come *on*! We need to—"

A footstep sounded behind her. Allandra looked up to see Pete in the doorway, dressed in a T-shirt and his underwear, his jaw hanging open. For one shocked second the two of them stared at each other.

Pete reacted first. He lunged forward and grabbed Allandra's arm, yanking her forward. Allandra stumbled, slashing at Pete's hand. She felt the claws catch and rip. Pete bellowed, throwing her against the wall.

Stars danced before Allandra's eyes as she shook her head, trying to clear it. Tav appeared at the door. Pete jerked his head, hand cradled. "It's her! Get her!"

Tav advanced and Allandra lashed out at him. The *shuko* flashed in the dim light, making him jump back.

"Watch it, she's got a blade!"

"Michael!" Allandra pulled herself to her feet, pointing at the window. "Get outside! I'll—"

Then Allandra froze. A new figure had appeared in the doorway. There, sleep fading quickly from his eyes as he stared at her, was her father.

Allandra dived for the window. The familiar voice rang out, sending ice down her spine. "Take her down, now!"

Hands latched onto Allandra's legs, dragging her to the floor. She twisted in wild panic, slashing with the claws.

"Watch the hands!"

"Choke her out!"

Then Pete's hands were at her neck, squeezing. Allandra ripped frantically at them. Blood ran in the darkness, trickling down onto her coat. Pete's grizzled face – only centimetres above her – twisted in pain, but he only gripped tighter. Her head was pounding. As blackness swallowed her, the last voice she heard was her father's: "Don't damage her! I want her whole!"

10

ALLANDRA ALONE

The driveway was silent and still. One by one, the house lights flickered on, casting the tarmac in a harsh yellow glow. Pete and Vargas stepped out of the door, moving left and right as they checked out the area. Tav appeared in the doorway as they returned.

"None of the other windows are touched," Tav said. "Looks like she was on her own."

"Check again." Vargas was tense but calm. "If she's here, Ignis will be too, somewhere. Pete, get Michael and have him help load the car."

"Uh, boss?" Pete said quietly. Vargas turned to look. An elderly woman was standing at the bottom of the drive-way, shielding her eyes from the light. "Mr Havelock? Is that you?"

"Get the car ready," Vargas said in a low voice. "I'll handle this." As the two of them turned away, he walked down the ramp, a surprised smile coming onto his face. "Mrs Gwynn! What are you doing up at such an hour?"

"Oh, Mr Havelock, are you quite all right?" Mrs Gwynn

was the next-door neighbour. Vargas had made use of her as a housekeeper in the past. Her sing-song accent was laden with concern. "I heard ever such a screaming."

"Yes, I know." Vargas shook his head. "I'm afraid my son had a nightmare. He's calmed down a little now, but I don't think he'll be able to sleep in the house. We're going to take him back to London."

"A nightmare?" Mrs Gwynn's face cleared in understanding. "Ah, but they're terrible things for parents, it's true. Why, only last month my dear daughter down in the city was kept up all night by the couple next door. The little one was only eighteen months, and they'd hired someone else to take care of it!" Mrs Gwynn peered up towards the house. "Is that your boy there? My, but he does look upset. Is that his luggage?"

Vargas glanced back. Pete and Tav were manhandling a one-and-a-half-metre wooden trunk into the back of the Land Rover. Michael was hovering nearby, anxious. "Yes, silly, isn't it? He insists on having everything in one box ever since some burglars tried to get into our Hampstead house. But, well, if that's what he wants . . ."

"Ah, burglars." Mrs Gwynn shook her head. "Terrible, they are. Why, only last year in the valley we had old Mr Williams's place up the hill broken into, and him an old man all on his own—"

"Exactly," Vargas cut in smoothly. "Mrs Gwynn, I

wonder if you could do a favour for me? We need to get back to London urgently. Could you watch over the house for us for the next few weeks? There's plenty of food in the fridge that you're welcome to use. I wouldn't ask this usually, but since we have to leave all of a sudden . . ."

"Why, you hardly have to ask, Mr Havelock. Of course I will." Mrs Gwynn accepted the keys, then paused as she was about to turn away. "Mr Havelock, I don't mean to embarrass you, but I have to say, it really is wonderful in these sad times to see a man who cares as much for his children as you do. They don't know how lucky they are to have such a father."

Vargas smiled. The lighting of the house painted his tall frame in yellow as he looked down on his neighbour. "Well, Mrs Gwynn, you know what they say. When all's said and done, your children really are the only thing that matters."

Vargas waved Mrs Gwynn back to her home. Then he turned to the Land Rover and settled into the driver's seat with a long sigh of satisfaction.

"No trace of the other one, boss," Tav said.

"Doesn't matter." Vargas smiled into the darkness. "He'll follow."

With a rumble the car turned out of the driveway and onto the road.

Allandra woke to darkness. She was curled up on a floor that was vibrating with a steady rumble.

She tried to stretch out and hit wood. She was in a tiny space, sealed on all sides. Suddenly she realised what the rumbling underneath her meant, and felt ice in her veins. She was in a car. They were taking her back to London.

In panic, Allandra hit out, up, sideways and down, her hands scratching on coarse wood. Nothing gave an inch. She screamed, but her voice sounded flat and muffled even to her.

The journey went on and on. After an eternity, the car began to slow, stopping more and more often. Finally it came to a halt, and the engine died.

Allandra was waiting for them when they opened the box, but there was nothing she could do. Hands held her down as she fought, while a needle was slipped into her arm. The world faded into nightmares.

Allandra opened her eyes.

Then she closed them again. The world was too bright, and too harsh. When she tried to move, pain stabbed at her from a dozen places, making her gasp.

Her neck hurt terribly. As she carefully sat up to massage it, pain flared along her spine. For a long minute she sat motionless, then she raised her head to look around.

It was as if time had been turned back. She was in her

253

old room. The white lampshade on the ceiling, the *Star Wars* quilt, the shelves next to the bed with all of her old books, the window that looked out onto the back garden. In Allandra's fuzzy thoughts, it wasn't clear what was real and what had been a dream.

Then, as her head began to clear, she noticed the differences. The door was metal now, instead of wood. The window was barred. As she pulled herself shakily to her feet, ignoring the ache in her neck, she saw a tray of food on the floor.

She looked down and realised her clothes had been changed. Instead of her *gi* and *tabi*, she was barefoot and wearing a pale blue tracksuit and top. When Allandra had first put on the black coat and trousers, they had felt heavy and uncomfortable. Now, without them, she felt naked.

She tried the door. It was locked. The bars in the window were cemented in, and tugging didn't loosen them.

Painstakingly, Allandra went over every inch of the room, moving the furniture and going through the cupboards for a way out or a tool that could break the bars. Then she tried the floor, looking for a loose board. There were none. Finally, with nothing else to do, she sat down and ate.

The sun was setting by the time footsteps sounded outside the door. Allandra sat up from the bed where she had been lying. There was the sound of a bolt being drawn, and Pete entered.

Allandra watched, eyes flat, trying not to let her fear show. Unlike Tav, who could be smooth and charming when he wanted to, Pete was only vicious. He was a stocky man, grizzled and scarred, with pockmarked skin and a cold, mean look, as though he blamed the whole world for all the things that had gone wrong in his life. Twice in the past, when Vargas had been really angry with the children, he had turned them over to Pete for punishment. The memory still made Allandra shiver. Pete removed the tray and replaced it with a new one. Then he advanced on her.

Allandra pulled back against the wall. Pete leaned in close. "See this?" he growled, holding up his right hand. It was heavily bandaged. "You did this to me, you little brat, and you're going to pay for it. You ain't leaving here for a long time, and you and me, we're going to have a good long while together." His unshaven face pushed in at Allandra, the muddy brown eyes ugly. "I've been waiting for this a long time. When I—"

A sharp, cold voice spoke. "Pete."

Pete jumped. Vargas was standing in the doorway, his eyes blue ice.

"Boss, I was just—"

"Get out."

255

"Yes, boss." Pete retreated quickly, shutting the door behind him.

Vargas stood watching Allandra for several minutes. Allandra held herself dead still. Vargas walked into the room, his pace leisurely. He took a chair, spun it around so that the back faced Allandra and sat down, resting his chin on his hands. "So."

Allandra said nothing.

"So. The wanderer returns." Vargas tapped his fingers. "Do you have any idea how much time I spent trying to find you, Allandra? I could have bought a yacht with the amount of money I put into searching. Every county, city, town, station and local government agency of Britain and Ireland. And after all that, you walk right into the same room you broke out of, nearly a full year ago. Like a homing pigeon." Vargas grinned, his face suddenly becoming friendly. "Maybe I should have just sat there and waited, hmm?"

Allandra stayed silent. Her father's good moods had always scared her far more than his bad ones. Vargas in a bad temper was dangerous, but as long as she and her brothers kept their heads down, they wouldn't usually be hurt. When Vargas was in a good mood, however, he would want to talk, and doing so set Allandra's nerves on a razor edge. Her father could go from high good humour to savagely vicious in a split second, with never any guarantee as to what would trigger the change.

Vargas reached into his pocket and Allandra tensed. "Oh, don't worry," Vargas said with a smile, producing one of the *shuko* Allandra had worn. "I just wanted to have a look at this. Interesting design. Most of the claws you see around are market-stall deals for Bruce Lee wannabes. These have a decent balance, and they're good steel, too, with an edge. Not a bad weapon. No match for a good knife, though. You just wouldn't have the range. And it's obvious you've never tried to hide a weapon from the cops. Flat and secure are the ways to go. These things would rip you up if you tried to run with them concealed. Where'd you get them?"

Allandra stayed silent.

"Well, let's see what we can put together, then." Vargas ticked off points on his fingers. "You show up at my house carrying these unusual little weapons and a few pieces of standard breaking and entering kit. You also make your entrance wearing some sort of martial arts outfit with a Japanese look. Then when we catch you, you fight like a cornered rat in a way I certainly never taught you." Vargas chuckled. "Though I might have if you'd asked. What do you think all this adds up to?"

Allandra couldn't stay silent any longer. "What are you going to do with me?"

"What do you think? It's time for you to start learning the family business, Allandra."

257

"Pete—"

"Pete does what I tell him to. And so will you."

Allandra met her father's gaze. "No."

She was ready for him to get angry. She wasn't ready for him to smile as though she'd just said something amusing. "No? Why not?"

"What? Because . . ." Allandra stopped. "You're a *drug dealer*!"

"And?"

"You sell people stuff that ruins their lives! Guns, crack, coke – it's all horrible! You've killed people yourself, I know you have, even if you and Tav try and keep it secret! You're a *murderer*!"

Vargas shook his head. "No, Ally. What I am is a professional."

"What's the—"

"I'll tell you what the difference is." Vargas sighed. "I should have had this talk with you a long time ago. I always thought of you as the most promising of my children, did you know that, Allandra? Ignis was strong and tough, but too undisciplined. Michael was obedient, but a little too weak. You were just right. Strong enough to be worth teaching, and smart enough not to kill yourself fighting back. It was why I put up with those constant ridiculous escapes of yours. How hard do you think it would have been to stop them? I let you fight me because

I knew it would make you stronger.

"A murderer kills for personal reasons. A professional kills for business. My business is supply, whether the commodity is drugs, weapons, money or people, and violence is a part of that business. And believe me, Allandra, I am very, very good at it."

Allandra couldn't believe what she was hearing. "That's it? You think it's OK to kill because it's your business?"

Vargas sighed. "Oh, for God's sake, Allandra, stop talking as though I hit a dozen people every day before breakfast. My business is supply, not assassination. If people don't interfere with it, they don't get hurt. It took a while for that lesson to sink in around London, but now that it has, it isn't necessary for me to kill any more. I do my business, people respect my rules, and everything runs smoothly. I work the same way the government does, except my organisation is much more efficient."

"You're nothing like the government."

"I am exactly like the government. A government passes laws and uses the police and the army to enforce them. If someone living in a country doesn't pay their taxes, or doesn't do what they're supposed to, then they'll be given warnings. If they don't listen to the warnings, they'll be destroyed. I work the same way. Just like the government, I prefer it if people obey the rules quietly, but just like the government, I occasionally have to make an example of someone. The government will send people in official uniforms with pieces of paper. My men are much less conspicuous. But the end result, if people don't obey, is the same."

"But the government doesn't sell *drugs*!"

"Really? What do you think alcohol is? Add up the deaths of everyone who dies from illegal drugs in a year and the number won't get anywhere close to the number that die from alcohol. The government oversees its production, slaps a big tax on it, sells it to people, and pockets the money. Same for cigarettes." Vargas shrugged. "One of these days, the government is going to legalise pot and coke and crack and most of the rest of the things that I sell, and when they do, they'll take over doing exactly what I do now."

"That's different!"

"The only difference is in your head. Learn this well, Allandra. The world is made up of predators and prey. Those who have the power take what they want from those who don't. The only quality that matters is the power to hurt and to kill. Because if you do not have it, you are at the mercy of those who do, and then nothing will save you."

Allandra shook her head.

Vargas raised an eyebrow. "Why are you putting up a fuss? What do you call what you've been learning?" He tossed the *shuko* into the air and caught it. "You've been learning to fight, to use weapons, to sneak around. What were you planning to do with those particular skills, Allandra? Help little old ladies across the street?"

The words struck to Allandra's heart like ice. "No!" She jumped to her feet. "I wasn't learning that! I was learning it to fight—" She clamped her mouth shut, but Vargas only laughed.

"To fight me. Of course. Haven't you put it together yet, Allandra? Everything you've done has been perfectly suited to make you the same as me. You've learned to hide, to escape, to fight, to kill – if you have to. Can you think of a better training course for a drug dealer?"

For the first time in her life, there was absolutely nothing Allandra could think of to say.

Vargas rose. "Well, I'll leave you to think it over." He paused at the door. "You're still my daughter, Allandra. I may hurt you, but it's only because I love you. In time, you'll understand why it has to be this way." He left.

Allandra lay down on her bed. Her thoughts were unwieldy, uncertain. The old picture of her and her brothers on one side and Vargas on the other, which had kept her going for so long, was suddenly fragile. Allandra didn't dare touch it, or look too closely, for fear of what she might find. For the first time, instead of seeing the differences between herself and Vargas, she saw the similarities, and it

261

terrified her. Was her father right? Had she been running away from him all her life only to become like him?

She tossed and turned on the bed as the sun vanished behind the horizon. Then, drifting up from the depths of her memory, came Mr Oakley's words. Ignis had told them to her, one evening under the autumn leaves.

A man who knows only how to fight is not a warrior, he is a thug. What you are given here is a real education, not a programme to turn you into a killer.

Ignis's response. *Why should I bother to do all this stuff!*

A ninja is not just a fighter. A true ninja is a warrior philosopher, an exemplar of the benevolent heart.

Dimly, Allandra began to see what Mr Oakley had been trying to say. If she knew only how to fight, then she *was* no different from Vargas.

Scraps of ninjutsu history and the essay on the wall in her room floated through her mind. Protection of the mind and spirit. Justice. A clear and pure heart.

But what did they all *mean*?

Allandra lay awake as the last traces of light faded from the sky and the moon rose in the east. The food grew cold upon the floor.

Allandra's time as a prisoner passed slowly. Whenever she asked to go to the bathroom, she was escorted by both Pete and Tav. After the long months under the open sky of

Rokkaku, Allandra felt hemmed in by the close walls. There was nothing to do between meals except exercise, read or sit.

On the third day of her captivity, the door opened in the early afternoon. Allandra glanced up, expecting to see Pete or Vargas.

Michael stepped through. Allandra bounded to her feet. "You!"

"Hi, Ally—"

"Don't you *dare* call me that, you little traitor! Why didn't you listen to me? We could have been out of here and I would have been safe, if you'd just done what I told you!"

"Ally—"

"What's gone wrong with you? Last year you were helping me escape, but now I come back and it's 'Yes, Father, no, Father, three bags full, Father'. I can't believe that I came back for you. I should have left you in this pit to rot!"

"I—"

"And you even help him with his meetings now? Has he taken you along on one of his drug deals yet, or do you help selling it on the—"

"*Will you shut up!*"

Allandra stopped, shocked. The two of them stared at each other for a long moment.

Then Michael sighed. He seemed to deflate, and suddenly he was the brother Allandra knew again. "I never thought you'd come back, Ally. I thought you were gone for good."

"I was always going to come back."

"You shouldn't have." Michael sat down on the bed and Allandra took a seat next to him.

"Michael . . ." Allandra touched his arm. "What's happened to you?"

"Dad was furious after you left." Michael wouldn't meet her eyes. "He nearly went crazy trying to find you. It was only a few months ago he finally gave up. I've been going to school the last year – you remember Emery Road?" Allandra nodded. "It wasn't fun. The kids there were worse than before. Tav started teaching me how to fight. In the spring, Luke – remember him? – stayed behind after school, waiting with a couple of his friends." Michael looked at Allandra, and suddenly his face was hard and alien. "I took him down with a pipe. The school suspended me for a month, but it didn't matter. Since then his gang does what I tell them."

Allandra's eyes went wide. "Jesus, Michael." Her brother had always been the compliant one, the one who tried to talk things out. When Luke had started picking on him in the Emery Road class, it had been Allandra who'd stood up for him. "Did you . . ."

264

"No, I didn't kill him. Just put him in the hospital. Dad started bringing me into his business after that."

"But . . ." Allandra shook her head. "Michael, it's wrong. How could you help Vargas?"

"What else was I supposed to do?" Michael's voice was bitter. "How many other people do you think there were to go to? You think the teachers cared about me? They remembered Ignis, and they thought I was the same. All they were worried about was whether I'd hurt any more of their prize students. They would have kicked me out of school if they could. I tried looking for something else, and there wasn't anything. I did what Vargas told me because there wasn't anything better."

"Don't you remember everything we did? We promised we'd never do what he told us! How could you betray—"

"Because you left me! You told me that you'd always be there for me, and you lied!" Michael jumped up, staring at Allandra, his fists clenched. "I waited for you, Ally. I waited and waited. I stopped waiting when I knew you'd never come! You said that we'd always be together, and you lied! You left me alone!"

"I'm sorry," Allandra whispered. "Michael, I didn't mean to. I'm sorry . . ."

Michael turned his face. "I've got to help Tav."

"Michael . . ." Allandra grabbed at his hand. Michael brushed her off, walked to the door and knocked on it.

"Michael, please!" Allandra stared at him desperately. "I did come! I was going to take you home!"

Michael turned back towards her. His face was hard and set. "I am home." The door clanged shut behind him.

The kidnapping, being imprisoned, Vargas's words, all these had been terrible, but they had hurt in a brutal, impersonal way. This was something far worse. As Michael's footsteps faded away down the hall, something broke inside Allandra. She lay down on the bed and began to cry.

"Hey, Ally, I'm home!"

Jennifer swung the door shut behind her and tossed her sports bag onto the bed. She sighed in relief. "Wow, it's good to be back. Hey, where are you? You've got to tell me what's been happening since . . ." Jennifer walked through into Allandra's room and stopped. "Ally?"

Damn.

Jennifer went into the bathroom, freshened up, then ran a comb through her hair, studying it critically in the mirror. She fetched her hairbrush and brushed it out thoroughly until she could toss her hair back and let it flow down her shoulders. When she was satisfied, she unpacked, throwing her books into a drawer and emptying the rest of the bag in her cupboard. She changed her clothes. She put her old clothes onto the laundry shelf. She got a glass of water.

Still no Allandra.

Jennifer sighed and flopped down on the bed. Well, until Allandra showed up, she would catch up on her History homework. She had a chapter and a half of the Industrial Revolution still to read.

The resolution lasted about five minutes before Jennifer tossed the book into a corner and lay with her head in her hands, tapping her feet together. Where *was* she?

For Jennifer, having no one to talk to was like having an itch she couldn't scratch. She bounded up and headed for the door. If Allandra wouldn't show on her own, she'd go and find her.

An hour later, a tired and puzzled Jennifer trailed back up the hill towards their room. Allandra wasn't in the *dojo*s, the kitchens, the canteen, Shiro and Ignis's room, Christopher's room, the storerooms, the classrooms, by the climbing face, the lake or any of the teachers' huts.

Disappointed, Jennifer curled up on her bed to have a second try at the History homework. She'd barely found her place when there was a knock on the door.

Jennifer opened it. "Ichiro?"

Ichiro bowed curtly. "Hello."

"Well, hey." Jennifer leaned against the side of the door. "What's up?"

Ichiro looked irritated, although, when Jennifer thought

about it, she wasn't sure if she'd ever seen him any other way. "Is Allandra there, please?"

"Well, that depends."

"That depends on what?"

"Are you really coming to see Ally?"

"What? Why else would I be here?"

Jennifer looked innocent. "Maybe you missed the melodious sound of my voice."

Ichiro scowled. "Where is Allandra?"

"First say you missed the melodious sound of my voice."

"I do not have time for this! This is the third practice she has missed. The High Hunt is in less than a week. She needs to train!"

Jennifer grinned inwardly, opening her mouth for another try at annoying Ichiro. Then she stopped as his words sunk in. Allandra *never* missed practice, much less three in a row. Suddenly Jennifer was worried. "She's not here. Wait, you mean you haven't seen her all weekend?"

"Not since Friday. Excuse me, I will look elsewhere." Ichiro stalked off.

Jennifer crossed the valley to Christopher's room.

"OK, I move four armies into the Ukraine, so now I control Europe. Ignis, I'm attacking Northwest Africa from Southern Europe as well, with everything . . . OK? I move another five armies into Northwest Africa and redeploy to guard Alaska." Christopher sat back. "Your turn."

Ignis looked at Shiro. The three of them were seated around the game board. "Why do we even play this game with him?"

Shiro shrugged. "I think we're going to have to gang up on him next time."

"Hey!" Christopher protested. "I don't do that to you."

The door opened and Jennifer walked in. "Ignis, have you seen Allandra?"

Ignis frowned. "I thought she'd gone on some sort of trip with you?"

Jennifer shook her head. "No. I was away on my own."

"I haven't seen her either," Christopher added.

"Wait a minute," Ignis said. "You mean she's been gone all weekend?"

Jennifer nodded. "She hasn't been at practice since Friday."

"What?" Shiro looked up sharply. "Friday?"

"Yes. Why?"

"Something happened during our Friday patrol." Shiro frowned. "It was right at the end. One moment Allandra was fine, the next she was white as a sheet and shaking."

"What happened?" Ignis demanded.

"Nothing," Shiro answered. "No alerts, no hikers, nothing. Only four people even passed us. It was after the last two that she was so shaken, and they didn't look special. A man and a boy our age."

A cold feeling went through Ignis. "A man and a boy? What did they look like?"

"Let me think. The man was in his thirties? Big guy, tough looking. The boy looked like his son, early teens, brown hair. The instant Allandra saw them she nearly had a heart attack."

Ignis's heart froze. "Oh my God."

"What?"

Ignis jumped to his feet. "I have to go."

"Ignis, stop." Shiro stood in front of him. "What's going on?"

Ignis looked around the room. Jennifer, Christopher and Shiro were all watching him closely, sensing something of what he was feeling. During the year, Ignis had grown close to the three of them, but he had never told them anything of his family's secret. But if what he feared had happened was true, things had gone so badly wrong that it didn't matter any more.

"It's Michael. She's gone to try and get him away from Vargas." And Ignis told the whole story, sketching it out quickly.

When he had finished, Jennifer and Christopher were staring at him open-mouthed. Even Shiro's normally impassive face registered disbelief.

"You mean this was going on all year?" Jennifer finally said in astonishment. "And she never said anything?"

"That's incredible," Christopher breathed. "A *drug baron*?"

"That was it?" Shiro's face was twisted with fury. "And I just let her go? I shouldn't have let her out of my sight!"

Ignis shook his head. "No. It was my fault." Throughout the year, Allandra had been saying that she'd do something like this, and he hadn't taken her seriously. If he'd only paid attention . . . A knife twisted in his gut. "If she'd managed to get away, she'd already be back here. Vargas has got her."

"What are we going to do?" Christopher asked, his bronzed face pale.

Ignis took a breath. "*We* aren't doing anything. I'm going after her."

"Wait, wait, wait." Jennifer hesitated. "What about the teachers?"

Shiro shook his head. "They can't leave the school, not now. But after term . . . "

"That's too late." Ignis walked for the door. "I've got to go now."

"I'll go with you." Shiro turned. "Christopher, go check the patrols. They should have seen her going out."

Ignis turned and stared at Shiro. "What?"

Christopher nodded. "On it." He walked out.

"I'm coming too," Jennifer stated.

"Wait a minute!" Ignis shouted. "What do you think you're doing?"

Shiro looked at Ignis, his eyebrows raised. "Did you think we were just going to let you go off and do this alone?"

"No," Ignis snapped. "You can't do this! She's my sister, not yours!"

"You'll need my help," Shiro stated, calm. "And she's my friend as well."

"And mine," Jennifer insisted. "If your father's as bad as you say he is, I'm not leaving her in trouble. Anyway, I'm going whether you like it or not."

"But—"

Christopher reappeared. "I asked the sixth formers. They saw Ally leaving on Friday evening, going in the direction of Rhosmaen."

"Oh, no." Ignis closed his eyes. "That's where the house is."

Christopher looked at him. "What's going to happen to her?"

Ignis was silent.

Christopher sighed. "Fine. Then I'm coming. I'm not leaving you three to do this on your own."

"All of you, you don't get it!" Ignis insisted. "This is dangerous! It's not your problem!"

"Wrong," Jennifer said, suddenly serious. "Ally's my

272

friend. That makes it my problem."

"And mine," Shiro added quietly.

"We're going to have to get some supplies," Christopher pointed out. "And clothes. If we try and do this in our *gis* we'll stand out a mile."

Ignis looked at each of them in turn, then threw up his hands. "I give up. You're all crazy."

Twenty minutes later, they were in their street clothes, picking through the storeroom.

Christopher took a *hanbo*, spun it, and put it in his bag. "You do know that we're breaking every rule in Rokkaku by doing this?"

"If you don't want to break them, don't take anything," Shiro replied, slinging a coil of rope into his bag before zipping it up. "Ready?"

Ignis and the others looked at each other and nodded. "Ready." They stepped out of the storeroom and came face to face with Ichiro.

Ichiro's face was ice. "What are you doing?"

The four of them were silent. Even Jennifer had nothing to say.

Ichiro looked at them with narrowed eyes. "This is against the rules. I will report you."

"Ichiro." Shiro spoke softly. "Allandra is in trouble. Bad trouble. I can't tell you all the details, but she needs help, and we're going to try and save her. If you stop us, she might never make it back to Rokkaku. We're not asking for help. Just let us go."

Ichiro looked at them. "Where is she?"

"She went to Rhosmaen. We don't know if she's still there."

For a long minute Ichiro studied them, his face unreadable. Then he stepped aside. He jerked his head towards the path out of the valley.

Shiro bowed. "*Arigato*."

Ichiro gave a curt jerk of his head. As the four of them passed, he called out, "*Shiro-san*." Shiro stopped. Ichiro nodded his head. "*Kento*." Then he turned away.

"What did that mean?" Ignis asked quietly.

Shiro glanced at him and smiled slightly. "It means 'good luck'."

In single file, they set off into the forest.

11

THE LONGEST NIGHT

"Is there anyone there?"

"I think it's empty."

"What if it's not?"

Tawelfan looked back at them, the windows shuttered and the doors closed. Rhosmaen was quiet in the summer afternoon.

Ignis shook his head. "We can't hang around all day." He stood up and crossed the road, walking up the same tarmac drive that he'd run down a year ago. The house loomed up in front of him.

The doors were locked. The windows were locked. The Land Rover wasn't there. Ignis did a full circuit of the house. It felt dead. Ignis's spirits sank. If Vargas had Allandra, and she wasn't here, then he could think of only one other place where she could be . . . the last place on earth he wanted to go.

He heard running feet and Christopher and Jennifer were next to him. Jennifer looked at him anxiously and Ignis shook his head. "Nothing."

"So where is she?" Christopher brightened. "Maybe she never got here?"

"Chris." Jennifer's voice was flat, and both Ignis and Christopher turned to look. Jennifer traced her fingers along three scratches in the brickwork. They were underneath the lower roof.

"*Shuko*," Christopher said softly. "So she was here."

Shiro appeared, quiet as a ghost. "I asked at the shop. The people in the house left between Friday and Saturday. No one knows where they went."

"I know," Ignis said quietly. "They went to London. And that's where I'm going, too."

Jennifer and Christopher exchanged a look. Going a few miles to Rhosmaen was one thing. Going two hundred to London . . .

But Shiro didn't blink. "In that case, I think I found us some transport." He pointed up the road. A red Royal Mail van was parked just a hundred metres away.

A few minutes later the postman, a grey-haired man of fifty or so, left the house he had been visiting and settled back into the driving seat of his van. Starting the engine, he put the van into gear and pulled out to continue his journey back to the post centre in Brecon. As the afternoon wore on and he drove steadily eastwards, over hills and through valleys, it vaguely occurred to him that his van seemed a little heavier than it ought to be with all the mailbags empty. He made a mental note to have the engine looked at.

The afternoon turned into evening and the evening into dusk as the four children worked their way across the country. Sneaking out of the mail depot, under the high peaks of the Brecon Beacons, they caught a lift to Abergavenny, and from there stowed away on a truck that took them to Bristol. They crossed the great suspension bridge that spans the mouth of the Severn, the vast darkness of the Bristol Channel stretching out on their right, fading into the black ocean. There in the huge port, the city lighting the night in smoke and sodium yellow, they became lost and wandered for hours before they found their way to the M4 motorway. It pointed east, and they started walking. Finally, at a roadside service station, Jennifer managed to convince a truck driver to carry them to the capital.

Dawn was breaking by the time they reached the outskirts of London. The vast city stretched out in all directions, stirring slowly with the morning light. The only people on the pavements were joggers and delivery men, out early to avoid the crowds that would start to fill the streets with the approach of morning rush hour. Jennifer waved goodbye to the truck driver as he pulled away, and they set off deeper into the city.

As the sun rose, London woke up. There was noise everywhere, the traffic, voices, shouts, horns and movement of countless people all blending together into one huge, endless, anonymous sound. Buses and cars blared past them, shaking the pavements as they took people to work. Ignis began to tense up as they crossed into Hampstead. He recognised the streets. Finally, at the bottom of one leafy avenue, he stopped.

Christopher blinked, tired. "Are we there?"

Ignis pointed at the house opposite them. It was three storeys high, surrounded by a large garden and a fence. A garage stood between rhododendron bushes. An expensive-looking house, but not an unusual one. "There," he said flatly.

"Ignis—" Jennifer began, but he was already moving. A three-metre wall surrounded the garden on the back and sides. Ignis tried to climb it once, then twice, falling back both times. He shook his head, trying to shake away his tiredness. He couldn't fail now! With a burst of energy, he took a grip on the wall, vaulted it, and dropped down into the garden.

He was around the back of the garage. The sun was beginning to cast the bushes, trees and house in bright summer light. Ignis straightened, and began to step forward.

278

"Stop!"

The hiss was urgent. Ignis froze. Christopher dropped from the wall and grabbed Ignis's arm, pointing. Ignis followed his eyes. A black object was planted on the ground a metre or so to his right.

"That's a motion sensor," Christopher said softly. Although fatigue showed on his face, his eyes were still sharp. "One more step and you'll trip an alarm."

"They weren't there before," Ignis muttered. Through the trees ahead, he could see the window of Allandra's room. "Fine. We'll go around."

Jennifer stepped forward from the wall she'd just cleared. "No, Ignis, wait. We can't do this now. I'm exhausted."

"We all are," Christopher said. "They're just waking up, and we've been going all night. Let's pull back and rest."

Ignis shook his head. "No! She's *right there!*" He could see that the curtains of the room up above were drawn. At any minute Allandra might appear. He shook off Christopher's arm. "I'm going in."

Then Shiro was in front of him. "Stop, Ignis."

"What is it with you?" Ignis snapped. "Get out of my way!"

"We don't know what's in there. We don't even know if she's in there. And even if we managed to get her out, we don't know how to get away." Shiro's voice was quiet. He took a glance at Jennifer and Christopher, then lowered his voice. "Ze'ev told me you'd learned discipline, Ignis. Have you?"

Ignis glared at Shiro, wanting to wipe the calm expression off the taller boy's face. His fist clenched, then opened. He took a long breath, then let it out slowly, controlling himself. "There's nowhere else to go."

Jennifer sighed. "Yes, there is." Christopher looked at her in surprise and she nodded. "I'll take you to my parents' house."

Even in the mid-morning, Mayfair was quiet. London's rich and poor districts are more interwoven than those of any other metropolis, but if there is any location that would qualify as uptown, it would be Mayfair. The houses here were no bigger than those in the rest of the city, but they were better painted, more sturdily built, more ornate. Most of the houses were split into apartments; a single house in Mayfair could sell for over three million pounds. Ignis stumbled as Jennifer led them to the end of a street. He'd been awake and on edge for more than twenty-four hours, and his energy reserves were almost gone. Jennifer stopped and Ignis bumped into her, nearly falling. Jennifer held up a hand, seeming not to notice. They stood in front of a big house, with white pillars holding up a front balcony. Jennifer walked to the steps, then pulled up the broken corner of a paving stone. There was a key underneath. Now that Ignis was closer, he could see that the house was less impressive than it had first appeared. There were cracks in the front pillars, and the paint was flaking. A sign was tacked up below the doorbell.

Collection agents: Documents left here will not be received!
Forward mail to PO Box 2069, Central Office.
Advertisers will be boycotted. Travelling salesmen will be shot.

Jennifer rang the bell and they waited in silence, listening to the sounds of the city. When no answer came, she turned the key in the lock.

The front hall was wide and spacious, painted in white. A staircase curled up the side of the hall towards the first floor. The furniture was unexpectedly small and splintered, and wide spaces of floor had been left bare. Two paintings, old and dark, looked down from the walls, but lighter patches between them marked where others had once been. Jennifer stepped over the letters on the mat and walked out into the hall. "Hello? Mum, Dad, it's me! Are you home?"

There was no answer. Jennifer seemed to relax a little. "OK, you guys can stay in the bedrooms on the second floor. Try not to leave any sign we were here, OK? I'm going to see if there's anything to eat."

Ignis yawned, despite himself. "Maybe I'll sleep. Just for a little while. Are you sure it's OK for us to crash here?"

Jennifer hesitated. "Yes. But it'd be better if they never find out, OK?"

"We'll sleep today, then go back tonight and check out the house," Shiro said. "We'll see who's there."

Christopher paused, one hand on the banister as he looked at Ignis and Shiro, his dark eyes drowsy. "There'll be some way to get in. We just need some time to study it."

Ignis nodded. "OK. This evening."

Another day passed for Allandra in her room, and another, and another. The only constants were her meals and the rising and setting of the sun beyond her window.

Vargas came to visit every day. Sometimes it would be in the morning, sometimes late, but once there, he would stay for at least an hour, questioning and talking. Allandra refused to answer at first, but Vargas would always manage to provoke her sooner or later.

When she did respond it was like fighting against the tide. She argued; she refused; she snarled; she shouted; she was unresponsive, sarcastic, insulting, mocking, petulant. Nothing made any difference. Vargas answered her arguments, ignored her refusals, smiled through her insults and shouts. No matter what she did, he would always come back again, tireless as the wind and the sea. Finally, Allandra ran out of energy. She stopped speaking, sitting through his visits in silence until her father gave up and went away. Her life started to slip into a dull haze, until Rokkaku seemed like a dream, a world away.

"You're going to have to come out eventually, you know."

Allandra was on her bed, hugging her knees against her chest as she stared down at the floor. She'd lost track of what day it was. Afternoon sunlight shone through the window, silhouetting the bars against the wall.

"After all, what else are you going to do? Sit up in your room until you die of old age?" Vargas's voice was gentle, reasonable. "What I'm asking you to do isn't so horrible, Allandra. You don't have to become a hitman. Just start helping out with the business, in small ways. Then you can see what it's really like. Michael'll be with you all of the time. As soon as you agree, you can see him again."

The words burrowed into Allandra's tired brain. She wanted to be angry, but it seemed more effort than she could manage to shake off her lassitude. All she could do was stare.

"Think about it, Allandra. You're a professional. You always have been. You didn't half learn a few things the way most do, you trained yourself seriously. Do you want

283

to waste all that lying up here in a bedroom? If you join your brother and I, you can be somebody. You may think you're tough now, but that's nothing to what you could become with some real experience. You could be one of the people with the real power in this world, not a fugitive sneaking around in the shadows." Vargas paused, and when Allandra didn't answer an edge crept into his voice. "I've been patient with you so far, Allandra. I've been taking account of the fact that you've had a long time learning to think differently, and you've needed to get over it. But my patience might start wearing thin in the near future. Pete's still looking for payback on that injury you gave him. If I were you, I'd think very carefully before deciding how long you want to keep me waiting." Vargas stood. The door slammed shut behind him.

Allandra closed her eyes in exhaustion. Every time Vargas came, resisting was a little harder. Doing as he said would be so easy. Allandra was tired, dead tired, and she was coming close to the point where she simply didn't have the willpower to push her father away any more. Tav would bring in her dinner soon, but she had no appetite for it. Allandra curled up on the bed and tried to sleep.

The Mayfair house was silent. Shiro and Jennifer were in Hampstead. In the living room, Ignis was lying on a moth-eaten sofa, vainly trying to relax. Christopher was sitting at a table, his head in his hands, looking down at a dozen sheets of paper. On the paper were diagrams of the Hampstead house: maps of the house and garden, floorplans showing the inside layout as well as Ignis could remember it, all drawn in Christopher's neat, precise hand.

That first night the four of them had returned to the Havelock family house, looking for a way to sneak in. They hadn't found one. Ignis would have been willing to break in anyway and take his chances, but Shiro, Christopher and Jennifer had refused. So, as dawn had broken, they had returned to Mayfair. Since then, they had been studying the house and the people living in it in shifts around the clock, waiting for a weakness to appear. They were still waiting.

To Ignis, it felt as though the possibility of rescuing Allandra was slipping further and further away with each passing day. They had accumulated information. They knew for certain from comings and goings that Vargas was there in the house, along with Pete and Tav, and also Michael. They had seen movement at Allandra's window. They knew that only those four – or five – were sleeping in the house, despite the other men who would regularly visit. They had mapped out the motion sensors and the system of alarms. But they still hadn't seen Allandra, and despite all their surveillance, they had found no way in – and no way out.

Ignis sat up, restless. "So how can we do this?"

"I don't know." Christopher made a note on one of the pieces of paper and reached for another.

"You're the strategy expert. Come up with something."

Christopher let out a breath. "I'm a strategist, not a magician." He tapped his fingers on the table, then pushed the papers away. "I think I can see how to make part of it work. I can see how we could get Allandra out, and all get away. But to do it, I need to get someone inside the house. And I don't know how."

"I think we should break a window."

"I already told you the windows are alarmed."

"Yeah, but if we're fast enough—"

Christopher let out a breath in exasperation. "No! No, no, no! Setting off the alarm will bring them all down on us in seconds. There are three of them, and you say they'll have guns. There's no way we could get in and find Allandra before they reacted, and all it would take would be for one of them to catch one of us. And even if we *did* make it as far as Allandra's room, where would that leave us? We'd have no way of escaping."

"We have to do something."

Christopher said nothing. Ignis sighed, dropped back onto the sofa, staring at the ceiling. Christopher went back to his maps. There was silence for a few minutes.

"What day is it?" Ignis asked eventually.

"Saturday." There was a wistful sound to Christopher's voice. "They'll be holding the High Hunt this evening. I really wanted to compete in that. I wonder how our partners are doing."

"Probably annoyed that we're not there."

Christopher made a face. "You know, the teachers are going to kill us when we get back."

"If this doesn't work, I don't think I will get back," Ignis said under his breath.

"What?"

"Nothing." Ignis sat up. "What's the story on this house, anyway? What's Jennifer worried about?"

Christopher hesitated. "It's . . . complicated. There are some problems with Jen's parents. It was her choice to go to Rokkaku: they didn't want her to. If they find us here, it'll be bad news for her. They might try to stop her from going back."

"What? Why?"

"It's personal. You'd better ask her."

"I'd rather know why she keeps calling me 'Neko-kun' all the time."

Christopher laughed. "There was an old TV show we used to watch together when we were younger. It was about a family who each had the spirit of one of the animals from the Chinese zodiac. There were twelve, and the thirteenth one was the cat. He didn't fit in. He'd always flare up whenever anyone made him angry, and then he'd go up to the roof to sit by himself. He was always fighting, especially with the mouse. *Neko* means cat."

Ignis stared. "You mean all this time, she's been calling me a *cat*?"

"Some people would think that was a compliment."

"I'm not a stupid cat!"

Christopher grinned. "I think she only did it because it annoyed you so much."

Ignis scowled and looked away.

"Ignis? If we try this, and we fail . . . what will your father do?"

Ignis looked up in surprise. Christopher's eyes were steady.

"As long as the three of you don't have anything he wants," Ignis said slowly, "he won't be interested. Just say that I made you come along and you should be all right, as long as you don't make him angry. For me and Ally . . ." Ignis was silent for a moment. "It's Ally Vargas wants the most, not me. Michael used to say that to make me angry." He laughed, an edge of bitterness underneath it. "It drove me crazy. But he was right. My father'll keep Ally alive, no matter what. I won't have so much slack. He'd prefer it if I stayed there. He'd like all three of us to join him. But if it comes down to a choice between me and Ally – or if he ever really thinks that I might be a serious threat to his

plans for his daughter-heir – he'll kill me in a second."
Ignis cocked an eye. "And that might go for you and the others, too."

"Oh."

"You still want to take the risk?" Ignis looked hard at Christopher. "You're not like me or Allandra, Chris. We've got nothing to lose. But you have. You've got a nice family, a nice life. Are you sure you want to be involved?"

Christopher gave a half-smile. "No, I'm not sure. I'm scared to death. To tell you the truth, I feel like running home, or back to Rokkaku. But I feel as though I have to help, as well. This might be the one time in your entire lives where you and Ally really need someone to stand by you. If I don't help you now, when you really need it, what kind of person am I? Even if it does terrify me out of my wits." Suddenly Christopher laughed, a little shakily. "Well, I did go to Rokkaku because I wanted life to be more interesting. I guess I got my wish, didn't I?"

Ignis looked at Christopher, surprised, then laughed. "You're all right, Chris."

Christopher tried to smile. "Thanks."

There was the sound of a key turning in the lock and Ignis and Christopher looked up. Shiro and Jennifer walked in, shutting the door behind them. Ignis jumped to his feet. "Any news?"

289

"No news on Allandra," Shiro answered. "But, Jennifer, you tell them."

"I've been looking at the trees," Jennifer said. She looked nervous, but wired. "I think I know a way to get into the house."

"And there's no sign of anyone visiting," Shiro added. "Tonight might be our best chance."

Ignis and Christopher looked at each other. "OK," Christopher said. "Let's hear it."

Working out the details took several hours. Christopher made them repeat every part of the plan until he was sure they knew it perfectly. By the time he'd taken them through every last contingency, it was after sunset. They gathered their equipment, tidied up behind them, and left the house. Jennifer locked the door, then placed the key under the flagstone. The unspoken message was clear: one way or another, they wouldn't be coming back.

London was alive with weekend traffic, streams of taxis and minicabs taking people to parties or back home, red and orange lights shining over the packed crowds, people out for a night on the town, their party clothes illuminated in the neon glow of the streetlights. No one noticed four children walking out of the city centre into North London.

The journey from Mayfair to Hampstead is two hours by

foot. There are several ways to make the trip that are safe and well-lit, even late at night. Unfortunately, none of them knew what they were.

Shiro was the first to notice. "Heads up," he said quietly as they turned down an avenue near Hampstead Heath. "Someone's following."

Ignis glanced back over his shoulder. Three figures were trailing them, ten metres or so down the street. One of them called out. "Wait up, man."

The four of them stopped. Their followers came closer. Under the orange-yellow glare of the sodium lights, Ignis could see that they were boys a few years older than him. The one at the front was about sixteen years old, with long arms and a hooded top that hid his face. "Hey, man," he said. "Wanna buy some catch?"

Ignis and the others looked at each other. "Buy some what?"

"Catch. You know, grass?"

"No. We haven't got any money," Christopher answered.

"Oh, that's right, is it?" The boy in the lead began to circle. "You hear that, guys? They haven't got any money."

"He's lyin'," a second one commented.

"Are you guys muggers?" Christopher asked.

"What?" The first boy's eyes went wide. "What did you say?"

Christopher looked confused. "I—"

291

"Hey, Kev," the second boy said. "You hear what he just called you?"

The first boy took a threatening step forward. The three of them were now in a semicircle around Ignis and his friends, backing them against a wall. "You little dipshit. You think we're letting you get away with that?"

Ignis stepped between Kev and Christopher. "Back off."

Kev stared down at Ignis. "Who do you think you are, you cocky runt?"

Ignis's eyes narrowed. "I'm not telling you again."

"Oh, you hear that?" Kev looked to the other boys. "He's not telling me again. Let's see what you got on you, dipshit." He reached down for Ignis's bag.

Ignis lost his temper.

Letting the bag fall, he stepped in and sideways, kicking up hard into the other boy's crotch. Kev gasped and bent forward, bringing his face down into a perfect position for Ignis to snap a punch into it. Kev backed away, swinging at Ignis. Ignis slipped the punch easily, moving in to finish him.

"Hey!" Kev grabbed at Ignis's left shoulder. Bad mistake.

Ignis took hold of the boy's wrist with his left hand. Reaching back over his left shoulder with his right hand, he closed his grip over one of the fingers on his jacket. Holding the wrist tightly, he yanked the finger back.

Crack.

"Aaaaah!"

Kev stumbled and fell, clutching his hand, face twisted in pain. "My hand! You broke my hand!"

"That was just a finger." Ignis took a step forward, the light of battle in his eyes. "Get up and let's finish."

Kev looked at him wildly. "You're crazy, man!" He scrambled to his feet and ran into the night.

Ignis turned to see Christopher, Shiro and Jennifer three steps away. The fight had been so fast they had not had time to reach him. All four of them turned to face the other two boys, who were staring at Ignis in disbelief.

"Boy," Jennifer said softly, "you *really* picked the wrong bunch of kids to mug, you know that?"

The second boy stared. "Who *are* you?"

"We," Shiro said quietly, "are just going about our business. Unless you want to try another round." He took a step forward. Ignis moved to his side.

The two boys looked at them. They looked at each other. Then they ran.

As their footsteps faded away into the darkness, Ignis crouched down. Suddenly, he was breathing hard and his hands were trembling. He heard a footstep and Christopher was next to him. "Ignis, are you OK?"

"I thought Ze'ev didn't teach nasty techniques like that," Shiro said, watching to make sure the boys were gone.

"He doesn't." Ignis drew in a breath, then straightened. "I figured that one out myself. Come on, we've got work to do."

The streets were empty by the time the four of them reached Vargas's house. One by one, they slipped over the wall and carefully wove their way through the motion sensors, Christopher directing them. They took shelter behind one of the rhododendrons by the garage.

A light was on in Allandra's window. "We're coming, Ally," Ignis whispered.

Jennifer was slipping on her *shuko*. "Sure you want to do this?" Shiro asked quietly.

"Stop asking stupid questions," Jennifer whispered. She slung on a light backpack.

Shiro smiled in the darkness. "Sorry. Are you ready?"

"As much as I'll ever be." They all looked up. Next to the house, a tall ash tree stretched up past the roof.

They crossed the grass to the base of the tree, avoiding the vision arcs of the windows. "Jen . . ." Christopher said quietly.

"I'll be fine." Jennifer tested the tree bark. "When's the last time you ever saw me take a fall? Hey, it's so easy I might do it twice. Or three times. Just for fun."

Christopher let out a breath. "Remember, when you get in—"

"The east window, I know. See you in a few minutes."

"Good luck," Ignis said quietly.

Jennifer took a grip on the tree, and started climbing.

The ash wasn't an easy tree to climb. Most of the branches were steeply angled, not horizontal, and often there was no footing at all. But the *shuko* gave Jennifer a grip even when there was nothing to hold, and balance and practice made up for the rest. She passed the first floor, then the second. She glanced into Allandra's room as she passed it, but saw nothing. Then the branches were dividing and becoming thin under her hands, and she was level with the roof.

Jennifer kept going up. The tree began to sway alarmingly beneath her. Only when she was level with the chimney did she stop and turn, carefully, to look down. The slope of the tiled roof, with the skylight in the centre, was before her.

Before her, but not beneath her. The tree didn't quite overhang the roof: there was a gap of a couple of metres. A small gap. Barely worth noticing if she was in Rokkaku with a safety line. With a ten-metre fall to the ground and no safety, it looked much bigger. Jennifer placed her feet against the thin trunk, and began to rock.

The tree groaned and swayed, swinging first closer, then further, from the house. The roof grew, shrank, grew, shrank. Jennifer watched it, judged the motion, breathed

295

in, and breathed out. Then, as she swept towards the roof, she pushed off from the trunk with all of her strength, throwing herself horizontally over the gap.

Jennifer turned a forward somersault as she fell. For one endless moment the roof, tree and sky whirled in her vision, the wind rushing through her hair. Then she came down with a flat *wham* on the roof tiles, hands and feet landing as one. For a moment she started to slide towards the drop, then she spread her weight and came to rest.

"OK," Jennifer whispered quietly. "I do *not* want to do that again."

Ignis gasped as Jennifer made her jump, then clenched his fist as he saw that she'd made it. "Go, Jen!" he whispered.

Christopher grinned in the darkness. "I knew she'd do it. OK, let's move."

Jennifer stayed motionless for a minute as her breathing steadied, then, spiderlike, she began to work her way across the roof towards the skylight. Once she could get a grip on it, she relaxed slightly. She reached down to pull it open. Nothing happened. She looked down through the glass at the catch.

Locked.

Great.

Jennifer thought of the tools in her backpack. Maybe

296

she could break the skylight. Surely it wouldn't be alarmed? No one could be so paranoid as to alarm even the roof, right?

Jennifer pulled out a torch and flashed it into the window.

Right?

The torchbeam lit on a wire.

Wrong.

Jennifer was stuck. She couldn't go in and she couldn't go back. She tried to think of what Christopher would do. She tapped a hand on a tile and then stopped to look at it more closely.

The tiles . . .

Jennifer took a grip on one and pulled. At first it resisted, then as she wiggled it from side to side there was a crack and it came away in her hand. Jennifer lifted it with an effort – it was surprisingly heavy – and looked at it thoughtfully.

OK, then.

Jennifer set to work.

In her room, Allandra tossed and turned, somewhere in the confused state between dreaming and waking. There was a monster outside in the corridor, creeping slowly towards her door. As it drew closer, she could hear its footsteps, echoing on the floorboards . . . tap, tap, tap . . .

Allandra sat up on her bed, shaking off sleep. She could still hear the footsteps: it hadn't been a dream. She heard Tav's curt voice. "Five minutes. No more."

The door opened, revealing Michael in the splash of yellow light. Allandra rolled over to face the wall. The door shut again, returning the room to darkness.

"Ally? Are you OK?"

"Fine," Allandra answered dully. "Go away."

Allandra heard the scrape as Michael pulled up a chair. There was a minute's silence.

"Dad doesn't want me coming here," Michael said eventually.

"Why do you call him that?"

"Call him what?"

"*That*. Dad. You never used to."

"Well, he is, isn't he?" Michael sighed. "I'm sorry I yelled at you. I still like you."

Allandra didn't answer.

"Why don't you just do what he says? It's not like he's asking us to go out and kill people." Michael paused, then went on. "We could – we could do stuff together. You could go to school with me. It'd be like old times again, except we wouldn't have to keep fighting him. I did miss you, Ally. I mean it. Can't you stay, this time?" Michael hesitated. "Please."

Allandra's insides curled up. She bit her lip, not letting

herself make a sound. Michael sat there in silence for a little while longer, then left.

On the east side of the house, Ignis looked at his watch. "What's keeping Jennifer?"

Shiro was still. "Wait."

Up on the roof, the skylight now had a pile of a dozen slates resting against it. Underneath was some kind of black rubber which Jennifer had ripped a hole in, and underneath that was a cross-hatch of wooden beams. The vertical beams were thick and strong, but the horizontal ones were thin enough that she had been able to break several of them – enough to give her a way in. She took a grip on two of the rafters, and slipped through.

Jennifer came down in an attic. A quick sweep of the flashlight revealed nothing except junk. She looked up: she could see stars through the ragged hole. The next time it rained, whoever was underneath this part of the house was not going to be happy.

There was a hatch in the floor. Jennifer eased it aside, then froze at the sound of footsteps.

In the brightly lit corridor below, a boy about Allandra's age walked past, so close that Jennifer could have reached out and touched him. He had Allandra's tilted blue eyes, but darker hair. Then he was gone, and she heard him speaking with someone. The voices faded into silence.

Jennifer remained motionless for five minutes. When she heard nothing further, she hung from the edge of the attic floor, and let herself drop.

The corridor was small and empty. There were doors on both sides, and a staircase at the end. Jennifer stood silently for a minute, listening. Nothing. She moved to the top of the staircase, and descended on cat feet.

The front hall looked deserted. To the right was an open door into what looked like a living room, and in a tray on the front table were several sets of keys. Jennifer darted to them, and selected the ones that looked right.

Footsteps sounded. In a flash, Jennifer was pressing herself against the wall. Somebody had just walked into the living room, and voices, clear and loud, were speaking through the doorway, just a few centimetres to her side.

"How long's this going to take, boss?" A grating, rough voice. The reply was cool.

"It will take as long as it takes."

Very cautiously, Jennifer edged along the wall. Holding her breath, she peered around the corner.

"The key is alternatives, Pete. If you control them, you can make people do anything. All you have to do is make sure that their best choice – or *only* choice – is to do what you want them to. And right now, Allandra has no alternative but to do as I say."

"I reckon you should beat it into her. That'd teach her."

The one who had addressed the other as boss was a short, grizzled man with a shaven head and pockmarked skin. He radiated an aura of viciousness. The second was taller and better dressed, with dark brown hair. He moved smoothly, and might have been good-looking but for the coldness in his eyes. He looked at the other with a gentle smile.

"Pete, Pete. You're good at what you do, but you don't understand anything about upbringing. Raise a dog and have everybody beat it, and it'll be vicious to everyone. Raise a dog and have one person treat it kindly, and have everyone else beat it, and it'll love that one person and hate everybody else. It would be easy to break Allandra, but I don't want her broken. I want her to be a trustworthy daughter that I can rely upon. That means she has to serve willingly."

Nerves on edge, Jennifer watched from around the edge of the doorframe. Neither of the two men was looking in her direction, but if she crossed the doorway one would be sure to notice her. Jennifer looked at the staircase longingly. It was less than two metres away, but out of her reach.

"Allandra is isolated." Vargas's voice was reasonable. "She has no one to turn to except me and her brother. If it were Ignis, he'd fight back until he killed himself, but Allandra won't do that. She has too strong a will to live. And the only way for her to live is to accept my authority. Sooner or later she'll realise that. And if she doesn't," Vargas shrugged, "then I'll arrange a session with you for her."

Pete grinned. "Yeah. I'd like that."

Vargas looked towards Pete thoughtfully. "You would, would you?"

"Yeah, boss."

Vargas moved so fast that Jennifer had no time to catch her breath. One moment he was on the other side of the room, the next he was standing over Pete, staring down into his face. Pete backed away, his eyes wide.

"Let us get something very clear, Pete." Suddenly, Vargas's voice was cold as death. "The point of all this work is for Allandra to become my heir. Not for you to indulge your sadism. When I tell you to hurt Allandra, you will hurt her, but you will hurt her exactly as much as I tell you to, and in the *way* I tell you to, and you will do nothing further. I want Allandra whole, healthy, and neither crippled nor insane. Should you go one inch beyond my instructions, should you lay a finger on my daughter in a way I do not approve, then I will see you dead, and it will not be a quick death. You will die slowly, alone in the dark, screaming."

Pete's face had gone chalk white. He stared up into Vargas's icy blue eyes, licking his lips.

"Allandra is mine. She belongs to me. And I do not like my property being damaged. At least," and suddenly Vargas was smiling cheerfully, as though the two of them were the best of friends, "not permanently damaged. You will keep that in mind, won't you?"

Pete nodded, the colour returning slowly to his face.

"Good, good." Vargas clapped Pete on the shoulder and turned away. Pete stared after him. For an instant both of them were facing away from the door.

Quick as a flash Jennifer crossed the doorway and sped upstairs, her heart pounding. What she had just seen had terrified her, and she had no thought beyond finding Allandra and getting out of this nightmare place as quickly as she could.

The sound of a window opening made Ignis, Shiro and Christopher look up. Jennifer's face appeared for an instant at the second-floor window before metal flashed in the night and the keys dropped into the grass.

"*Yes!*" Christopher grabbed them. "OK, Shiro?"

Shiro nodded. "I'm coming. Ignis, you wait for them."

Ignis nodded and the two of them ran into the night. He looked up at the open window above. *Hurry up, Jen . . .*

Allandra stared up at the dark ceiling. She couldn't get Michael's words out of her head. *Like old times again. Together.*

She could do as Vargas said. It would be so easy just to stop fighting. The future unfolded before Allandra. Agreeing to help her father. Learning Vargas's business, succeeding him, in time becoming the ruler of his organisation, powerful and terrible, her brother at her side. She and Michael against the rest of the world, together again, for ever. It hovered before her, tantalising. All she had to do was say *yes*, and it would become real.

Allandra got off the bed and paced, nervous energy rippling through her veins. The world was split into two paths, both dark and uncertain. She halted at the window. The full moon shone down from a clear sky, pale light falling on her face. She stared up at it through the bars. *Show me what to do . . .*

Footsteps, soft and uncertain, sounded in the hall. Allandra turned to face the door. There was the sound of bolts being pulled and the door creaked open. "Michael?" Allandra whispered.

"Nope. Guess again."

Allandra stopped dead.

A figure stepped forward into the moonlight. For a minute, Allandra thought she was dreaming.

"Jennifer?"

"Who were you expecting, Luke Skywalker?"

The familiar voice swept through her, blowing the suffocating cobwebs away. All of a sudden, Allandra was wide awake. "*Jen?* How did—"

"No time to explain. Come on!"

Jennifer dragged a dazed Allandra into the hallway. Pulling a coil of rope from her backpack, she tied one end of it to the radiator. "OK." She threw the rope out of the window, the black nylon uncoiling into the darkness. "The others are down below."

Allandra hesitated. "But Michael—"

"There's no time." For the first time Allandra could remember, Jennifer's face was deadly serious. "Ally, some day I'll tell you all about what I just overheard, but right now, trust me, you do *not* want to stay here! Let's go!"

Footsteps sounded on the stairs below, and with a single quick motion, Allandra took the rope and swung herself out, sliding down through the darkness. She landed in a flowerbed with a soft thump. The night breeze blew in Allandra's hair, and she looked up with a surge of joy to see the stars. She was free.

"Ally!" A dark figure enveloped her in a hug.

"Ig?" Allandra gasped. Jennifer landed behind them. "How did—"

"She's gone!" The shout from behind them was Tav's.

"Come on!" Ignis grabbed Allandra's hand and started

running. He led Jennifer and Allandra at a sprint towards the flat-roofed building between the bushes.

"But that's the garage!" Allandra called as they ran.

"We know!" Jennifer called back.

Vargas, Pete and Tav poured out of the front door, fanning out. "She's in there!" Pete shouted, pointing to the lit window of the garage.

Vargas yanked at the bottom of the garage door, and snarled as it didn't give. "Pete, get a sledgehammer! Tav, cover the back door! We'll trap them in here and—"

There was the growl of an engine from inside. For a moment Vargas and Tav paused. The growl rose to a roar.

"Look out!" Tav yelled.

Vargas dived sideways as the Land Rover smashed through the door, shards of plastic flying in all directions. For a moment, he had a glimpse of Allandra's face at the window, looking out at him, then it was gone, the Land Rover shedding pieces of door from its roof and sides as the four-by-four powered down the driveway.

"Chris!" Ignis yelled. There was a crunch as a rose bush went under the wheels, throwing the five of them around inside the vehicle.

Christopher yanked the wheel left. The Land Rover clipped a parked Ford with a screech of paint, sending the car's alarm wailing. They swung to the opposite side of the street, ran up the bank and down it again, missed a lamppost by centimetres, and sped away into the night.

"After them!" Vargas shouted, scrambling to his feet. Pete raced into the garage towards the other car, then skidded to a halt. "What the—'

A second later, Vargas saw why. All four of the Mercedes' tyres were flat.

For a moment, blind, incredulous rage enveloped Vargas. How *dare* anybody do this to him? How *dare* they?

Tav saw the tyres and swore. "I can call a car."

"No." Suddenly Vargas was icy calm. He walked to the Mercedes and studied it closely. Apart from the tyres, it seemed undamaged. "Tav, call a mechanic. Tell him I want this car ready to drive in fifteen minutes or they'll be picking his body out of the Thames. Pete, get Michael. We leave as soon as you have your tools."

Pete blinked. "Huh?"

Vargas turned to them and smiled a very cold smile. "I know where they're going."

12

WITH THE DAWN

The night streets of London were all but empty, and they wove through them at breakneck speed. Only after a dozen turns did Ignis look back. "We lost them."

"Ignis, Jen . . ." Allandra shook her head, dazed. "How did you get here?"

Ignis grinned. "Well, I tried to ditch them, but they just wouldn't stop following me. And then Christopher decided that he could plan everything out, and—"

"But how did you get into the house? Everywhere's alarmed."

Shiro smiled. "You can thank your roommate for that one."

Jennifer waved a hand. "Ah, it was easy. I'll do it again some time."

Allandra hugged her tightly. "Thank you," she whispered, blinking back tears. "You don't know what it was like back there. I was about to give up. Ignis, Shiro, Chris . . . thank you, all of you."

Ignis reached across and ruffled her hair, his voice gruff.

"We weren't going to leave you."

Jennifer grinned. "Hey, I didn't want to lose my double room."

"Anyway, we're not safe yet," Shiro said with a smile. "We still have to survive Christopher's driving."

"Hey!" Christopher looked back. "Welcome back, Ally—"

"Chris, the road!"

The Land Rover ran a red light with a screech of tyres and headed north.

They drove all through the night, working their way out of London and east on the A40 as they passed through cities and towns. There was time for Allandra to hear the story of her friends' journey: Brecon, Bristol, Mayfair, the muggers, and the final raid. In turn she told them her own story. Her voice began to waver as she reached the part with Michael.

"Ally," Ignis said. "It was his decision. It's not your job to look after him."

Allandra dropped her eyes. "I should have come back earlier."

"If you had, you'd probably still be in there," Ignis replied.

Allandra didn't answer. She felt Jennifer's hand on her shoulder and was grateful for it, but the memory of her brother was an ache that she knew would not soon pass.

Conversation flagged as they crossed the border into Wales. Twice they had to stop and look at a map as they worked their way through the dark country lanes. By the time the sign for Rhosmaen flashed green in their headlights, the first traces of light were showing in the eastern sky.

Allandra yawned. Jennifer was propped up against her, asleep. Ignis and Shiro were drowsing against the doors. Allandra wanted to join them, but somehow she needed to be awake for her return. "Hey, Chris," she said, stifling another yawn. "How'd you learn to drive?"

"Uh, I used to practise on a driving simulator."

"A driving simulator?"

"Yeah. It was called *Carmageddon*. I'll show it to you some time."

Houses swept by as they wove though Rhosmaen village. Christopher was driving more slowly now. Headlights pulled out behind them. "Huh," Christopher said, glancing in the mirror. "They're up early."

Allandra looked back over her shoulder. She frowned, then her eyes widened as the lights grew closer. "Oh, no!" She shook Jennifer and Ignis. "Wake up! Chris, drive!"

"What is it?" Jennifer asked, drowsy.

"It's them!"

The Land Rover's steady pace suddenly accelerated. "They've seen us," Tav said from the back seat.

Vargas pressed harder on the pedal and the Mercedes leaped forward with a growl. Slowly, the Land Rover's brake lights began to grow in their windshield.

"They're gaining!" Ignis shouted. "Chris, go faster!"

"I can't! We'll go off the edge!"

They were on the road that ran the length of Rhosmaen valley, the ground sloping sharply down into the Tawi on the left. Somewhere in the darkness ahead was the dam, Allandra knew, and if they could get to that, the steel barrier at the bridge would stop the cars . . . but then what?

Shiro was rummaging in his bag. "Ally, open a window!"

Allandra hit the button and her window slid down, letting in a rush of air. Shiro leaned over her with a black pouch that clinked in his hands and emptied it out of the window. Slivers of metal flashed, falling away into the night.

"What the—" Vargas muttered under his breath as a shower of glinting stars bounced away from the Land Rover and into the glow of the headlights, spreading themselves over the road.

The Mercedes sped over them with a *thunkthunk*. The

car lurched. Vargas fought the wheel, pulling the car level again.

"Caltrops!" Tav called.

"I noticed," Vargas answered tightly. "Pete, we've lost a tyre. Even things up."

Pete grinned. "You got it, boss." He rolled down his window.

Jennifer and Allandra cheered as they saw the Mercedes fall away. Then there was a glint of metal above the lights.

"Get down!" Allandra shouted, pulling Jennifer flat. The gunshot echoed off the valley sides and the Land Rover shuddered. Two bullets slammed into the bodywork before the third caught a tyre.

The Land Rover slewed sideways. For one horrible moment they were speeding straight towards the edge of the road and a sheer drop into the darkness. Then with a heroic effort Christopher dragged the car to the right, wheels bumping on grass as they pulled back onto the path. The speedometer dipped and fell. "They're going to catch us!" Christopher called.

"I know." Shiro had been staring off into the shadows; now he was suddenly calm. "Listen to me, everyone. This is what we're going to do . . ."

The brake lights of the Land Rover glowed red as the Mercedes drew closer. It seemed to be slowing. Then, as they pulled around an S-bend, the door swung open and a figure jumped out, rolling over and over down the slope towards the river.

Vargas stamped on the brake. "Tav, get after her!"

"On it." Tav didn't wait for the car to stop before swinging out. Pete slammed the door, and they roared into pursuit again.

Shiro slid down the slope, grabbing at branches to slow himself as he approached the river. With a splash he landed in the wide, shallow waters of the Tawi and ran across, his shoes kicking up spray.

Tav reached the river's edge and saw in the half-light a dark shape scrambling up the bank on the far side. With a curse he jumped in after.

"It worked!" Ignis turned back. "Ally, go after me. We'll all meet up on the far side of the bridge."

Allandra's throat tightened as she looked at her brother. "Ignis . . ."

"Don't worry." Ignis grinned. "Let him try and catch me. Chris, go!" Christopher stamped on the brake and Ignis jumped out, rolling into the night.

"Hey, *that's* her!" Pete turned to Vargas as the figure disappeared over the edge of the slope. "Boss, stop and I'll—"

"Wait." Vargas studied the shape as it scrambled away. "It's Ignis."

"Huh?"

"They're using decoys. Stay with the car."

Ignis came up out of his roll to hear the Mercedes flash past above him without stopping. He swore, then started running after the cars.

The hawthorn branch blocking Tav's way snapped with a crack as he stamped into it, a thorn tearing the silk sleeve of his shirt. He cursed. The figure ahead was cutting through the undergrowth and gullies. Tav was lean and tough, in good condition, but his size made it harder to duck under the obstacles. He scrambled up the slope, keeping a steady pace. Sooner or later, his quarry would tire.

"Ready?" Christopher asked tightly.

Allandra pulled on the jacket of Jennifer's *gi* and tied the belt tight. "Ready."

"Go!"

Allandra gave Jennifer one last look. Then as they

314

skidded around a bend, she leaped out. For an instant Allandra was falling through the darkness, air rushing past her, then she hit grass. She rolled into the bracken and ducked down, covering her head just as the Mercedes' headlights swept over her hiding place. Then it was roaring past in a cloud of noise and smoke, and Allandra was left coughing on the exhaust fumes.

She peeked up as the sound of engines faded away up towards the dam. When she was sure neither was stopping, she cut down into the trees and began cautiously to follow them. *Jen, Chris, please make it out safe . . .*

Jennifer slammed the door. Through the back window, she saw the Mercedes pass Allandra without slowing, and a wave of relief swept over her. Then another gunshot sounded from behind them, and Jennifer ducked. Underneath her, the car jerked as a second tyre blew out, throwing her hard against the door. "Chris!" Jennifer shouted as she struggled into Allandra's clothes.

"Nearly there. Please, car . . ." Christopher said under his breath to the screeching engine, "just a little longer . . ."

Pete frowned as the Land Rover pulled left at the fork, heading up the dam path. "That's a—"

"Dead end," Vargas interrupted. "They're going to run. No guns, Pete. I want them alive."

Limping and smoking, the Land Rover cleared the top of the hill with one final effort and then its engine died with a wheeze, sending them coasting into the empty car park. Christopher grabbed his *hanbo* and jumped out, Jennifer a second behind him. They vaulted the barrier and raced out over the bridge that crossed the spillway.

Pete and Vargas were less than ten seconds behind. The Mercedes slewed to a halt next to the stricken Land Rover. Past the barrier, they could see a boy and a blonde-haired girl in Allandra's tracksuit, sprinting.

"I've got 'em!" Pete yelled. He ducked under the barrier and ran. Vargas took two steps, then stared after the disappearing shapes, frowning.

Shiro burst into the open to see the quarry face before him. Once upon a time it had supplied stone for the houses and lead mines in the hills around, but now it was deserted. He took a flying leap onto the cliff and scrambled up, hearing a shout behind him as he reached the top.

Once there, he saw what he had been looking for. All the students at Rokkaku knew every inch of the terrain around them, and Shiro's memory was better than most. He took his position, drew a deep breath, and waited. *So,* a detached voice said from somewhere inside him, *this is what a real duel feels like.*

Tav's head appeared at the top of the slope. He stopped dead as he saw Shiro. "Who the hell are you?"

"I was out for a walk," Shiro replied.

Tav's face darkened. He walked towards Shiro, his eyes fixed upon him. Shiro stepped smoothly sideways, leading Tav.

"I'm in a bad mood, little boy," Tav said quietly. "You've messed my clothes and you've wasted my time, and those are two things I don't like. Now, I think you know where those two kids are going. Take me there right now." He stepped forwards. There was barely a metre between them.

Shiro looked at him steadily. "They don't want to see you."

"I don't care what they want. And I don't care what you want, either." Tav's voice was soft. He threw open his jacket to reveal a shoulder holster. "Vargas wants her alive. But he didn't say anything about her friends."

As Tav reached across his body for the gun, Shiro struck with all his speed. His palm slammed into Tav's chest, fingers spread wide in the *shako ken* strike with all of his body weight behind it.

The impact sent Tav staggering backwards, his eyes going wide in surprise. His foot stumbled onto a thin crust of earth that broke beneath him. With a shout, Tav plunged down into one of the ventilation shafts of the old mine, his yell vanishing down into the earth to finish with an echoing thud.

Shiro let out a long breath. The shaft was silent. Cautiously, he approached it. He leaned forward, about to stick his head out over the hole to look for Tav, then something made him stop. He paused, then took hold of a branch and poked it out over the hole instead.

Two gunshots crashed. Splinters flew and the branch spun out of his hand, clattering down the mineshaft. Shiro jumped away, tripping and falling. He stared at the hole with wide eyes, his heart going cold as he realised how close he had just come to being killed.

"I'll remember that trick for next time," he said when his nerves had steadied.

There was silence for a few minutes, then a voice floated up, cold as ice. "You're dead, kid."

Shiro didn't answer. He could imagine Tav lying at the bottom of the hole, his gun trained on the patch of blue sky at the top of the shaft. Quietly, he crawled back across the clearing, then, once he was out of earshot, rose to his feet and began running for the dam.

Jennifer risked a brief glance back as they sprinted along the causeway to catch a glimpse of Pete. "He's after us!" she gasped.

No, you think? Christopher would have called back if he had the breath. Having Jennifer switch clothes with Allandra had seemed like a good plan when Shiro had explained it; now, he was having second thoughts. The dark waters of Llyn Garedig rippled to their right, but swimming would make them a sitting target. As they cleared the dam and began climbing along the lake, Christopher looked quickly back over his shoulder to see that their pursuer was fifty metres behind and closing. They needed an idea, fast.

The path wound uphill around the lake's inlets. Jennifer was panting now, and the man behind them was gaining steadily. As they ran down towards the first stream, Christopher grabbed Jennifer's arm. "Jen, there!"

Ahead, Pete saw the two children he was chasing cut left into the trees. With a burst of energy, he jumped the stream and sprinted after them. His boss's daughter wasn't getting away from him this time.

He turned the corner to see the girl curled up in a ball on the grass. The boy was nowhere in sight. Pete slowed to a trot, panting. "Freeze!"

The girl didn't move. She was shaking in fear, and this sent a glow of satisfaction through Pete as he walked towards her. "Well, well. Don't move a muscle, girl. Vargas wants you alive, but he didn't say how many bones yer still had to have. Run from me, will yer? I've been wanting to give you this a long time, you little—" He grabbed the girl's hair and yanked her head back, and the smile died on his lips. It wasn't Allandra.

Pete shook her, his good mood turning to murderous rage. "Where is she?"

"Please don't hurt me!" Jennifer's eyes were filled with tears.

Pete dragged her up by her hair, shaking the girl until her teeth rattled. "Where is she? Tell me right now or . . .!"

"I don't know! She made us switch, it wasn't my fault." Jennifer sniffled. "We were just going to get away! Ally made us switch clothes and run. The other boy ran when you got close. I don't know where she's gone!"

"Like hell you don't." Pete tossed her down and reached into his jacket. A long knife gleamed in the dawn light.

Jennifer's eyes went wide in panic. "No! Please!"

Pete stared down at her, his eyes cold. "I'm gonna make this real simple. Tell me where she is by the time I count to ten, or I start cutting bits off. One. Two. Three—"

A voice spoke from behind him. "Hey, Pete. Look up."

Pete turned. Thirty-six inches of Japanese red oak *hanbo*, travelling at fifty miles an hour, caught him squarely between the eyes. He hit the ground like a fallen tree, the knife spinning away across the grass as he slid to a halt. His hand twitched once, then he was still.

Christopher lowered his weapon. Jennifer pulled herself to her feet, and the two of them stared down at Pete's unconscious form.

Jennifer let out a long, shaky breath. "I think I just gave the performance of my life." She looked up. "Thanks, Chris."

Christopher looked down at his hands. They were trembling. He dropped the *hanbo* and put both arms around Jennifer.

Jennifer held on tight to her friend. Behind them, the first rays of sunlight reached up over the hills.

The rising sun painted the dam complex in bleak grey. To the left, the spillway plunged down towards the spraying jets of water at the bottom. To the right, the lake rippled in the early morning breeze. Ahead of them, the bridge ran over the spillway into the woods.

Ignis was crouched behind a concrete bastion, Allandra by his side. He looked longingly at the inlets on the far side of the lake. In one of them was Rokkaku. "If we could just get across . . ."

Allandra's eyes searched the bridge. "Where is he?"

Two shots rang out from somewhere downriver, echoing through the valley. Ignis looked at Allandra. Her eyes held the same fear that he knew was in his. *Shiro*.

They waited motionless for ten minutes, but no further sound came. The dam was silent and still.

"I'm going to check it out," Ignis said at last. "Wait here till I'm across."

"No way. I'm coming too."

Ignis glared at her. "I said no. Stay here and don't come out, no matter what." Ignis jumped the barrier and ran out into the car park, passing the still-smoking Land Rover. He ducked under the barrier and came out onto the bridge across the spillway. Water spray from the pumping station far below misted the air.

For a moment Ignis thought that the sun rising over the hills in front of him was playing tricks with his eyes. Then as the figure stepped out onto the other end of the bridge, he slowed and stopped.

"Well, well." Vargas walked forward, his shoes ringing dully on the concrete. "The prodigal son returns."

Ignis watched his father. Vargas came to a halt three metres away, his stance calm and relaxed.

"So, where's your sister?" Vargas asked when Ignis didn't respond.

"None of your business."

"Oh, it's very much my business. Allandra is going to be my successor."

"Dream on."

Vargas cocked his head with a smile. "What's the

322

matter, Ignis? Jealous?"

Ignis narrowed his eyes. "You wish."

Vargas shook his head sadly. "I'm afraid you're not going to be the heir, Ignis. Allandra is. She was always better than you, right from the start. Without her, you would never have amounted to anything. But don't worry. Once she's joined me, there'll be a place for you in my organisation, too. Then you can go back to being second fiddle again, just like always."

A wave of fury rose up within Ignis. He took one step forward, clenching his fists. Vargas stood watching him, calm. Ignis looked at Vargas. His father's stance was loose and relaxed.

Ignis stopped and let out a breath. "No."

Vargas raised his eyebrows. "Hmm. Once upon a time, you could never have controlled your temper like that. What have you been up to this past year?"

Ignis started to speak, but suddenly Vargas shook his head. "No, don't answer that. Sorry, Ignis, but I can't stand around talking to you all day, and I don't have time to beat some sense into you, either. I'm on a deadline here." His hand flickered down and up. Ignis's eyes went wide. Suddenly Vargas was holding a gun.

Vargas's expression was calm. "So let's just cut to the chase."

Ignis stared down the barrel. The 9mm automatic

suddenly seemed very big and very dangerous. "I'm . . ." He swallowed. "I'm not going to tell you where Ally is."

Vargas smiled. "Who said you had to?"

Ignis heard running footsteps from behind him, and his heart sank. He turned to see Allandra running towards him.

"Why won't you *ever* listen to what I tell you?" Ignis shouted at his sister as she drew closer. "Get out of here!"

Allandra came to a halt, her eyes defiant. "Not without you."

There was the crash of a gunshot, the sound of the 9mm deafening in the early morning stillness. Concrete chips flew between Allandra and Ignis as they jumped, the bullet whining away into the distance. They both turned to look at Vargas.

"Touching," Vargas said. All of a sudden, his voice was steel, and his eyes ice cold. The gun was pointed at the centre of Ignis's forehead. "Now, Ignis, your sister and I are going to have a talk. You and I have a lot to discuss, but we're going to have to save it for later. For now, get out of here. Walk away and I'll deal with you next. Make one move towards me, and son of mine or not, I'll shoot you right through the head and leave your body lying on this bridge."

Ignis held perfectly still, staring into his father's eyes. He knew Vargas meant it.

Allandra grabbed her brother's arm. "Go on, Ig!"

"I'm not leaving you alone!" Ignis snapped.

"It's OK." Allandra's voice dropped to a whisper. "I won't be."

Ignis looked at his sister, torn. To stay was death – yet running away, leaving Allandra behind . . .

Allandra's eyes were steady. She spoke softly. "Ig, I've never been more serious in my life. If you've ever trusted me, trust me now. Go."

Ignis took a deep breath and backed away, his eyes on Vargas. The gun tracked him as he circled around Vargas and towards the Rokkaku side of the bridge. With a final look back at Allandra, he ran.

Vargas holstered his weapon and turned to Allandra with a smile. "Now. Where were we?"

Allandra looked steadily at her father. "I'm not going back with you."

"That's a pity. I told Michael you'd be home this evening."

Allandra shook her head. "That's not going to work on me any more. You're not using Michael to catch me again."

"Catch you? What I want is for you two to be with your father." Vargas cocked his head. "I brought Michael with me, you know. He's waiting at the house in Rhosmaen. He thinks you're going to be returning with me. I wonder how he'll react when you don't come back for him and leave him all on his own? Not that it'll be the first time—"

Allandra attacked with a wordless snarl. Vargas took the arm that slashed at his face, knocked the breath out of her with a punch to her stomach, and spun her into the stone with stunning force.

"Now," Vargas whispered into her ear, "you see what happens when you lose your temper?"

Allandra gasped for breath. Vargas was standing over her, holding her arm twisted up behind her back. "Get off me!"

"I could teach you to use those attacks properly. Real combat, not martial arts. You could be so much more—"

"I . . . said . . ." Allandra forced out.

Vargas leaned in. "What was that? I'm having trouble hearing you."

Allandra took a breath. "I said *get off me!*"

She swept her leg across – the gymnast's muscles earned through long hours on the mat – lashing up to sweep Vargas's ankle from under him. Vargas fell heavily, yanking Allandra with him as she tried to rise. Allandra went with the flow, broke her father's grip as she rolled past, and flipped to her feet. Vargas was up almost as fast, striking like a snake. Allandra ducked and dodged, trying to find an opening.

✺

On the far side of the bridge, Ignis turned to see Allandra and Vargas fighting. A blow from Vargas slammed Allandra to the concrete, and Ignis winced. Allandra was hitting Vargas with everything she had, but it was obvious that she was losing. He took a step back towards them.

"Ignis!"

Ignis looked back. Christopher and Jennifer were hiding in the bushes, beckoning. He ran up to them.

"What are you doing?" Ignis demanded. "Ally's on her own!"

"No, she's not." Christopher pointed. "Look."

Ignis looked. Running along both sides of the bridge was a thin ledge, just over a metre or so below the level of the railing. Halfway along it, right underneath where Allandra and Vargas were fighting, was a small figure, balancing above the spillway. It was Shiro. Wind whipped at the tall boy, trying to pluck him from the edge, but he held on. Ignis frowned: Shiro was tying a rope to the underside of the bridge.

Allandra rolled away from a punch and came to her feet, keeping her distance. A thread of fear snaked up through her anger. She'd landed a dozen blows on Vargas, but he didn't even seem to have felt them. Where was Shiro? Blood trickled down her forehead, and she shook it away quickly.

"Ding, ding," Vargas said with a smile. "Round four."

With a kind of dull, weary surprise, Allandra realised that she had lost. Her rescuer from Junction Pool had been right; she wasn't ready to face Vargas. Every part of her body was battered and bruised. Her back and shoulders ached where she had hit the concrete, and her ribs hurt when she moved.

"Give up, Allandra," Vargas said quietly. He wasn't smiling any more: instead, he sounded almost pitying. "Stop this pointless fight and we can all go home."

"No!" Allandra snarled. She charged. Vargas slipped her attack, spinning her into the railings. Allandra crashed into the steel bars, then again onto the ground, gasping for breath.

Vargas waited as Allandra pulled herself to her feet. "It's over, Allandra. I've given you long enough outside of the family. It's time you came home."

Allandra looked up as the spots faded from her vision. A figure seemed to dance in the morning sunlight behind Vargas's shoulder, beckoning to her. Strength surged through her and she stared up at her father.

"I am home." Then she vaulted up onto the railings behind her. She wobbled once, then caught her balance, the sheer drop at her back.

Vargas's eyes went wide. He ran for her, reaching out.

Allandra jumped. Not back, but forward. She turned a

complete somersault in midair, flying over Vargas's grasping hands, and landed on both feet. Vargas turned to see her sprint across the bridge and leap the railings into Shiro's arms, taking them both backwards off the edge.

Allandra clung tight to Shiro's chest as they fell down and away. Behind them, the rope attached to the underside of the bridge snapped taut, almost jerking Allandra loose from her grip. Shiro tightened his hold on her. For one moment they were swinging in space, the bridge above them and the spillway below, then they were sliding downwards, Shiro holding Allandra with one arm and the rope with the other.

They hit at a steep angle, kicking off to bounce twice down the steep concrete. As they touched down for the third time Shiro let go and they rolled down the spillway channel, dead leaves crunching beneath them as they scraped to a halt.

Vargas stared, hands on the railing, as the two children dropped away out of his reach. His face went white. He drew his 9mm from its holster, a fine tremble starting along his jaw as he lowered the sights down upon the figures below.

Allandra saw the flash as the gun caught the sunlight. She moved between it and Shiro. "Stay there," she whispered. Shiro saw the look in Allandra's eyes and was still.

Allandra's golden-blonde hair was a bright dot between the sighting notches on Vargas's barrel. Despite the tremble in his muscles, he held the weapon perfectly still. Vargas's teeth showed in an animal snarl. The first knuckle of his trigger finger went white, then the second. Then the tremble stopped. Vargas's lips closed as he stared down at the shape of his daughter standing far below. Slowly, he lifted the gun off its target. "You are mine, Allandra," he said quietly. "No matter how long it takes."

Allandra saw Vargas pull out of his shooting stance. She and Shiro scrambled down the spillway, until the sprays of water from the pumping house began to hide the valley in a white mist. She looked back and had one last glimpse of her father, a distant figure watching them from high above, before the haze of vapour drifted in around them, hiding everything from vision.

"We can loop back from around the hills," Shiro said.

Allandra was exhausted, but shook her head. "No. There's somewhere I have to go first."

She expected Shiro to argue, but he only studied her for a second before replying. "Then I'm coming with you."

Together they set off down the valley. Allandra looked

back one last time once they had cleared the pumping station, but the bridge above them was empty.

The sun was high in the sky by the time they climbed down into the junction of the two valleys. Shiro waited under the trees while Allandra clambered wearily down the rocky peak.

The cleft in the rocks was cool from the night's breeze. To the left and right, the Tawi and the Garedig ran together into Junction Pool, where everything had started, so long ago. With one finger, Allandra traced the X carved into the rock. It was faded and weathered, but still easy to make out. She sat against the stone, waiting.

She waited as the sun rose high into the sky, bathing her and the valley in golden light. Lower down in the valley, the rumble of engines drifted up as the farms got on with their day's work. She waited as the birds sang in the forest on both sides and the heron flapped down into the pool to fish for its dinner. Finally, her head bowed, she rose and climbed up the ridge towards where Shiro waited to take her back to Rokkaku.

From behind a tree on the far hill, Michael watched her go. "Goodbye, Ally," he whispered, as the yellow dot of her hair vanished into the bracken. Then he turned away to find his father.

EPILOGUE

It was Sunday afternoon. Rokkaku was sleepy with the sun and the end of term, the students relaxing after the High Hunt. In places, boys and girls sat together, reliving the successes and failures of the night before. For the five students who had spent the night in a far more deadly hunt, the day had been spent sleeping.

Now, up on Rokkaku's north hill, Allandra and Ignis were looking out over the lake. They had reported back to the teachers, and now they were waiting to see what would happen to them.

"So who won the Hunt?" Ignis finally asked.

"I don't think anyone knows." Allandra's new *gi* had yet to shed its stiffness, and she worked at the sleeves as she sat. "They all got eliminated too quickly. Seems like the sixth formers really are good. But Ichiro came top of the first year."

"There's a surprise."

Allandra sighed. "I still haven't seen him since I got back. He is going to be *furious* that I left just before the biggest Hunt of the year."

"Actually, he's not. Shiro saw him and Hiroshi just an hour ago."

Allandra looked at Ignis in surprise. "They're not angry?"

"No. Mostly, they just wanted to make sure we'd got back safely." The news had taken a weight off Ignis's mind. He hadn't been looking forward to explaining why he'd let his partner down. Coming up with a convincing story to tell the teachers had been bad enough.

A sound from behind made them both turn. Mr Oakley was climbing the hill towards them. He waved. "Hello, you two. Feeling better?"

Neither of them said anything. Ignis didn't want to speak first, and Allandra looked drawn and tired. Mr Oakley settled down between them and they sat quietly.

"It is a beautiful view, isn't it?" Mr Oakley suggested after a few minutes. Below them, the lake wind blew the dark water from north to south in white wavelets. "Llyn Garedig's less than thirty years old, you know. The valley wasn't always a lake: it was flooded when the dam was built. That's why the hills slope as steeply into the water as they do. An odd look, don't you think? Most people find it eye-catching, but it takes them a while to see what it is that's different. Somewhere underneath all that water, you'll find the riverbed, the roads, and even what's left of the houses the farmers lived in all those years ago. That's why Llyn Garedig is empty. A lake needs the mud and weeds and algae on its bottom to support life. Eventually, with enough years, it'll become a live lake, if the dam doesn't erode first. Coots and moorhens will nest in the inlets, and fish will stock the waters. And with the fish will come fishermen, and with the fishermen will come boaters. And when that happens, we in Rokkaku will have to leave this valley of ours, and find a new place in which we can train in secrecy." Mr Oakley sighed. "Ah, well. Nothing lasts for ever."

Ignis couldn't stay silent any longer. "What's going to happen to us?" he asked.

"Hmm? Oh. Well, let's see. You ran away, missed a week's worth of classes, and left your partners for the Hunt. Not to mention visiting London without permission. Strictly speaking, we ought to hold you responsible for that car accident down at the dam, added to whatever else you did in Hampstead. However, as far as I know, Vargas Havelock hasn't reported any crimes to the police, so until he does, the most we can hold you for is putting yourselves and your classmates at risk. All added together . . . well, it's just as well you're both staying in Rokkaku over the summer. With the amount of chores and detention duties you've earned, it would set your studies back a good deal if you didn't start them until the next term."

Ignis and Allandra stared at Mr Oakley open-mouthed. "You know about Vargas?" Ignis finally said in disbelief.

"My dear children, I've known all about it for a very long time."

"And you let us stay here?" Allandra asked.

"Of course. What did you think we would have done?"

Ignis hesitated. "We thought, if you knew, you wouldn't let us stay."

"Good heavens, of course not. Did you think Rokkaku vetted students on their backgrounds? It's whether you can handle the training that counts, not where you come from. No, if we were going to expel you for anything, it would be for going on such an insanely dangerous escapade. But it isn't the school's place to pass judgement on your relations with your family. In any case, given the amount of time we spend here trying to teach you to use your abilities for the sake of others, it would be a little unfair of us to expel you for trying to help your family, no matter how foolish it might have been."

Ignis looked at Allandra. "So we're OK?"

"Except for the matter of your incredible foolhardiness, yes. You might say that your real punishment for doing this is to have used up however many of your nine lives it must have taken to get you all the way to London and back without even getting injured. The two of you survived by ten per cent skill, ten per cent determination, and eighty

335

per cent dumb luck. Don't expect to be so fortunate again."

"But what else could we have done?" Ignis asked.

Mr Oakley sighed. "Perhaps nothing. Perhaps I am being too harsh on you. But it is important that both of you understand that you were entirely outmatched. Neither you nor Allandra could possibly overcome someone like Vargas at the age and level of training you are at now."

Allandra shook her head. "I didn't try to fight Vargas. That wasn't why I went back. It was to get—"

"Your brother, I know. But he didn't want to leave. He's growing up now, Allandra, and with growing up comes responsibility, the right to make one's own decisions. The two of you are apart, now, two separate people living their own lives, as perhaps you were always meant to be."

"But he was the *reason*." Allandra stared at Mr Oakley. "That was why I stayed here. That was why I persuaded Ignis to stay, too. Oh, I know it was to be safe, and to learn – but that wasn't the *real* reason. That wasn't what kept me going through all those classes and training sessions and days and nights, no matter how tired or hurt I was. It was because of Michael. He's the reason I'm here."

"Is he?" Mr Oakley looked at them with eyebrows raised. "Allandra, the reasons that start us on a journey are very rarely the same ones we finish it with. Ignis, perhaps to begin with you remained here only because Allandra asked you to. But is that why you are staying now?"

"No," Ignis answered slowly.

"Then, Allandra, if Michael really is all that matters to you, why haven't you already left?" Mr Oakley raised himself to his feet. "I'll leave the two of you to rest for what's left of today. See you both tomorrow." He walked back down the hill.

Allandra stared out over the lake. Ignis nudged her. "Hey, Ally."

Allandra turned to Ignis. Her eyes were lost. "He's never coming back, Ignis. I knew that, at the end. He's chosen to be with Vargas, now."

Ignis was silent. "Maybe Mr Oakley's right," he said at last. "Michael was always like our shadow when we were together. He needed his own life. And if the life he wants is to be like our father . . . it's his choice. Maybe he was always a little like Vargas, and we never saw it."

Allandra hung her head.

Ignis grinned. "Hey, you've still got me."

Allandra half smiled. "I guess I have."

Ignis looked at her, suddenly serious. "You said a few months ago while we were sitting up here that we might be able to make this work. Stay in Rokkaku. Make a new life here. Well, I'm going to give it a try. How about you?"

Allandra looked up, studied her brother for a minute, then took Ignis's offered hand. "It's a deal."

Ignis laughed. "Now you just have to tell me why you

told Mr Oakley all about Vargas and our family even though you promised me not to."

Allandra frowned. "Me? I thought you must have told him?"

"Huh? No, I didn't."

"Neither did I."

Allandra and Ignis looked at each other, puzzled, then turned to look back down into Rokkaku, where the voices of students mingled with the sounds of the coming evening.

Fishing rod on his shoulder, Mr Oakley shut his door behind him and started to walk up and out of the valley. He nodded to the home ring patrols as he passed them, and they gave him a wave as he went by.

Once out of the spotter ring, Mr Oakley set off along his usual path. He was in no particular hurry; it was a warm evening, and he kept to a steady amble as he picked his way down towards the Tawi and Junction Pool.

Junction Pool was lower than usual with the hot summer, but the waters still mixed and churned. Mr Oakley settled himself down on the shore and set to unpacking his reel and tackle box. When he was satisfied, he cast the red and white float out to land with a gentle plop in the swirling water.

He sat quietly, his eyes half closed, for twenty minutes.

A dipper scooted out from the rushes on the far side of the pool, submerged with barely a sound, and dived and surfaced five more times before riding the current downriver. A pair of buzzards circled lazily on the evening thermals high above, their *kew . . . kew . . . kew . . .* cries echoing through the hills. Finally Mr Oakley opened his eyes and stretched. "You can come out now, Jessica," he said to the evening.

There was a soft laugh from the undergrowth behind him. A figure stepped out into the evening light, wearing close-fitting black clothes. Hands rose and the hood over her head was tossed back, revealing the face of a young woman.

She looked to be around twenty-five years old, with pale skin and tilted blue eyes. Her hair, as she shook it loose to fall around her shoulders, was fine and golden-blonde, shining in the sunset, and her steps were graceful as she walked towards Mr Oakley, smiling. "I wondered if you'd noticed me." Her voice was quiet and clear. Allandra would have recognised it.

"My dear, I may be old, but I am neither blind nor deaf." He studied the young woman appreciatively as she sat beside him. "Overseas travel seems to have agreed with you, Jessica: you look even more beautiful than before. The resemblance is quite striking, you know. You could pass for Allandra's older sister."

Jessica smiled, but only briefly. "How are they?"

"Allandra seems to be taking Michael's loss very hard. Still, she'll recover. Ignis has settled in the best. The changes in him over the year have been amazing. Rokkaku suits him very well."

"I wish I'd been there." Jessica watched the dipper reappear and scoot across the pool. "When I got your message that Allandra and Ignis had vanished I was on assignment. If I'd been in the area I could have helped them, somehow."

"You're not their guardian angel, Jessica, no matter how much you may act like one. In the end, no harm was done, and it may have been for the best. Better that they got themselves out of the trouble they had put themselves into than that you did it for them. In any case, if Vargas had recognised you, the consequences would have been far worse."

"I know," Jessica sighed. "I tried to warn Allandra, but she just wouldn't listen. There's a lot of my sister in her."

"Neither of them is the sort to be put off by something as sensible as a warning. They learn the hard way. It seems to be a family trait." Mr Oakley raised an eyebrow. "For that matter, I don't recall *you* being exactly an obedient student yourself."

Jessica laughed. "I know. I was worse than Ignis when I came to Rokkaku. But I learned." One of the buzzards

340

glided overhead. *Kew, kew* it called, kittenlike, and began circling for height.

"He'll never give up, you know," Jessica said finally. "As long as Allandra and Ignis are still alive, Vargas'll be after them."

"I know."

"What are we going to do?"

The dipper swam close to Mr Oakley's float and he twitched the line aside. "We will help them as we can, Jessica, as we do for all our students," he replied eventually. "We will shelter them and teach them, and give them time to grow. Beyond that, it is up to them."

Jessica nodded. The two of them sat quietly, the float bobbing in the currents. This was a problem to be turned over in their minds, and in time it would be discussed again. But the river of time is a wide one, and no one can predict its flow with certainty. A day would come for action, but that day was not now. The buzzards glided away into the west as the sun set, laying darkening shadows across Junction Pool and the man and the woman at its side. The creatures of the forest above paused briefly to study them, then turned back to the concerns of their own lives, following the cycles of day and night, food and sleep, predator and prey, as they have always done and always will.

POSTSCRIPT

Ninjutsu's practice was confined to Japan until the early 1970s, when Masaaki Hatsumi, the grandmaster of the schools of ninjutsu, founded the Bujinkan, a worldwide organisation for teaching ninpo. At the time of writing, Dr Hatsumi is still teaching at his home *dojo* in Honbu, Japan. Ninjutsu *dojo*s can now be found in nearly every country in the Western world, including most cities of the United Kingdom. Please do not ask any of the instructors there about Rokkaku, as most have no idea it exists, and those few who *do* know are required to deny all knowledge of the subject.

A list of registered *dojo*s can be found online.

GLOSSARY

arigato	thank you (casual)
baka	fool
bokken	wooden sword
dan	level, grade for black belts
do	way
dojo	training hall
gaijin	foreigner (impolite)
gi	training uniform (slang, proper name is *dogi*)
hanbo	one-metre staff
jutsu	art, method
kancho	senior instructor
kata	form, arranged series of movements
kento	fight well
Kihon Happo	Eight ways: the fundamentals of *taijutsu*
kohai	junior
-kun	suffix used to one of lower status (friendly, affectionate)

kyu	degree, grade for green belts
kyusho	vital points, pressure points
mu-kyu	no-*kyu*, ungraded
nani?	what?
neko	cat
ninpo	the way of persistence, (literal) endurance
omote gyaku	"front reverse", outward wrist lock
-san	suffix added to names, equivalent to Mr or Sir
sempai	senior
sensei	teacher
sente	striking the first blow, having the advantage
shikanken	strike with extended knuckles
shimewaza	choking techniques
Shinden Fudo ryu	one of the schools of *daken-taijutsu*
Shinobi no Ho	Shinobi methods (early name for *ninpo* or ninjutsu)
shitan ken	strike with middle three fingers
shuko	hand claws used for climbing and fighting
shuto	strike with side of open hand
tabi	training shoes (shorthand, full name is *jika tabi*)

taijutsu	body movement, unarmed fighting techniques
tongyo	hidden/evading form
tori	defender, "doer of the technique"
uke	attacker, "receiver of the technique"
yame!	stop!
<u>*sanshin no kata*</u>	three hearts form
chi	earth
sui	water
ka	fire
fu	wind
ku	void
<u>*kamae*</u>	stance, posture
ichi mongi	"straight", first stance – side on with one arm extended, the other over the heart
doko	as *ichi mongi*, but leaning backwards with one hand back and raised in a fist
jumonji	"crossed", side on, leaning forwards, arms crossed
seiza	kneeling

fudoza	sitting with one leg folded underneath
ichi	one
ni	two
san	three
shi	four
go	five
roku	six
shichi	seven
hachi	eight
kyu	nine
ju	ten

Shikin Haramitsu Daikyomyo – said before and after training. Literal translation: "The sound of words, the perfection of wisdom, the great light."

ABOUT THE AUTHOR

Benedict Jacka is half-Australian, half-Armenian, and grew up in London. He attended Cambridge University where he practiced ninjutsu and was a member of the university's ballroom dancing team. He has worked for the Ministry of Defence and the Northern Ireland Office, and as a bouncer in Camden and Islington. When he isn't writing, he reads, practices ninjutsu and boxing, plays computer games, dances street jazz and rollerblades around London. Still only 24, he's currently hard at work on the sequel to *To Be A Ninja*.